Goodnight and Goodbye

Timothy Harris is an American who was educated first in France, then in a tough New York City school and later at an English public school and Cambridge. He currently lives in Los Angeles, where *Kyd for Hire*, his fourth novel, is set. His second novel, *Steelyard Blues*, has become something of a cult movie in this country, starring Donald Sutherland and Jane Fonda.

Also by Timothy Harris
in Pan Books

Kyd for Hire

Timothy Harris

Goodnight
and
Goodbye

Pan Books London and Sydney

First published in Great Britain 1981 by Pan Books Ltd
Cavaye Place, London SW10 9PG
2nd printing 1983
© Timothy Harris 1979
ISBN 0 330 26096 0
Printed and bound in Great Britain by
Hunt Barnard Printing Ltd, Aylesbury, Bucks

to my friends,
George Ganchev and Gina Medcalf

one

The first time I saw Laura Cassidy, it was four in the morning and she was trying to drive a fire-engine red Volkswagen out of the underground garage of a Harper Avenue apartment building. She nearly sideswiped the stone entrance, knocked over a garbage can at the end of the driveway, and turned right up the hill towards Sunset Boulevard. What held me rooted to the pavement wasn't her driving; it was the man spread-eagled on the hood of her car. A Volkswagen bug has a sloping hood and the man was having a hell of a time hanging on. His back was arched, his legs struggling to straddle the hood, his hands desperately clawing at the windscreen wipers to prevent his sliding off. He was middle-aged, overweight, and his face had the horrified, windswept look of someone who has just been pushed off a tall building.

The car weaved up the steep hill, paused at the top, and then vanished over the rim into the neon brilliance of Sunset. You had to feel sorry for him. He was trapped on the hood of a speeding automobile driven by a woman who looked like she'd got her driver's licence playing bumper cars. Sunset was one of the most brightly lit and heavily policed boulevards in Los Angeles. And he was stark naked.

I stood there for a moment completely awed by the bizarre sight I'd just seen. How had the man ever got himself into such a totally helpless position? It was like one of those humiliating childhood dreams where you suddenly find yourself sitting in a classroom without any clothes on.

The background hum of city traffic had died out hours ago, and in the silence I could hear the sound of the Volkswagen coming back into focus. It was straining, going too fast in low gear. I knelt beside a parked van and waited, mouth open, eyes wide with excitement, waited like a fool to see what would happen next. The Volkswagen came churning up the street; the nude man was still splayed across the hood, gripping onto the windscreen wipers. I got a good look at him as the car turned into the underground garage, and suddenly it wasn't so amusing any more. Eyeballs rolled back, lips foam-flecked and snarling, he looked mad enough to bite through the windscreen. The girl behind the wheel was in a state of terror. Laura Cassidy had the kind of face that you didn't want anything to happen to, no matter what she'd done, or how many times she'd done it. She had the kind of beauty that always finds the world on its side.

In that one brief instant, based on nothing more than the glimpse of her face through the window, I wanted to get her out of trouble. Without even trying, she had me on her side the way the electric light has the moth.

I followed them inside and went for the cover of the shadows along the right-hand wall. Very slowly the Volkswagen wound its way through the maze of pillars and parked cars. She was obviously driving slowly so the man could jump off, but he wasn't cooperating. The car made another slow twisting round of the garage. When it reached the area furthest from the entrance, the man leaped off, dodged through the parked cars to the wall, and pulled the switch activating the electronic gate. The girl hesitated too long. By the time the car started accelerating, the gate had already begun its clanking, whirring descent. She never made it. The gate banged down and she had to hit the brake so hard, her engine stalled out. A second later the man had torn open the passenger door and dragged her by her hair onto the garage floor.

'*Freeze!*' I shouted, holding up my black loafer between both hands the way they teach you to hold your weapon on the police firing range. I was in the shadows and I had the element of surprise. Neither of them had been expecting a third party and from twenty yards the black polished leather would seem to gleam like gun metal.

'Now do I put away my gun or are you going to give me trouble?'

There was a dead stunned silence. Neither of them moved. The bare bulbs in the ceiling cast a harsh light over the raw concrete and black pipes. They could have been posing for the cover of some true adventures magazine: the naked psychopath gripping the prone girl by the hair deep in the Gestapo cellars, his fist raised to strike; the girl cringing helplessly in his grasp, her breasts bursting through her torn blouse. I WAS DEFILED BY A GESTAPO INTERROGATOR. And then the pulp-fiction tableau dissolved. The man let go of the girl's hair and slowly raised his hands above his head. The girl got off her knees and brushed her skirt free of dust.

I put my loafer behind my back, dropped it to the ground, and wriggled my foot back into it.

'She tried to kill me.' The man's voice cracked with emotion. 'I coulda died.'

I approached cautiously with my hand on my back hip as if I was ready to draw and fire at the slightest suspicious movement.

'Anything could have happened out there.' The man swallowed, panting, trembling. 'I coulda got killed.'

'Shut up,' I said, getting right up close to him.

'Jeezus . . .' he wailed. 'Wouldya just let me . . .'

'What's your name, buddy?' I pulled out my address book.

'Fieldman.' His face struggled against tears, eyebrows woefully raised, mouth turning down at the corners. 'Morris Fieldman. But if you'd just . . .'

'Address, Morrie?' I snapped.

'Here.' He sobbed, looking around as if it was yet one more injustice. 'I live in the building.'

'Doesn't look like you're carrying any identification to prove it.'

'I haven't got any clothes on . . .' His hands had dropped until one was nervously fingering the gold coke spoon on a chain around his neck. Attached to it was a jewelled Pisces symbol and a gold Star of David. His wrist and fingers were ornamented with silver and turquoise Indian jewellery. He'd lifted weights once, before taking up cocaine and astrology; his arms and chest were covered in artificially enlarged muscles which had sagged with age and neglect. It wasn't too hard to read Morris Fieldman: the ageing matinee idol face coarsened by drinking, the expensive hairpiece wrenched out of line by the drive, the too bright porcelain caps, the desperate keeping up with fashion – he was trying to shore up the illusion of youth with every trick and trinket on the market. I'd seen him before. It was a city full of Morris Fieldmans: grown men driven by the kind of anxieties which traditionally haunt ageing actresses staving off the approach of middle age. Each new fad a new indignity to be endured. I felt for him; there is nothing as sadly human as a hairpiece knocked out of place, but he was also a guy who'd been ready to beat a girl's face into a bloody mess. I kept playing it like a cop.

'What's the big idea running around in your birthday suit, Morrie? You can't do that. That's breaking the law. You just broke the law, buster. Keep 'em high. *High!*'

'I don't believe he's armed,' the girl said dryly. She was standing with her foot planted on the running board and her hand on her hip. It was an elegantly defiant pose but she held it a little too stiffly. I had a feeling if you took the car away she might just keel over.

'I'm armed, lady,' I said.

'I was referring to Mr Fieldman.' She ran a pale hand through her black hair and shook it out.

'Let's hear it. What's Fieldman doing on your car without his Jockey shorts?'

'I met Mr Fieldman this evening at a painting exhibition at Melrose. Mr Fieldman is an art dealer.' She smiled to herself at the thought, with a trace of impish amusement. For someone who'd narrowly escaped a beating she seemed to have incredible self-possession. She detailed the story with light sarcastic touches. 'I had a drawing to sell. Mr Fieldman professed an interest in buying it. He was kind enough to offer me dinner and I was naïve enough to accept. Over dinner we agreed on a price. Mr Fieldman suggested we adjourn to his apartment where he would pay me for the drawing. I think Mr Fieldman misinterpreted my willingness to have dinner with him and return to his apartment as some kind of romantic interest in his person. You see before you the results of that misinterpretation.' She said it with a deadpan face.

'In any case, since he'd told me he was a married man, I expected his wife was going to be present. She wasn't. And I wasn't sexually interested in Mr Fieldman. The feeling unfortunately wasn't mutual. Mr Fieldman, against my protests, insisted on removing his clothes and I ran out of his apartment.

Mr Fieldman pursued me and jumped onto the front of my car. I didn't ask him to jump naked onto the front of my car. Now that I've returned him safely home I hope we can just forget about it.' The speech seemed to have exhausted her. She gazed steadily forward at nothing in particular and then could not repress a large yawn.

'Is that your story, too, Morrie?' I asked.

'I'd like to talk to my lawyer.' He tried to sound dignified but it was hard going, standing there naked with nothing to hold on to but his gold coke spoon.

'All right, Morrie. Indecent exposure. Disturbing the peace. Attempted rape and assault, not to mention cheating on your wife if you have a wife. Does the lady want to press charges?'

'Not at all,' she said. 'If I just don't ever have to see Mr Fieldman again, I'll be perfectly satisfied.'

'It looks like I'm going to have to let you off the hook this time, Morrie.'

'Thank you, officer.'

'You better go back to your apartment now and put some clothes on and think about why you feel you have the right to rape and beat up a woman just because you paid for her dinner. I want you to think about that. You were ready to smash this lady's face in just because she hurt your feelings. Don't be getting so damn sensitive, Morrie. It's not worth it. Now get out of here.'

He walked stiffly away, passing behind the line of parked cars towards the staircase. The girl watched him until he disappeared from sight and then turned to me.

There are girls with blue eyes: blue eyes so dark it can take ages before you even notice they're blue; so vividly blue they seem like brilliant minerals; or so glittering and pale they don't look human. Laura Cassidy's eyes were metal-blue, a misty silver-blue like the radiance that glows around gun metal. Set wide apart in a finely boned face, they seemed to hit me with a soft dizzying force right in the centre of my chest. The pallor of her skin, the bluish suggestion of veins around her temples gave her a hothouse look: sensitive, high strung, a little overbred. She was wearing a pearl grey crêpe de Chine skirt, a skintight brown silk blouse, a brown velvet choker, and platform heel espadrilles. Every inch of her face was as carefully and sharply painted as an enamelled Oriental doll.

'Well . . .' She let out a pent-up breath. 'Thank you.'

'It was a pleasure.' I felt suddenly awkward now that I was no longer pretending to be a policeman.

'I'm not used to the police . . .' She smiled to herself. '. . . being on my side.'

'I'm not a cop,' I said.

'But your gun .. .' Her eyes widened in alarm.

'That was my thirty-two calibre Italian loafer.' I slipped my shoe off and aimed it like a gun. 'Freeze!'

'Oh, boy.' She shook her head slowly. 'That is wild. If you knew how wild that is . . .' Her eyes had a lacquered shine and there was a dreamlike, disassociated quality to her speech. I had the eerie impression that I was little more than a blurred presence to her, vaguely perceived through a fog of pills or booze. She drew her hand back through her hair and carefully removed her foot from the running board. She tottered perceptibly. She smiled at her own lack of balance and then made a regally pathetic attempt to pull herself together, rearranging her face into an expression that she might have used to see a guest out after a dinner party.

'It was very kind of you to rescue me.'

She smiled with serene vagueness. 'I think I'll be wending my way home now.'

'Better let me take you.' I gently gripped her arm but she immediately removed it.

'I can drive.'

'In your shape,' I took her arm again, 'you won't get three blocks. You'll end up in the hospital or the drunk tank.'

She sagged a little against me, smelling of wine and perfume and face powder. 'You're probably right.'

I led her by the arm outside to my car and poured her into the passenger seat. Then I went back for her Volkswagen and parked it around the corner. The white slip in the glove compartment was made out to a Laura Megan Cassidy domiciled in San Francisco. The interior smelled very much like I imagined her bathroom smelled: scented, perfumed like the toiletry counter of an expensive department store. I collected a pack of Gauloises cigarettes, a full-length white fox coat, and a circular crocodile-skin purse with a heavy silver clasp in the shape of a bird.

By the time I returned to my car, she was asleep with her forehead pressed against the side window. I draped the white fox over her and started the engine.

'Where to?' I shook her arm.

Not even a flicker of reaction. She was gorgeous, she looked and smelled like a million dollars, and she was as out of it as a skid-row bum. The shimmering fur coat looked out of place in my dusty Mustang. A girl with her style should have had the leather upholstery and hand-tooled interior of a Stutz to pass out in, not cracked, nine-year-old vinyl seatcovers from Sears. But that loaded you don't notice fine distinctions like where you are. She would have been just as oblivious if I'd put her in the trunk. Anyway the city at night was full of gleaming expensive cars a girl could get into and stagger out of an hour later feeling as if a brood of snakes had laid their eggs in her guts. Or maybe she couldn't even stagger out because of the things that had been done to her; she could just be dumped like a sack of garbage on the side of a dark road. She could have done worse than me.

I shook her some more and finally slapped her cheeks a little. Her eyes opened just long enough for her to give me a Missouri Avenue address and then slid shut.

I eased the car west along the silently glittering Strip, past the electric arrows, exploding signs, and looming billboards of musical stars. Limousine showrooms, tricked-out boutiques and restaurants alternated with massage parlours and institutes of palmistry and hypnosis.

Laura mumbled something in her sleep about wanting to go to Missouri. She said it wistfully, as if going to Missouri was something great she'd always dreamed about and now she knew it wasn't ever going to happen.

'I've never been there either,' I said, and that was about it as far as our conversation went.

Abruptly the pinball machine landscape of the Strip dipped

into the dark green flat of Beverly Hills. I opened it up and made all the lights along the foothills until UCLA and the glow of Westwood Village appeared like another world in the distance. Fog had rolled in across the basin In the drifting mist you couldn't see the skyscrapers, only the occasionally illuminated floor, hovering like a spacecraft over the deserted streets. It was an eerie, beautiful sight; up and down desolate Wilshire Boulevard the sky was alive with disembodied bars of light shining through the fog.

I followed Westwood Boulevard south, over the train tracks, past the islands of concrete dotted with park benches covered in mortuary ads, into the anonymous maze of West Los Angeles.

Everything about the streets near Missouri Avenue was so similar you could live there a year and still get lost two blocks from home. Laura Cassidy's apartment was one of a thousand two-storey stucco boxes with a flat roof and metal-framed windows. It had its own birdbath of a pool and its own postage stamp of a lawn, and the mandatory number of macramé hanging plants and coloured garden lights. Pets were tolerated in some of the apartment buildings but children were generally not allowed to live in that part of town. It was a stopping-off point for the rootless singles, the students, the young couples biding their time before they moved up the economic ladder and into another neighbourhood, or else for the elderly making a last stand before the move into what's euphemistically called a retirement hotel.

I parked, took her house keys from her purse, and went to open the door. Then I returned and woke her up. I don't think she remembered who I was, but it didn't seem to make much difference. She leaned heavily on me while I negotiated her up the short flight of stairs to her living room.

When I turned on the lights, she blinked and then smiled at me as if I'd done something sensational in bringing her to such an interesting place. She dropped her coat, offered me coffee, and walked towards the kitchen. The only thing that swayed was her hips. I couldn't figure her out at all.

The place was unfurnished except for a leather sofa and a chipped Danish coffee table covered in the remains of a party:

14

dead champagnes and Guinness bottles, ash-trays choked with butts, a silver ice bucket with a cork floating in it. Tacked on the wall over the sofa was a Picasso drawing of a matador fighting a bull with an audience of sad-faced women looking on. It was signed in pencil and dated. The bedroom was just a smaller version of the living room, only there was a bed instead of a sofa, and clothes lay in mounds on the floor, along with half-finished take-away food containers and Styrofoam coffee cups. Being beautiful the way she was beautiful is a job. It takes time and care. As far as I could see, most of the discipline she had went into her personal appearance.

I'd pulled her out of a jam but I would have poked around anyway. The tiny bathroom was strewn with wadded-up towels and open bottles and jars of makeup. The medicine cabinet was loaded with pills. She took her looks and her pills seriously. The bottles were neatly organized according to type: German pain killers; English sleeping pills; French tranquillizers; American mood elevators, muscle relaxants, and diet pills. The prescriptions on the foreign drugs were written in foreign languages so she'd been abroad recently. From the dates it looked as little as two months ago. On the bottom shelf there was a vial of brown powder, two twists of paper containing white powder, and a nearly empty cardboard box of disposable syringes. Suddenly a lot of things about Laura Cassidy became clear.

When I came out of the bathroom, I went into the kitchen. The kettle was whistling, and there were coffee things neatly laid out on a tray, but my gracious hostess was passed out on a barstool. I turned off the stove and lifted her up in my arms and managed to get her into the bedroom without banging her head too many times against the doorjambs. I didn't undress her. I straightened her limbs on the bed and covered her with a quilt. She was lovely and looked thoroughly innocent lying there, a sweet, placid princess of a junkie.

I left her car keys on her bedside table and wrote a note with a map to show her where her car was parked. I was going to leave my card but in the end I just scrawled T for Thomas. In a very unchivalrous way I was sore about the whole thing even though I had no right to be. She hadn't asked for my help. I'd

15

forced myself on her. Still I felt let down. It had started out on as high and bizarrely promising a note as any relationship can between a man and a woman. Now she had slipped into a cold, stoned oblivion.

I turned off the lights and let myself out. All the way home I was aware of the scent of her perfume in the car and I kept recalling how her body had felt lying slack in my arms, and those arresting silver-blue eyes and the way they seemed to do something to the centre of my chest. And another part of me kept recalling her medicine cabinet and the syringes and the slackness in her face. I'd been around long enough to know there was no percentage in falling for a junkie. I had my own self-destructive tendencies to deal with, there was no way I needed hers. I told myself to forget about Laura Cassidy and decided I wouldn't try and see her again.

two

The next afternoon I cruised by Harper to see if she'd collected her car. The red Volkswagen was still there with a ten-dollar parking ticket under the windscreen wiper. Maybe she hadn't woken up yet, or was stoned out again, or maybe she had other things to do. It wasn't any of my business and I had things to do myself.

Around eleven that night I checked by Harper again on my way home, and Laura Cassidy's car was gone. I felt a little jolt of disappointment; the last conecting link between us had been removed. The city had swallowed her back up again. Sometimes you can feel nostalgia for things that never even happened. I suppose that's how I felt about Laura Cassidy.

Over the next few weeks I'd think about her occasionally and toy with the idea of dropping by her apartment but I didn't do it. She was trouble and I didn't want the responsibility. Then in late June I was in Westwood to deliver a summons to an actor's agent and I thought I was so close I might as well pay a visit to Missouri Avenue.

It was a clear, windy, blue day and for once the city looked sharp and in focus. The palm trees lining the streets seemed to belong there instead of looking like some realtor had flown them in from Arabia to give the place atmosphere.

When I got to Missouri Avenue I parked and smoked a cigarette in the car. From the street I could see the living room drapes of her apartment were drawn shut and there was no sign of her car. I finished the cigarette and ground it out in the ashtray. Then I got out and climbed the stairs to her landing and pressed the doorbell. There's something distinctive about a buzzer resounding in a deserted apartment; it has an echo as it rattles off the bare walls. It's almost like sonar; you can sense furniture and the presence of people through closed doors by listening to the doorbell noise being absorbed. There wasn't a damn thing inside that apartment except a shag rug and a disconnected fridge. I knew it but I rang the doorbell again. On the second ring a woman popped her head out of a door further down the corridor and said Laura had moved three and a half weeks ago without leaving a forwarding address.

'You a friend of hers?' the woman asked. 'Or selling something?' She was a wizened, feisty little character with blue-rinsed hair and watery, indignant brown eyes. She had a cross, pug-nosed face and a high, sharp yelp of a voice. From her apartment came the *yap-yap* of a small dog who I imagined probably looked a lot like her.

'Just a friend,' I said. 'I don't know her that well.'

'That girl did awfully well for herself. Awfully well.' She took a step further out of her apartment but kept her hand protectively glued to the doorjamb in case I tried anything funny. 'A fellow came looking for her just before she moved. I had a long talk with him. At first I wouldn't speak to him about the girl because the way I see it, everyone's got a right to privacy. But when I heard what he wanted her for, I knew I was doing that girl a service.' The old woman abruptly clamped her mouth shut and stared at me, smugly delighted. It was a game. She was trying to manipulate me into asking a question.

17

'Gee, what happened?' I cooperated.

'I'll tell you.' She took another step out into the hall, letting go of the doorframe. 'The Cassidy girl won a lottery. Thousands of dollars and prizes, houses, and trips to Rio de Janeiro and God knows what else. This fellow just had to check she was the right girl. He showed me pictures of her and asked a little about her. I'll tell you, I was the one identified her. I was the hand of fate. Never thanked me, the girl, just packed up and left the same day. Probably on the other side of the world now, on some yacht.'

Her small brown dog came out and stood at her feet, barking at me.

'You won't see her now,' she said happily. 'She's got a whole new life for herself.'

I thanked the woman and made my way around her snarling pet and down the stairs. I was pretty sure there had been no lottery, no cash prizes. Lottery stories were old standbys in my business. The man looking for Laura had simply used the old ploy on her garrulous neighbour. He might have been employed by a collection agency, or making a credit check, or been a plain-clothes cop. There were a million ways she could have been in trouble and countless agencies and departments who might have an interest in locating her. From what the old woman had said, Laura Cassidy hadn't waited around to find out what it was about.

three

I saw her again in the second week of July coming out of a piano bar on Western near my office. There were two drunk soldiers trying to get her to go with them. She walked around them, but they tagged along, one on either side of her, urging her to change her mind. When she just kept walking and showed she was going to ignore them, they started getting abusive. They asked her who the hell she thought she was, and then who the hell she thought they were. They told her they didn't take that kind of stuff from anyone. They asked her if she didn't want to have some fun and then they figured out she had to be a dyke.

The Laura Cassidy I remembered would probably never have been approached by the two soldiers but this was a different girl. She'd lost weight and the street had left a soiled mark on her. Her clothes obviously hadn't been changed for days and her face was glazed with sweat and fatigue. The soldiers sensed it; she was in a tail dive. They sensed it the way sharks sense the presence of a weakened fish struggling in the water hundreds of yards away.

I crossed the street and came up behind them. I was about to say something when the soldiers abruptly veered off into another bar. I dropped back then and followed her from about thirty yards. She was trying to project an unconcerned air, but her body language gave out a different message. She was rigid with fear and the men passing her on the pavement obviously frightened her. The Hollywood flora and fauna – big black glitter-queens, motorcycle greasers, pimps, transvestites, hustlers, winos, junkies, street-gang punks. It was Mutant City and she was wandering through the heart of it in search of something. A cap of M? A safe trick?

She turned left on Hollywood, walked half a block, and turned into the doorway of an empty storefront next door to a joint called the PussyMania Club which did a big trade in watered drinks and oral love. I watched her from across the street. She was standing inside the entrance of a vagrants' hotel, just standing there, leaning against the wall, with her arms wrapped around herself.

On that stretch of the boulevard, for a woman to loiter in a doorway meant only one thing. Passing cars slowed down and pulled to the kerb, but she wouldn't get into any of them. A few pedestrians window-shopping for whores stopped in front of her but they all got the brush-off. It didn't take long before she came to the attention of the oral-love crowd next door, and they didn't like independents working their part of the street.

An Arab-looking pimp in a canary-yellow three-piece suit and a black-and-white headdress came out and shook his fingers at her, raised his voice, shrugged, and went back into the Pussy-Mania Club.

A few minutes later I saw a squad car pulling up on my side of the street. By the time the two cops stepped out, I'd already started walking toward her. At first she didn't know me, and then an exasperated look of recognition crossed her face.

'Let's take a little walk around the block,' I said. 'We've got company.'

She saw the cops coming over my shoulder and quickly stepped out of the doorway. As we started walking towards Western, I put my arm around her shoulder and pulled her close to me.

'Hold it there.' The voice was like a hand tightening on your neck.

I turned around, with a look of vacant surprise on my face, keeping my arm around her.

'What's the problem, officer?'

'We just received a complaint. Call it a tip-off. Why don't you get lost, friend?'

'Come on, sister.' The other cop made a move for Laura.

'This is a friend of mine,' I protested.

'You and plenty of others. Get lost.'

'I'm meeting this lady to go to the movies. I can prove it.' I kept a tight grip on Laura.

'Prove it,' the cop said. 'Prove it some other time. Now blow!'

'Her name is Laura Megan Cassidy,' I said. 'She's down here from San Francisco. Look at her driver's licence.'

'Who's he?' the other cop asked Laura.

'His name is Thomas Kyd. An old friend. We were to meet here but he was late. I don't see what the problem is . . .' She rummaged in her bag and produced her driver's licence. I brought out mine.

'Just old friends, huh?' The cop unwillingly studied our licences and took in Laura's bedraggled clothes.

'Ask me, Henry, I'd take a look at the little lady's arms. She got the look.'

'This is swell,' I said in earnest imitation of an outraged liberal. 'We have to pay taxes so we can be harassed and abused . . .'

'Be quiet.' The cop waved his hand.

'What kind of tip-off did you get? Some slime merchant from the PussyMania Club getting nervous about his territory? Boy, you guys sure hit the scene fast when a pimp puts in a call.'

'Back off, mister.' The cop's hand dropped to his weapon, slipping off the leather loop. 'Turn around nice and easy and put your hands against the wall and spread those legs wide. *Wide.*'

He frisked me and then emptied the contents of my pockets on the pavement while his partner looked through Laura's purse.

'She's clean,' his partner said. 'You've got lovely arms, sweet-heart.'

'Friend here's a private sleuth,' the other one said, fanning through my wallet. 'Okay, friend, you can go. But the next time I hear you shooting your mouth off, I'm giving you nine from the sky with my stick. Talk nice. And do something with her. She don't look right. Not looking right around here gets you busted.'

They looked at me, then each other, shrugged, and ambled back to their wagon. A message was crackling over their radio. They accelerated the squad car from the kerb with a roar, made a squealing U-turn, and gave it the swift towards West Hollywood.

I didn't ask Laura Cassidy what she'd been doing in that doorway, or where she'd been, or why she looked so beat. I knelt down and collected my things from the pavement and said:

'Do you have a place to stay?'

She shrugged, keeping her eyes averted.

'How are you fixed for money?'

Her mouth was pained, her jaw locked tight, her eyes expressionless.

'At least,' I got to my feet, 'you remembered my name.'

'I don't think we have a lot to say to each other, Mr Kyd.' She eyed me with a kind of sulky violence. 'I'm sure you're just doing your job, but I don't want to see him. Okay?'

'Can I ask you something?'

'Sure.' She folded her arms. 'But don't expect me to answer it.'

'What in hell are you talking about?'

'Come on.' She scuffed her foot impatiently. 'I know who you are. After that setup on Harper I looked you up in the phone book to thank you. You're a private investigator. You were following me then, and you've obviously been following me ever since.'

'Did anyone ever tell you you're paranoid?'

'This is embarrassing.' She sighed. 'I really don't have anything to say to you. I'm sorry. I just don't.'

'Okay,' I said. 'Then I'll do the talking.'

She fell into step unwillingly, her eyes scanning the people lurking in doorways, keeping a good yard between us. I wondered how many men had offered to protect her in the past month. Probably dozens. Men offering to protect her from other men. She was just too good-looking to last very long out on the street on her own.

'Harper was just an accident. I saw you giving Fieldman a ride in the raw – I stopped to look just the way you look at a building burning down. That probably would have been the end of the story. Except that my office is above that store over there.' I pointed at the BOLTON SAFE AND VAULT COMPANY show window. She looked suspiciously at the stained yellow brick building rising above the store. An old woman was squatting in the entrance with brown paper bags of garbage arranged around her in a defensive wall like a child in a sand castle. I considered telling Laura that I'd returned to her apartment in Westwood and then decided it would only trigger her suspicion. 'This is my territory.' I smiled. 'If you insist on hanging out in front of my office, chances are I'm going to run into you.'

She didn't say anything. Her silence made my explanation sound like a lie, but I continued anyway.

'I saw the soldiers bothering you. I just wanted to check you were all right. When the pimp called the cops, I figured they were going to Mickey Mouse you on a soliciting or vag charge. No one's paying me to look out for you, and I don't have to apologize for doing it. Anytime you don't like the help, just hiss.'

'How did you know my name was Laura Megan Cassidy? How did you know I had a San Francisco address?'

'When I parked your car that night I looked at the registration. I would have asked you, but you'd passed out.'

'Maybe I'm wrong,' she said truculently. 'If I'm wrong, I'm sorry.' She frowned to herself and then gave me a swift sideways glance, trying to make up her mind. 'Only, why me?' she demanded. 'Why do you waste so much kindness on someone you don't even know?'

'Do I ask you questions?'

She crossed her hands over her breasts and chafed her bare arms, staring ahead with a look of miserable confusion. 'I suppose you don't. You sort of pop up out of the blue and fix everything. Why *don't* you ask me questions?'

'Okay,' I said. 'How the hell did you know my name? I never told you.'

'While you were checking my car registration, I looked at yours. You'd lied to me about being a policeman – I wanted to know your name.'

'Why didn't you just ask me?'

'Why didn't you ask me mine?' she countered.

'I don't know,' I said. 'It doesn't seem very important now. This is my car, remember?'

I opened the side door and walked around and opened the driver's side. 'I'm going to drive it home and cook some dinner and have a couple of drinks. You're welcome to come with me. There's a spare bed if you need a place to crash, or I can drive you somewhere else if you have another place to stay. Or I can just go away period.'

'It's not that I'm not grateful,' she said. 'It's just this town is swarming with very helpful people who expect you to go to bed with them in return for their hospitality. I just don't swing like that.'

'You'll have to take my word no one's going to make you do anything but take a shower and eat what's on your plate.'

She looked at me very carefully and then without saying anything got into the car. 'I have some things at the Greyhound station,' she said.

'We'll get them.'

'I think you're going to regret this,' she said wearily. 'I'm not a very good investment. People don't get much out of knowing me.'

'You're not quite as frightening as you think,' I said.

At the bus station I waited in the car while she went inside to collect her things from a locker. She took a long time over it, and I started to think she'd given me the slip. Finally she came out with a pigskin suitcase and a black leather artist's portfolio. Her hair was brushed and she smelled of that liquid soap they offer you in public toilets. Cleaning her face and hands seemed to have given her back her edge a little. She leaned back in the seat, took lipstick and a mirror from her purse, and began applying it with a shaky hand.

'Did you think I was looking for a trick in that doorway?' she asked casually.

'Were you?'

For a while she didn't say anything but she was obviously debating something with herself. Finally she blurted out, 'I was high that night at Fieldman's. I was under a lot of pressure. I was using smack.' She waited for me to react but I didn't say anything. 'I don't do that any more,' she said.

'What's that like?' I asked.

'Not using?' She shrugged. 'It's cool. I never really had a bad habit. I don't like it. It turns you into a slob. Well, you saw me.' She chewed at the freshly applied lipstick and stared at her hands which were balled into fists. 'My life is rather a mess at the moment. Complicated. I'm not saying it hasn't been a mess before but it's never gotten this bad.' She talked excitedly and chain-smoked and the muscles in her jaw bunched regularly. She was speeding, entering the ragged, nervous stages. Her story poured out in intense spurts of words as if there wasn't nearly enough time to explain everything. Then she'd fall silent, spent and depressed. She hadn't slept for two days. She hadn't had any money for a hotel or food so she'd been popping diet pills. She couldn't afford to sell any more clothes, or she wouldn't have anything left to wear. She supposed it was a kind of vicious circle.

'I have some tranquillizers at home,' I said in a lull. 'If you want to come down off the diet pills.'

24

'That would be great. I haven't slept, you know . . . but I already told you that, didn't I? Oh God, the ravages of drugs. I'm turning into a vegetable.' She stubbed out her cigarette and hugged herself, leaning against the door with a glazed, hopeless look in her eyes.

'You don't add up,' I said. 'A girl with your looks, your clothes, would have friends. Why the starving-vagrant trip on Hollywood Boulevard? Why not sell that Picasso drawing you had?'

'It's my insurance.' She shrugged. 'As long as I have the drawing, I feel special. I know I'm not but I'm good at kidding myself.'

'You're good at running yourself down. Who convinced you you were such a cripple, Laura?'

'It was a gradual realization. I assure you, I resisted the verdict for a long time, but the evidence has become overwhelming.'

'That's cute,' I said. 'Cute, but not so funny. You can get out of this mess if you want to.'

'I'm very tired,' she said wearily. 'When I hear that kind of thing, it all sounds like something I heard Kathryn Kuhlman say on television.'

We'd arrived at my house at the end of Bundy Drive. I brought her luggage in, handed her a towel, soap, and shampoo, and showed her the bathroom. Then I popped a bottle of white wine in the freezer, put on some potatoes, and defrosted two steaks. After making up the couch as a guest bed, I sat in the living room and nursed a tumbler of Scotch, and asked myself what I thought I was doing, or hoped I was doing by bringing her home with me. It didn't take much self-examination to come up with the answer: In a circuitous, friendly, Samaritan way I was hoping to go to bed with her. If it didn't look like it was going to happen naturally then I wouldn't press it. But the idea was there; you couldn't be near Laura Cassidy without imagining what it would be like to know her better.

After the shower stopped, I could hear the buzz of a portable hair dryer and, nearly drowned out by it, Laura singing in a soft, tentative vibrato. I called in to her that the tranquillizers were in the medicine cabinet if she wanted them.

'Already found them,' she sang out cheerfully and laughed. It was quite a different sound to the resigned, scornful laughter I'd heard so far.

She came out with black hair still damp and a splash of cherry lipstick on her mouth. It was hard to believe she'd been scuffling on Hollywood Boulevard an hour ago. She'd put on a pale, raw silk robe that buttoned from the throat to her ankles, and pointed yellow Arab slippers; she could have been on a *Vogue* photographer's shoot in Morocco. It was damn hard not to stare at the contours of her breasts and thighs as they slid beneath the robe, hard not to speculate on what she would be like in bed if she wanted you.

It remained speculation. Dinner was a pretty silent affair. She was too hungry to talk and by the time she'd demolished her food she could barely keep her head up. She made a valiant attempt to ask me about my work and put up a good fight to have the honour of clearing the table and washing the dishes, but in the end I won out. She went straight from the table to the couch, closed her eyes, and that was the end of her for the next fourteen hours.

It seemed the mark of our strange relationship that I watched her sleep; I was someone with whom it was safe for her to fall asleep.

four

'I have a friend in San Francisco,' she told me the following afternoon over breakfast. 'An ex-business partner. I was thinking of going up there.'

'Someone who can help you?' I asked.

'He'll put me back in business.' She gave me a flat, level stare and her mouth hardened defensively. 'They're not quite the same thing,' she added with a shrug.

'There's no rush. Maybe you should call him first.'

'Eric doesn't have a phone.' She watched me closely. 'He's

easy to find but you have to find him in person. The people Eric knows don't give out much over the phone.'

I thought she was trying to impress me with what an outlaw she was so I didn't ask her what business Eric was going to put her back into.

'Why don't you give yourself a couple of days to unwind?' I said.

'I can't.' She stared into her plate. 'I'm going to sell the Picasso.'

'What for? I can stake you to a plane ticket to San Francisco.'

'You've done all these things for me. I can't keep sponging like this.'

I blew on my coffee and said: 'You can't divide life up like a restaurant check. I suppose there are a few sorry bastards who don't owe anyone anything, but that's because no one ever liked or trusted them enough to lend them anything.'

'You trust me?' she said.

'Sure.'

'Why?' She acted almost annoyed

'I distrust people for a living. Once in a while I like to indulge myself. Like a lady breaking her diet with half a gallon of ice cream.'

'Don't you want to know what business I'm talking about?' she said after a moment.

'I'm a private detective. If you want to tell me, I'll listen. If you want me to help you on something, maybe I'll help. But don't tell me about something illegal you're going to do.'

She slumped in her chair and made a studied production of taking several drags on her cigarette and blowing smoke at the ceiling. Her whole body seemed to contract and become tense and purposeful. Finally she leaned forward over the table and very slowly crushed out her cigarette in the middle of the remains of her scrambled eggs.

'I could go to bed with you,' she said in a thin, unnatural voice. The second she said it, you could see she would have given anything not to have said it.

'You could go to bed with almost anybody.' I laughed to conceal my surprise.

'God knows why I said that.' Her face was pink. She let out a pent-up breath, the kind of breath that comes out in a controlled hiss but would really like to be a wail of pain. 'I've never offered to do that in my life.'

'Forget it.' I poured her some more coffee. 'You worry too much.'

'It's just that I don't know what you want. It's as if you're sizing me up all the time and never saying anything.'

'I am.' I laughed.

'I don't know what you expect of me. I'm not what you think I am.' She shut her eyes tightly and faintly moved her head from side to side. 'I've ruined it now.'

She seemed at that moment very callow, very young, and neurotically self-absorbed. She was attractive, but I suddenly had a guilty twinge that I was dealing with a child, a vivacious, sadly damaged child. It was her beauty that confused and poisoned my reactions. It would have been the same for any psychiatrist treating her as a patient, or any medical doctor giving her a physical examination: it was impossible to treat her objectively. You could pretend she was ordinary, but all the time your heart pounded at the sight of her. At the time I told myself I was following the right course, offering her help but not taking advantage of her. In retrospect I was simply afraid. With looks like hers and that neurotic personality she was a dangerous proposition. That face was a lethal weapon; that body had the power to dissolve judgement, or drive a man into all manner of crazy self-destructive behaviour. She was as dangerous as a little kid toying with a loaded shotgun, aiming it at people, not aware or responsible for what she had. So I gave her a pass – to save myself from injury, though I told myself it was really for her own good.

'You haven't ruined anything.' I patted her hand. 'We both understand what you meant. If you want to do something for me, try liking yourself a little. I like you.'

She nodded, swallowed, her eyes moist and red, and blew her nose with the paper napkin.

I couldn't get her to stay another night. She made a resevation for a nine o'clock flight and packed her suitcase. When she was ready to go, she insisted on leaving the Picasso drawing with me as security for the loan she had finally agreed to take. I argued, but she wouldn't budge. It finally went up into the attic, pressed between the leaves of her portfolio.

I bought her dinner at a Mexican restaurant in Brentwood and the conversation was mainly about her business in San Francisco. It was an import-export business, she said, mainly clothes and antiques from North Africa and India, which involved her travelling a lot. I acted like I believed every word of it, which was more than you could say for her. A couple of times it was so obvious she was making it up, I almost thought she wanted me to call her on it. Some Zen wise man once said, 'It's by not believing people that you turn them into liars.' For what it was worth, I tried to act like I believed her. Towards the end of the meal she became silent, chewing on her shiny red lower lip, plainly troubled by something.

'You've been so cool about not asking me questions, Thomas. I feel I owe you an explanation,' she finally said. 'You see, there is someone following me. A private detective. I'm from New York originally. My family has hired this man to locate me. To bring me back – they're spending a fortune to get me back. I don't get on with my parents very well. They're incredibly rich – they want me to marry this guy – a stockbroker. It's a long story. I'm going to write them and tell them I'm okay, but I'm not going back. I just don't want that kind of life.' She smiled at me sadly, sentimentally, and I expressed suitable amazement at her tale, again wondering what, if any, truth was in it. Before I paid the bill, she insisted on checking it and discovered a two-dollar discrepancy in the waiter's arithmetic.

'I knew it wouldn't add up.' She laughed, pleased with herself. 'The way he looked – I've got a sixth sense for that kind of thing.'

It reminded me of her presence of mind in checking my car registration when I thought she was unconscious; the impertinent way she'd explained away Fieldman's presence on her car when she thought I was a real policeman. Behind the wistful, lost little girl there was a sharp, worldly intelligence that didn't miss a trick. It was all right with me – helplessness had never

seemed any more attractive in women than it was in men. I liked
that bright, canny, suspicious streak running through her personality. Lies were the stock in trade of my profession; I
couldn't help being attracted by someone who knew how to recognize and wield them as she did.

At the United terminal I brought her a one-way ticket to San
Francisco and handed her an envelope with two hundred-dollar
bills in it. She had a look that you see on young children being
sent off to school the first time. Her face was white and stiffly
composed but her eyes seemed to protrude too much. I touched
her shoulders, tried to plant an encouraging smile on my face,
and bent forward to give her a dry kiss. Her body leaned into
mine and then we were suddenly kissing each other with un-
ashamed hunger, all the dammed-up moments of the last
twenty-four hours going into it.

A voice cut through the airport Muzak, announcing her flight
was boarding at a distant gate.

'Come back,' I said quietly. 'I want you to come back.'

'Why do the men I like always wait so long to say these
things?' She pressed every contour of herself against me and I
felt a warm wetness where her face buried itself in my neck.
Then she withdrew, smiled gravely, ducked her head, turned,
and walked quickly away towards the security-checkpoint.

On the drive home the air cloaking the freeway was raw with
chemicals. You had to work to breathe it, and the harder you
worked, the worse headache it gave you. Visibility was about
fifty yards. On either side the neon-lit wilderness of junk-food
stands and body-repair shops softly glowed and winked in the
haze. I drove fast, changing lanes, trying to make time, hurrying
out of habit, though I knew there was nothing waiting at home
except a half-read novel, an open bottle of Scotch, and an un-
made bed.

I stayed with the San Diego freeway to the Sunset exit and
turned west. I wondered why I'd told her to come back when
I'd really wanted her to stay. I tried to imagine who or what she
was running away from. If I'd asked her, she probably would
have told me. Perhaps I'd been afraid to ask just as I'd been un-
willing to press her to stay in Los Angeles. She was young, dis-

turbed, and obviously in some kind of trouble and I hadn't been ready to get mixed up in it.

When I got home, I sat in the living room for a while and studied my shoes and burned my lungs with a few cigarettes. There was only one light, the desk lamp turned to the far wall, and the house was quiet, not a peaceful quiet, but the other kind, where you feel something is missing. I didn't care for it. It bothered me the way her presence had stayed behind in the house.

After a while, I went into the bathroom to wash. The porcelain in the sink and bath and the white shower tiles all sparkled. The towels hung neatly on the chrome racks. The mirror over the sink was brightly polished. It was all cleaner than it had been for months. She must have scoured the whole thing while I was making breakfast.

I washed my face and hands, brushed my teeth, and tried to keep my eyes off my face in the mirror. There'd been a possibility of something with Laura Cassidy, and I'd backed away from it. It was nothing dramatic. It was just an old law that says, either you gamble emotionally and grow, or the little spirit you have imperceptibly shrinks. I'd wanted her but I'd held back.

Maybe if I'd followed my real impulses towards Laura Cassidy, a tragedy could have been averted. Maybe not. In the silence of that spick-and-span bathroom I found myself definitely regretting that I'd let her leave town. The feeling didn't even entirely go away when I saw the metallic glint of a broken needle lying at the bottom of the toilet. It was all that she'd left behind. She'd told me she was through using drugs but she'd shot up before leaving. I didn't know if that also was something that could have been averted if I'd behaved differently.

five

A client was waiting in my reception room when I came in for work the next morning. He was a big broad-chested man in his early fifties gone soft around the jowls and midsection. He wore a square-cut, thin-lapelled brown suit, a white button-down collar shirt, and a satiny, green tie with too much shine to it. He had a flushed, crafty face, thin dourly curved lips, a blunt alcoholic nose, and disturbing yellow eyes the colour of cloudy urine. His eyes, set deep under his brow, were like animals crouching watchfully at the end of a tunnel. His hair was thin, pale, and oiled; his small furry ears were set close to his head, and lacked lobes. I noticed his shoes; they were the thick-soled, faintly orthopedic kind often favoured by people whose jobs involve a lot of walking. Cops on the beat do a lot of walking, but so do postmen and salesmen. There was also the possibility he just had corns.

'Larry Craig.' He wheezed up out of his chair and put out his hand. It was a firm grip he offered, but when I let go it lingered a little, as if he hadn't quite finished with my hand. He reached into his suit, removed a wallet, and withdrew a business card from it. I took it, glanced at it, and ushered him into my office. The card said:

Lawrence Craig – Counsellor-at-Law
2006 Avenue of the Stars
Suite 2255
Century City

He settled himself in the client's chair with a kind of wheezing self-consciousness and gave me a glib, flashy smile. 'It's a nice old building you've got here,' he said. 'I like an old-world atmosphere in an office.' He made a production of looking around, his teeth bared in approval. '*Funky*, that's the word, isn't it? You hear a lot of realtors describing houses that way. *Funky-emotional*. All those shacks up in Laurel Canyon, they used to be dilapidated. Now they're all funky-emotional.'

'It's a goofy town all right,' I said. 'Could you excuse me for a moment, Mr Craig? I've just got to use the bathroom.'

I shut the door and ran the tap lightly and pulled out the West Los Angeles phone directory from behind the john. There was no Lawrence Craig listed in either the White or Yellow Pages. I flushed the toilet and stepped back into my office.

'What can I do for you, Mr Craig?' I said as I settled down at my desk.

'It's a pretty routine matter.' He paused to light a plastic-tipped cigar, took enough puffs to fill the air with smoke, and get it burning way too hot, and then rested it in the ashtray. 'I got a call recently from a New York law firm I do a lot of business with – Powel and Raymond and Sobel. They're representing a Mrs Antonia Duval.' He crossed his legs and fiddled with the knot of his tie. 'Mrs Duval's sister recently passed away and Mrs Duval's been appointed executor of her late sister's estate. One of the beneficiaries of the will is Mrs Duval's niece, a Miss Laura Cassidy. I understand you know Miss Cassidy personally. Mrs Duval wants me to locate Miss Cassidy. She's got quite a sizable inheritance coming to her.'

'Laura Cassidy?' I pulled on my ear. 'Someone I know personally?'

'I got that information from a friend of Miss Cassidy's. This friend said that you'd got Miss Cassidy out of a jam.'

'A friend of this Cassidy woman said I'd got her out of a jam.' I looked puzzled.

'That's correct.'

'What's his name, the friend who told you this?'

'Paul Sassari.' Craig's cloudy, yellow eyes watched me closely. 'You may have read about Paul Sassari. He's something big in movies. His mother is Peaches Romaine.'

'Peaches Romaine the actress?' I whistled. 'No kidding. So this guy says I got this Cassidy woman out of a jam.' I shook my head. 'Someone's pulling your leg, or else you got the wrong Kyd.'

'I don't think so,' Craig remarked a little impatiently. 'In a matter like this I naturally looked into things. I'm not equipped to locate a missing person and so I was interested in hiring an investigator to find Miss Cassidy.'

'I wish I could help you.' I smiled. 'But I just don't hear any bells ringing when you say those names.'

'Any information pertaining to Miss Cassidy's whereabouts is worth two hundred dollars.' His thin, dourly curved lips slid back from his teeth. 'I often need the services of a reliable investigator on the cases I handle. I think I could push a significant amount of business your way. Sassari told me you saved Miss Cassidy from being assaulted by someone and then got her safely home.'

'Oh, *her!*' I laughed. 'The nutcase with the naked guy on her car. I never found out what her name was. Sure I know her. How much did she inherit?'

'I wasn't informed of the details of the legacy but I understand it's a sizable amount. I'm really more interested in her present whereabouts.'

'Westwood.' I took a cigarette from the box on my desk and lit it with a kitchen match struck on my steel watchband. 'Somewhere in Westwood. All those damn streets look the same to me. Kentucky Avenue . . . Mississippi . . . Ohio . . . the whole place sounds like a grade-school geography test.'

'Missouri Avenue?' he said. 'Was it Missouri?'

'That was it,' I nodded. 'Not a very funky-emotional pad. It was more . . . sterile-crummy, or modern-blah. Why don't you try there?'

'She's moved.' Craig expelled a savage sigh. 'And you haven't seen her since?'

'Listen, that girl is very unforgettable.'

He stared at me for several seconds and then moistened his lips. With a tired gesture he pulled out his wallet, slid out two one-hundred-dollar bills, and pushed them across my glass-topped desk.

'I *know* you saw her last night.' He flared his nostrils as if the air in my office bored him.

'Who's looking for her?' I asked.

'Her aunt. I told you.' His face was getting red.

'First she wins a lottery and then she inherits a big wad from her aunt. Come on, friend. I'm not Joe Schmoe, and you're not a lawyer. You've probably got cards in your wallet proving you're everything from a TV repairman to a county building inspector.'

'What's it worth?' He gave me a nasty, lopsided grin. 'Just where the girl is. I'll make it three bills and as far as anyone's concerned I've never been here.'

'Can't do it.' I stood up. 'One place she isn't is my house, so don't bother questioning my neighbours.'

'You're a pain in the ass,' he said wearily. 'Someone just wants to see her. Nothing's going to happen to the girl.'

'But she doesn't want to see that someone.'

'What is this? You screwed her? She paid you to keep quiet?'

'We've got nothing to say to each other and I've got work to do, and you're starting to rub me the wrong way. I suggest you find some accommodating moron to listen to your story. The door's right behind you.'

Maybe I was a bit hard on Mr Craig but his style annoyed me. He hadn't even bothered to paper over the cracks in his story, simply assumed I'd be too dumb to catch them, or too greedy for an easy three hundred dollars to care.

He rose heavily from the chair and looked contemptuously around my office, taking in the faded Oriental carpet, the hairline cracks in the plaster. He smoothed his tie with a slow, loving gesture and then glanced at me, slack-jawed, vacant-eyed.

'This operation isn't worth a one-line ad in the Yellow Pages,' he said. 'You want to be a loser all your life, is that it? I'm making you an offer . . .'

'I declined it.'

'You're an asshole,' he said meditatively. 'You're really some kind of an asshole.'

I sat down, leaned back in my chair, and eased open the desk drawer with my foot. Inside, at hand, was a small aerosol dog-repellent.

'Okay. I'm an asshole.'

'You just gonna sit there?' he leered. 'I said you're an asshole.'

'So you did. Why don't you leave before I get annoyed?'

'Make me.' He turned himself sideways in a faint crouch, moistening his lips, watching me in expectation.

'I don't believe this.' I stood up. 'Wouldya please get the hell out of here?'

He grinned with an absurd craftiness, lifting his fists in readiness, loosening up his shoulders. He was over fifty years old, a fat man gone to seed, wanting to have a fistfight in the middle of my office.

'Look,' I said. 'You're bigger than me, okay? I'm impressed. What more do you want?'

'How's this impress you, hotshot?' He whipped a snubnosed .22 revolver out of his suit-jacket pocket and levelled it at my face. 'You didn't think I had a piece.' He crowed. 'Naw, I'm just some old fart you can give the runaround to.'

I didn't think Craig was likely to shoot me out of rage. He was flamboyantly unbalanced but not someone who'd get so mad he'd gun you down. On the other hand, he was one of those thin-skinned, unhappy characters who might pull the trigger just because he couldn't figure out how to get out of my office without looking like a horse's ass.

'Put that damn thing away, for Christ's sake.' I waved my right hand, while my left closed on the aerosol can in the desk drawer.

At that moment the phone rang.

'Don't answer it,' Craig said.

I snatched up the receiver. It was someone called Frederick Bliss soliciting for the Eternal Rest Funeral Home which he informed me was one of the San Fernando Valley's leading Episcopalian mortuaries. There was a complete staff of directors ready to assist me should I be interested in reserving a plot in their new family garden. Terms were guaranteed.

'Like death,' I said.

'Death,' Mr Bliss told me with a grave geniality, 'is a subject we prefer not to reflect upon, sir, but it comes to us all.'

'All the world's a customer, eh, Mr Bliss?' I smiled encouragingly at Craig and then said into the phone: 'Did you just drift into this kind of work, Mr Bliss, or is it something you wanted to do ever since you were a little kid?'

Mr Bliss hung up with a muttered remark about how sick he was of creeps like me.

'That was a funeral home, Craig. You can shoot me first and then leave, or just leave. Take your choice. The suspense is killing me anyway.'

He snickered unsuccessfully and pocketed his weapon. 'A real smart number,' he said. 'I've seen your type before. All mouth and no action. We'll see how smart you are, buster. You got a couple of surprises coming to you from quarters where your mouth rates a pair of busted kneecaps.'

'Spare me,' I said. 'Let it be a surprise.'

He backed up to the door, crimson-faced, blinking, and with an inarticulate snarl, turned and slammed it shut behind him. There was the inevitable sound of the reception door slamming shut followed by the sound of his footsteps receding down the corridor.

I was just leaning back in my chair to digest what had happened when I heard footsteps returning. The outer door opened, then my office door, and Craig walked back in again, with the .22 in his hand. He approached my desk, leaned his left hand on it, waved the gun in my face, and blinked his disturbing eyes.

'I forgot to tell you something,' he said.

'Okay,' I said.

'No, I'm not going to tell you. Why should I tell you? You can just sweat it out, sucker.'

He strode out, violently slamming both doors again. A good exit line is worth a hundred banged doors. Craig's life had been all banged doors. I was so amazed by his behaviour it took me several moments before I realized he'd come back because he'd left his two hundred dollars lying on my desk.

six

Detectives don't have to be brave, or tough, or even have that many folds in their brains. Your average private investigator might be an ex-cop, ex-soldier, ex-bill collector, ex-door shaker, but always an ex-something with a personality profile somewhere between a night watchman and a vacuum cleaner salesman. He can be a coward, a cheat, or any number of other things. None of it matters much so long as he can tell a good lie and make it stick. In that department Craig was uninspired; he had a line but he didn't vary it to fit his audience, and when it didn't come off his only recourse was to lose his temper. Chances were his gun wasn't loaded, had never been used; it just sat in his pocket and gave him the feeling he had an edge on the world.

Just to be on the safe side, though, I put in calls to the American Bar Association and the Bureau of Collective and Investigative Services. For all the flimsy padding, I had an idea Craig's story might just have contained a few threads of real information. He was just the kind of overcute ham to believe that a lie was harder to detect if it was woven around some actual fact.

Of course it turned out to be pure fabrication: no law firm called Powel & Raymond & Sobel was registered in the United States, nor was an investigator called Lawrence Craig licensed with the bureau. The only information that checked out was Paul Sassari. There was such a person and he was listed in the privately published Beverly Hills directory as living at a San Ysidro Drive address located between Pickfair and the Harold Lloyd estate. Peaches Romaine, his mother, was listed under the same number and address.

Craig's visit buzzed around in my head for a while like a fly caught in a car and then I let it go. I was just glad Laura had escaped whoever had been misguided enough to hire him to find her.

The rest of the morning I drank beer from the office fridge and read an anthropological study of a tribe of New Guinea headhunters. Some of the members of the tribe reminded me a lot of some Hollywood types I knew. Around noon I got a call from a woman who wanted her husband found. He'd been gone two days. She wanted to know how much I charged for locating people. I said I charged one hundred dollars a day plus expenses. She said her husband wasn't worth nearly that much. She was obviously a daytime drinker.

'Hell,' she said, 'every day the bastard's gone, I'm saving a hundred bucks.'

'You've already saved two hundred since he left.'

'That's right. When he hears how much money I'm saving, he'll come back all right.'

I told her that the sooner she hung up the phone, the less it would cost her, and she told me I was a bastard just like her husband and started screaming down the line. I hung up. A few minutes later I got a call from a man who introduced himself as Dix Landau, Mr Paul Sassari's literary agent. Mr Sassari would like a word with me at my earliest convenience, on a matter of some urgency. Landau had a deliberate, mechanical manner of speaking that was like a legal contract; he talked in numbered clauses, leaving nothing to chance.

'Mr Sassari would like to speak to you in his home. The matter is a private one. You will be compensated for your time. Because of the urgency he'd like to see you right away and he understands that he may have to pay more for immediate service.'

'He doesn't have to pay anything unless he hires me.'

There was a whispered flurry of conversation on the line, then Landau said, 'Could you come right now?'

'Where are you?'

'He's at the new house.' Landau gave me a Malibu address on the Pacific Coast Highway and added that Mr Sassari was just now purchasing the place.

'I'll be about an hour.'

'Perfect,' he said. 'Mr Sassari should be through with the realtor by then. You won't have any trouble finding the house. It's on the ocean side, brown, very big place. There's no number. It cost half a million.'

'I'm glad.'

'There's a dog, but it won't bother you,' he added meticulously.

'Half a million bucks worth of brown house and the dog doesn't bite. Got it.' I hung up.

seven

The sun was shining in Hollywood, but a thick fog had wrapped up the coast. It was no great loss. The best thing about Malibu is the name. Once you get past the name and all its associations of movie stars taking moonlit swims, it's just a bare, uninspired stretch of sand fronted by a lot of overpriced beach shacks, tract houses, and quickie condominiums. The beach is narrow and the water is cold and the flimsy houses are too closely packed together. Most of them aren't much more than stucco fruit crates on stilts with a view of the ocean which you can't see for the fog. The Pacific Coast Highway runs right by everyone's front door so you've got the roar of traffic all day, not to mention hideous rush-hour congestion and sea gulls ruining the paint job on your Rolls.

Sassari's place was a vast, dark brown, two-storey Swiss cottage, with window boxes, carved lintels, and endless gingerbread motifs. In the Swiss Alps it would have been perhaps one quarter the size. Here on the coast of southern California it looked like the architectural equivalent of one of those tragic characters whose hormone imbalance gets them into the *Guinness Book of World Records* for being eight and a half feet tall. There was a wooden bridge over a circular stream and various painted trolls and gnomes were standing up in the weeds. The trolls and gnomes were also large, the size of real village idiots, and reminded me obscurely of the sinister playing-card characters in *Alice in Wonderland*.

In the driveway were three cars: a white Aston-Martin DB4 convertible with lipstick-red upholstery, a yellow Porsche, and a silver Ferrari. I eased my Mustang between the Porsche and Ferrari and got out.

There was a stooped elderly chauffeur with a dark blue, peaked cap pulled down around his ears, leaning against the Aston-Martin. He was grey-faced, with a protruding jaw and a mouth like a snapping turtle. Arms folded, he watched me approach out of the corner of his eye. Looking into his eyes was like staring at a motel-room wall.

'I'll watch it for you.' He nodded towards my Mustang. 'Someone might want your hubcap.'

'Which one of these is yours?' I asked.

'I drive, bub.'

'For Sassari?'

'I drive. You want to know something, dial information.'

I leaned over and laid a five-dollar bill under the Aston-Martin windscreen wiper. His hand snaked out and the bill disappeared. He didn't smile but his lips opened up enough to show me a pair of cut-rate dentures. For another five bucks, I thought, he'd sell me his teeth.

'You guessed right,' he said. 'I drive for Sassari. You collecting bills?'

'Private detective.' I stuck my hand in my pocket and rattled some change together. 'Who's inside?'

'His mother ain't.' The chauffeur spat and then carefully wiped his mouth.

'I guess Napoleon isn't here, either.'

'But his mother *was* here. Napoleon wasn't never here. That's the difference.'

'She was here and she left. Why did she leave?'

'Time's up.' He turned and started polishing the windscreen with a chamois that looked like it doubled as a handkerchief. I slipped a one-dollar bill folded up tight into his breast pocket and he stopped polishing and started talking. He should have had a slot in his forehead to stick the quarters through; it would have been simpler.

'Peaches is mad at the boss. She don't like one of the girls he runs with.'

'Laura Cassidy?'

'You know everything, don't you.' He gave me another bonus look at his teeth.

'Who else is in there?'

'In there?' He gazed over at the house like he'd never seen it before. 'Couple of hookers. The boss's agent. My memory ain't so good.'

'I got the same problem,' I said. 'I can't remember which pocket I keep my money in.'

'There's a realtor.' He lifted his cap just enough so he could get his hand under the visor to scratch his head. Maybe he kept rabbits inside and he didn't want me to see them. He was very secretive about the whole manoeuvre. 'There's a young typist fella called Kepler trying to get money from the boss. Kepler's desperate but he ain't gonna get his money 'cause the boss don't like desperate people.'

'It's Kepler's dough, but he doesn't get it because he's desperate? That doesn't sound right.'

'Shit on right!' He sniffed. 'Nothing in this life is yours until you take it off the other guy. That's my philosophy.'

'It's done wonders for you.' I said.

The front door was wide open. I rang the buzzer, and a moment later a tall redhead in a green bathing suit undulated down the hallway. She had a slinky, high, rolling walk and the kind of immaculate tan that comes from a daily regimen of careful lying around. She really got a kick out of her own mouth; she kept pursing and puckering and licking it like it was lined with candy.

'So you're the dick.' She delivered the innuendo with a lazy undulation of her shoulder, pouting in mock provocation. 'I never met a private detective before.' Her eyes added me up from shoes to haircut in one swift disappointed glance like a line of figures whose total wouldn't keep her in nylons. 'Paul's with the realtor. Everyone else is in the kitchen.'

I followed her down a long spotlighted corridor with a mural on its walls vaguely reminiscent of Salvador Dali. It was full of nautical motifs like lesbian mermaids, decomposing scuba divers, sunken U-boats, and swarms of jellyfish.

In the kitchen the redhead joined another woman in a bikini who was sitting at a table drinking white wine. A man was standing by the window with his back turned to me. The kitchen was brown, too, and the mural was repeated over its walls. It looked like something an art student might have painted on a three-day drunk before hanging himself.

The woman in the bikini was saying:

'Yeah, Tallulah owned it but she never lived here. Then some producer had it and Dylan bought it from him. I think Aldous Huxley lived here too for a while.'

'It must have been before he went blind,' I said.

The woman turned slowly in her chair and stared at me. There was irritation on her face which was rapidly replaced by a smile. It was supposed to be a smile anyway. Sometimes when very beautiful women sneer, it looks like a smile.

'And this is . . .?' she said.

'Thomas Kyd.'

'Thomas is a private detective.' The redhead tapped a cigarette smartly against the tabletop. 'That's Louise, and that's Morris. Morris is a stunt man. Louise does private stunts but we won't go into that, okay?'

The man at the window turned around and froze when he saw me. It was Morris Fieldman, wearing clothes this time, hairpiece glued in place. He said nothing, just scowled at me apprehensively. He was definitely in no rush to say anything about our previous meeting.

'Any idea how long Sassari's going to be?' I said.

The redhead wet her lips, placed the cigarette dead centre, rolled it around like a cigar and then lit it. She blew smoke across the table towards the other two. 'Paul just closed a big deal,' she said. 'He's taking a couple of days longer to see everyone. Louise has been waiting for two days. Morris has been hanging around for months. Morris is a stunt man. Morris is hoping that Paul will hire him to fall out of a window in his next picture because no one has asked Morris to fall out of a window for a very long time.'

'Shut up.' Morris snatched up a glass of wine. 'Can't you just shut up?'

Another man entered the kitchen and walked quickly to the wall phone. He was thin, with a nervous fine-boned face and unkempt, curly auburn hair. He had the high-domed forehead and dark, burning eyes you associate with writers whose careers are cut short by tuberculosis. He was dressed oddly in a striped, blue shirt with a boiled white collar and a silk tie, and floppy grey flannel slacks, with monogrammed green velvet slippers peeking out from under the wide cuffs. Everyone else in the room was bronzed, opulently healthy; he was bone-white, high-strung, somewhat tortured-looking. He paid no attention to the others. He sat on a barstool and studied a racing form with one hand poised on the telephone.

'And that,' the redhead said, 'is Kepler. Kepler is Paul's secretary. Aren't you, Kepler?'

Kepler didn't take his eyes off the racing form.

'Kepler doesn't talk much,' the redhead explained. 'He's a *thinker*. He won't have anything to do with riffraff like us. He looks down on us, don't you, Kepler?'

'It can't be helped.' Kepler kept his eyes on the racing sheet. 'You spend so much of your time on your back.'

'Screw you,' the redhead hissed. 'You think you're so damn superior. You're nothing but a lousy typist.' She angrily stubbed her cigarette out and looked around the table. 'Look at him,' she said. 'He's calling his bookie. How much did you lose his week, Kepler? What are you going to tell your wife?'

'Passions are running high today,' he said, smiling in my direction.

'Don't bother crawling to me for a loan,' the redhead cried. Her face was ugly with emotion, a little drunkenly blotched now. She turned her eyes on me. 'How do you like it so far?'

'Leave him alone,' Kepler said.

'He doesn't need your protection. He's a cop. I don't like cops.'

'I'm going to find Sassari,' I said. No one had asked me to sit down or offered me a drink. As far as rooms went, it was very easy to leave. I walked along the hallway and down three steps into a vast room panelled in oak. Four men were kneeling in the far corner around a packing crate which was the only thing in the room except for some books and oil paintings piled against the wall. I stood at the bottom of the steps for a moment watching them. A shaving mirror covered with lines of cocaine rested on the packing crate and they were taking turns, snorting it up through a short straw. As I tried to figure out which was Sassari, a giant wolfhound entered from the sundeck through the sliding glass door. It paused, looked vacantly around the room, and then walked over to the wall and streaked it with a brief spurt of urine. Considering what had happened so far, it didn't seem an inappropriate piece of behaviour. It wagged its tail. It yawned and then approached the crouching men and stuck its head between them. I watched in fascination as it sniffed experimentally at the white powder and violently sneezed, scattering what looked like several hundred dollars worth of cocaine in all directions.

No one was pleased: someone swatted the dog in the jaw and sent it yelping out the door. There was a lot of shouting and bad temper as the men crawled around on all fours searching for the scattered powder. They were sniffing it off the floor of this half-a-million-dollar beach-front property like a pack of disgruntled hounds. It was not the right moment to introduce myself, but I couldn't resist.

'Mr Sassari?' I said.

One of the men glanced up. He was in his late twenties, with a dark, petulant face framed by black curls. He had a prominent nose, a strong, sullen mouth, and pale, glassy blue eyes. Staring out of such a dark face, they had a startling effect.

'What is it?'

'You wanted to talk to me. I'm Kyd.'

He got to his feet and dusted his hand off. He was short, his chest thrown out, with that bristling posture you see in short, ambitious men. He gave me a lazy, charming smile and I showed him some teeth in return.

'I'm Laura's fiancé,' he said. 'You didn't know that.'

'No.'

'I didn't think you did. You gave Craig kind of a hard time. Don't worry – he's a jerk, I know.'

'He's not easy.'

'We'll forget about him.' He was smiling broadly now. 'What I want to know is . . . where is Laura?'

'I have no idea about that.'

Sassari shook his head, still smiling. 'Okay,' he said, 'I didn't expect to get it for nothing. Write him a cheque, Dix.' He nodded at one of the men, an older man dressed unlike the others in a suit and tie, the literary agent who had called me.

'I meant what I said. I don't know where she is.'

'You're all right.' He ambled over to me. 'We're going to get along.'

Louise, the redhead, Fieldman, and Kepler drifted into the room, holding glasses. Sassari paid them no attention but you could see he was used to an audience, liked playing before one.

'Now I could be mad,' he said, taking my arm. 'I could be jealous. I don't even know how you met Laura. Some jam you got her out of. Laura's a beautiful lady, right? She spent the night at your place. Now don't I have the right to be concerned?'

'Sure, but I still don't know where she is.' I smiled politely into his face and carefully removed his hand from my elbow. 'She slept on my couch – one night. The day after I drove her to the airport. She wouldn't tell me where she was going. It didn't seem to matter to her – her big thing was to get out of L.A. That's free information and all I know.'

'Bullshit!' he exploded.

'Sounds like Laura to me,' Kepler said.

Sassari ignored his remark, turned his back, and walked away from me. He stood alone for a moment, hands in his pockets, scuffing his shoe at the floor. When he lifted his face it had a cruel, slack-jawed look.

'I'm going to tell you this once. I don't need to argue with you. I don't need to write a cheque. I'll just have your fucking arm twisted. You don't know who you're dealing with, mister. Tell him who he's dealing with, Morris.'

Fieldman cleared his throat, ill at ease, watching me with an expectant, pleading look in his eyes. Laura had claimed he was an art dealer; it now appeared he was an out-of-work stunt man, a hanger-on. I no longer had any idea what had really led up to the incident on Harper, only that Sassari didn't know anything about it, and that was the way Fieldman obviously wanted to keep it.

'Do what he says,' Fieldman growled at me. 'He isn't kidding.'

'What Paul is trying to tell you,' Kepler said in disgust, 'is that he's not averse to having you professionally slapped around the earhole, if you get my drift. As a neutral observer I'd advise you to take the money and run. He means it.'

'I'll take my chances.' I started for the door and Fieldman lumbered across to cut me off.

'Do yourself a favour,' he said, blocking the door. 'Tell him where she is.'

'Is this really wise?' The older man, the literary agent, was shocked. 'I know you're anxious, Paul, but surely . . .'

'He doesn't go until he tells me where she is,' Sassari said quietly.

I walked towards Fieldman. He was considerably bigger than me, and with clothes on seemed much more of a threat. I thought, if he doesn't get out of my way, I'll make a run for the sliding glass door. The whole business seemed incredibly stupid. I had a mental picture of Fieldman, Sassari, the hookers, all of them, chasing me along the beach. I wasn't particularly afraid; I thought I could run faster than them. Fieldman backed up as I approached and suddenly threw a long overhand right at my face. It had no power or speed behind it. I saw it coming and easily blocked it. He threw the identical punch, a little slower this time, as if he was trying to tell me something. I stepped inside it, and countered weakly to his chest. It wasn't too bad a shot; he grunted and sagged against me. We were jammed together against the doorframe; he was making a lot of gasping noises, growling and struggling, but nothing was really happening: he had my arms expertly tied up.

'Beat it,' he whispered in my ear. He let my left arm go and I threw some hooks into his body. He started going down. I hurt my hand hitting him on the top of his head and he dropped as if he'd been felled with a tyre iron. Either I'd missed a great career as a ring knockout artist or Fieldman was a phony. I stepped over his prostrate body and glanced once back at the room; they were all standing there, frozen in startled poses, convinced they'd watched a genuine struggle. I couldn't think of anything to say; I was as shocked and bewildered as any of them.

The old chauffeur leered at me as I came out of the house.

'Didn't get the job, huh?'

I ignored him, heading for my car.

'That last bill you gave me wasn't a five,' he shouted. 'You ain't so smart. I got a motor home in Mexico all paid for and waiting for me anytime I want. What you got?'

I couldn't think of any answer.

'I could be retired right now if I wanted to,' he shouted.

He didn't even sound like a human being. It felt like I was being talked to by a yak in Outer Mongolia.

I reversed out on to the shoulder of the road and was about to

47

put my shoe through the floor when I heard my name being called.

'Kyd! Wait for me.' The redhead was running over the bridge, trailing a beach gown and a purse into which she was trying to stuff her sunglasses. She pulled open the side door and got in.

'I'm going with you,' she announced breathlessly.

I glanced sharply at her, shrugged, and accelerated so quickly she was knocked back in the seat. After a moment she fished in her bag for cigarettes and lighter and remarked in a bright, astonished voice, 'You know, you really should have taken the money. I mean, what do you care?'

'Where am I meant to be taking you, lady?' I said. 'Just tell me where.'

'Sunset Plaza Drive would be ideal.'

'You got it.' I shifted into high gear and put my foot down.

'You're going to get a ticket, you know.'

'After your friends, a traffic cop would be light relief.'

She laughed a high, brittle, sophisticated laugh. 'Do you always treat your clients that way?'

'That Hollywood brat isn't my client.'

'That was some wallop you gave Morris.'

'Do you find that kind of thing interesting?' I sneered.

'Your reaction,' she shrugged, 'was interesting.'

I glanced at her. She had the kind of coked-out eyes that would find the cracks in the wall interesting.

'What do you do for a living?' I asked her.

'Well, honey, what do you *think?*'

'I think you probably make it on your back like your friend Louise.'

'That's about it.' She lit a Camel and picked a speck of tobacco off the tip of her tongue. 'With my clientele, though, the job is mainly done on your knees.'

'Sounds like hard work.'

'*Tacky,* darling, not hard. Being a waitress is hard. But you look like the kind of guy who gets it free.'

'A lot of weirdos floating around these days do seem willing to do it for nothing.'

'Like Laura Cassidy?' She snorted with laughter. 'Oh dear, do excuse me. But it does amuse me how two characters as different as you and Paul end up going for the same soulful piece of ass.'

'Who says I go for it?'

'Your face is a picture. You get this stern look every time any-one mentions her. It never ceases to amaze me how everyone goes for Laura and how Laura doesn't go for anyone. Her big secret perhaps.'

Was it idle personal curiosity that had prompted the redhead to come along for the ride, or was she trying to pick my brains on Sassari's orders?

'You see,' she continued, 'I've been digging this chick's act a long time now. And it really knocks me out how she works it. I mean without fail. Every john looks at her and sees this unat-tainable *thing*, this sensitive troubled *soul*. And you all think you're going to be the one to get through to it. Well, I hate to tell you, but Laura is layers within layers. She's the killer onion. She makes all the boys cry. You think I'm kidding, don't you? Take it from a pro, sugar, it's all done with mirrors.'

'What makes you think I give a damn what you say about any-thing?' I smiled.

'You know.' She stroked my cheek. 'I dig hostile men.'

'You know, I don't care what you dig or don't dig at all. You make me feel like a block of ice. Like you chill me. Like we might as well be two ice cubes sitting in this car here.'

The redhead didn't work with mirrors; she was about as subtle as a car accident. She stubbed out her cigarette, turned sideways toward me, folded her legs under her bottom, and unbuckled my belt. You could say that having to drive put me in a difficult posi-tion. But it wouldn't mean much. In a detached, dizzying way I was horny, but mainly I was just sort of morbidly curious to see how outrageous she could get. She could get pretty outra-geous. Any shyness, reserve, or even fear had been burned out of her. She unzipped me and her hardened baby face assumed that look of glassy desire which is *de rigueur* for the act in any pornographic performance. As I slowed for a red light, she lowered her face into my lap.

And that's how it went, along the scenic Pacific Coast High-way, past the new J. Paul Getty Museum, onto Sunset Boulevard's looping twisting curves, a hard cold bizarre ride straight out of a low-budget sixteen-millimetre skin epic. The road unfolded before me, the trees and houses swept by. I noticed the dark roots in her glossy, copper hair, the pure white skin at the back of her neck which the sun had missed, the scent of her perfume and sun cream. I noticed trucks and schoolchildren crossing and road-construction warning signs. After about ten minutes, when I showed no sign of coming, she tried talking dirty to me in a kind of Muzak stewardess voice.

We went through Beverly Hills up to the Strip and climbed Sunset Plaza Drive into the hills.

'What number?' I asked.

'Oh, fuck the number,' she said thickly. 'Just stop anywhere.'

I pulled off under some trees in front of a house, killed the engine, and groaned aloud. Almost at once I exploded in her mouth.

Afterwards I sat there for a while with my head slumped on my chest, wondering how I'd ended up in such a freaky situation. She was sitting up, a cigarette between her lips, with a bored, irritated look on her face.

'When you've recovered,' she said dryly, 'I have to go to number fifteen thirty-four.'

'Thanks,' I said. 'Thank you very much. It was . . .'

She shrugged. 'Can we go now?'

I turned the car around and drove the few blocks to number 1534. Out of some desire not to leave it at just that, some guilty hope I could salvage something better out of it, I asked if I could go inside with her.

'I don't *live* here, sweetheart.' She twitched her shoulder. 'I'm seeing a trick.'

'Take a day off.' I tried to kiss her.

'Are you for real?' She turned her face aside and firmly removed my hands. 'I can't lose this client.' She checked her face in the car mirror. 'Hell, you ought to be flattered.'

'I'm flattered but I don't get it.'

She opened the door and slid her long bronzed legs out.

'Call it revenge.' She smiled. 'Laura doesn't like me, sugar. I get a kick out of turning on her admirers.' She got out of the car and checked her purse.

'What's your name?' I leaned sideways over the seat to keep her in view.

'That going to make you feel better, knowing my name? How pathetic. Please drive your crummy car away. You're a sentimental sap, Kyd, and men like you make me nervous.' She turned and moved in that slinky, high, rolling walk across the lawn, swinging her purse, trailing her beach gown in the other hand. Before she reached it, the front door swung open and a bronzed, wizened man in a terry cloth robe stepped out to greet her. He put his hand, which held a cigar, on her shoulder, and his other hand on her hip, turned her from side to side, then possessively steered her inside. Just before she vanished into the house, I heard her laughter ring out like the mechanical squeak you get from squeezing a plastic doll. Then the door banged shut.

I thought I was tough. I drove back to Hollywood feeling like something the dog had coughed up.

eight

Dix Landau got to his feet as I entered my small waiting room, his face screwed up into an expression of pained concern. He must have driven straight from Malibu.

'Are you all right?' he asked. 'This is a terrible thing . . . terrible.'

I unlocked my office and he followed me inside. I could see him taking it all in, the lone, dented filing cabinet, the leather client's chair with the cigarette burns, the bald patches in the carpet. There was no striplighting, no colour-coordinated walls, and my desk was littered with books, papers, and two empty beer bottles. I was in an ugly mood and I made no effort to hide it.

'May I sit down?' he said.

I waved at the chair and went and opened the windows as wide as they would go. A great wash of heated dead air came off the street and into the room: overheated engines, gas fumes, frying onions. It was as noisy as if we were standing on a street corner. I slumped into my chair and rested my feet on the rim of the wastepaper basket.

'Firstly, let me apologize,' he said.

I dismissed that with an eloquent grunt.

'And secondly, allow me to explain my position to you.' He folded his legs carefully and let out a soft, silvery chuckle. 'Paul Sassari is an extremely important client of mine. I handle lots of writers. Famous writers. Paul is the most important. Every page he writes turns into a great deal of money. I don't know if you realize . . .'

'I know what money is, Mr Landau.'

'It would be useless to try and persuade you that Paul is actually a nice human being – he isn't. Personally I think of him as an oil well – very ugly, a blot on the landscape, but extremely profitable. Without screenwriters the industry dries up just as a machine grinds to a halt without oil.' He paused for a moment like a teacher allowing a student time to absorb some complex piece of information. 'That is how I have to look at things. Now this girl Laura seems to be of vital importance to Paul. Since she's left, he hasn't been able to work. Things have been set in motion, you understand, actors contracted, financing set up. We're nearly through preproduction on his next movie, Mr Kyd, and we don't have a finished script. A multimillion-dollar motion picture is about to go into the toilet.'

'There's only one thing I have to say about that – who cares?'

'Yes.' He nodded sadly. 'Your annoyance is justified. If I may say so, however, I think you're unwise to take an emotional stand on this matter. Presumably you know where Miss Cassidy is, and you wish to protect her. You have perhaps some interest in her yourself? Is that realistic, though?'

'A few hours ago Craig was sitting where you are, waving a gun in my face. One of your client's goons tried to beat me up. The redhead tried the same thing in a different way. You people behave like hoodlums. It's more than bad manners. I don't think I care for your idea of what's realistic, Mr Landau.'

'But can you afford not to?'

'I've gotten by for eight years in this business without your kind of money.'

'Can I tell you something?' he said. 'I admired what you did back at the house. I admire your position now, but I think you're wrong. Laura Cassidy may not end up with Paul, but she'll gravitate to a man like him, a successful man, a man who wields power. I don't think you're right for the part. She's not suitable for you.'

'Are you her agent, too?'

'I've offended you. I'm sorry,' he said. 'The girl is a pathological liar and has a drug problem. I can't imagine a reasonable man wanting to have anything to do with her.' He realigned his tie and tried his glasses on several times in a fussy, irritated manner. He didn't look like a Hollywood type, a wheeler-dealer, a media pimp. His suit was soberly cut, he had an old-fashioned haircut; a definite eastern look, what you would expect from a man in banking or chartered accountancy. His face was grey, with prim, unremarkable features; people were probably always not remembering who he was.

'I suppose you don't think much of me,' he said wearily. 'But handling artists isn't as simple as you think.'

'Sassari's a very unpleasant guy. Art's got nothing to do with that.'

'Writers are crazy.' He frowned. 'When you get a guy like Paul who can turn his craziness into money, you've got to make allowances. Personally I don't know how he does it. I'm always looking for that sensitive side which comes out in his writing. Where is it? It's a contradiction to write so well and behave so badly.'

'There were German officers who ran the death camps in the last war. Guys whose idea of light entertainment was letting guard dogs tear children to pieces. Off duty they read Shakespeare, listened to Mozart, that kind of thing. Some people don't have trouble with contradiction.'

'Yes.' He looked thoughtfully at me, with a trace of irritation, as if he hadn't given me credit for having a brain and my possession of one offended his sense of order. 'Do you have a card?' He rose abruptly from the chair.

I took one from the drawer and handed it to him.

'You've inconvenienced me, Mr Kyd. You're obviously a stubborn person. Perhaps one day I can make use of your stubbornness in some other context.'

'If someone dear to you runs away, or you think your neighbour is poisoning your goldfish, call me.'

It was intended lightly but I could see our moods weren't connecting. He thanked me for giving him my time and looked at the card and thanked me again and we finally managed to part with a lot of teeth showing.

I stood for a while by the window, watching the late afternoon action on Hollywood. I could see the PussyMania Club where the cops had tried to take Laura in, and the Arab in the canary-yellow suit was limbering up for the evening trade.

My hand ached from banging Fieldman on the top of his skull and the redhead had left me feeling flat and squalid and sad. I remembered Laura's warning to me: 'People don't get much out of knowing me.' She might not be wrong at that. She had lied to me about Fieldman; he wasn't a stranger to her, or an art dealer. She had lied about Craig; her parents hadn't hired him, it was her jilted fiancé. I thought of Sassari with that cruel good-looking face, shrewd and hard as a jockey's, and the swaggering, tough-guy manner. Was that the kind of man she liked? What really annoyed me was that she had me lying for her now: staging bogus fights for Sassari's benefit, pretending not to know where she'd gone. I didn't mind lying; it was what I did for a living. But I liked to know the purpose behind a lie. With Laura I was acting in the dark, and all the information she'd given me was apparently false. I didn't need to know the details of any of it. Really, I thought, she was pure trouble. Her drugs, her cover stories, her fugitive behaviour; it all smelled of disaster. Yet she'd been truly lost that night I'd found her on Hollywood Boulevard. She'd left a valuable drawing with me and I was sure parts of her story were true. If she told me lies, I sensed, they were told to spare me something, not to dupe or exploit me.

The phone rang as I was on my way out of the office.

nine

'*Thomas Kyd?*' It was a heavily stylized voice, one of those husky, sexual voices that are meant to hit you below the belt. A full, throaty, come-hither voice. It was about as real as a wooden leg.

I said: 'This is Thomas Kyd.'

'My name is Peaches Romaine.'

'I know.'

'Oh . . . how do you know that?' She exhaled as she spoke, bending and sustaining the words.

'I'm an old fan of yours, Mrs Romaine.'

'Not too old, I hope. The only people who recall my movies look ancient to me and they're my contemporaries.' There was a clink of ice sliding about in a glass. 'But you sound like a young man to me, Mr Kyd.'

'I'm in my thirties.'

'*And* a private detective . . .'

'That's right.'

'Are you married?'

'Divorced.' My wife was actually dead but that was my business.

'Do you have hobbies, Mr Kyd?'

'Are you interviewing for a pen pal, Mrs Romaine, or just slow warming up?'

'Impatient,' she said to herself. 'Yes, you're impatient. Why not? You're young. All right, Mr Kyd, let us talk. I understand you and my son had a little chat today.'

'You could call it a chat. He shouted and I didn't listen.'

'I wonder why you didn't get on.' She sounded as if it really intrigued her.

'I think we're from different planets.'

'Oh, but you're great fun, Mr Kyd.' She laughed. 'They didn't tell me you were great fun. Now Paul isn't fun at all and I was happy to hear that you'd stuck to your guns. You're obviously a man of strong principle. But you see,' she paused, 'I think it was more Paul's bad manners than anything else that made you refuse the job. I imagine someone like Dix Landau might well convince you to reconsider.'

'You have a nice way of putting things, Mrs Romaine.'

'Now you're flattering me.' She chuckled. 'Anyway, dear boy, I don't want you to work for Dix because I want you to work for me.'

'I'm not working for him.'

'Fine. I've got a cheque here with your name on it. Tell me what he's paying you and I'll double it.'

'We're not communicating, Mrs Romaine. I'm not working for Landau.'

'You refused?' She didn't sound like she believed it.

'I refused.'

'Well, that is kind of you to tell me. I am sorry. It must get depressing going about refusing money all the time. In that case I won't be requiring your services.'

'Your son and Landau wanted me to find Laura,' I said. 'As far as I can make out, you were just willing to pay me twice as much to sit in my office and count the walls. I guess you really don't want her found.'

'You've understood me perfectly.' She chuckled in that whispery, velvet voice. 'It's been very pleasant talking to you. If you happen to see Miss Cassidy tell her to stay away from my son. You might tell her that I am not a person to trifle with. She's made one deal and broken it. She won't get off so lightly next time.'

'I don't know what you're talking about, and I don't know where Laura Cassidy is, and I don't expect to see her but apart from that, sure, I'll relay the message.'

'Thank you.' The line went dead.

And so did the whole thing.

People quit waving hundred-dollar bills in my face. No one pulled a gun on me or threatened to beat me up. Movie stars stopped calling. I saw no more red Volkswagens with naked men on their hoods.

It was all right with me; I'd made up my mind to steer clear of Laura Cassidy. But as the weeks and months passed, and I didn't hear from her, I found myself thinking of her in a kinder light, sentimentalizing her a bit in memory. She became that *beautiful kook* I'd met late one night in Hollywood under bizarre circumstances. The passage of time allowed me to domesticate her memory. Gradually I airbrushed out the doubtful aspects of her, and emphasized everything that was desirable. When I thought of her, I conjured up her eyes, her grave, sulky mouth, her pale, satin complexion. Even if she had lied to me, I would tell myself, she told me more than most people, and with a liar, perhaps that's a perverse sign of love. It seemed at the time just a harmless kind of daydreaming. After all, she had moved me by her sheer loveliness and there weren't many people who'd managed to do that in my life.

The truth was I was like a cured alcoholic unconsciously preparing to go back on the bottle.

The letter I received from her in early August put me right back where I'd started. It was covered in Moroccan stamps, contained two crisp one-hundred-dollar bills, and a note.

Dear Thomas,
    You must think very poorly of me for taking so long to pay back your loan. It was the kindest, cleanest thing anyone ever did for me. I expect to be back in California soon. I'm glad I left the Picasso with you because now I have a perfect excuse to ask you for a date when I return. Did you mean what you told me at the airport that night ? It was only a kiss, but I can remember it and play it back to myself like a piece of music. Please don't think of me as a child. Thank you – for everything.
Much love.
    Laura

If there'd been a return address on the envelope I would have answered her. As it was, I spent the next month expecting her back in Los Angeles. In the back of my mind every time the phone rang, a part of me hoped it would be her calling. When I went through my mail in the morning, I always checked first to see if there was a letter from her. But there was nothing. It disappointed me. I felt that, with some difficulty, I'd cured myself of an interest in her only to have it inflamed by her note. Why had she bothered? Had something happened to her in Morocco?

I got my answer late in September when I saw a photograph

of her and Paul Sassari in a magazine I'd picked up at the check-out counter of my local market. It was one of those throwaway rags that run features on Siamese twins breaking up, the drinking problems of famous actresses, and invasions of killer frogs in Idaho. On the inside page there was a blurred shot of Paul Sassari dragging Laura through a crowd of paparazzi.

Concerned friends of writer-producer, Paul Sassari and his blue-eyed bride, the chic Laura (née Cassidy) are laying bets that the marriage won't weather its stormy honeymoon. After a whirlwind courtship in Tangier, the much photographed pair's public quarrels have raised eyebrows in one European watering spot after another. To compound the Sassaris' woes, last week in Rome their private bodyguard, Morris Fieldman, was arrested at the airport for possession of heroin and cocaine. Rumour has it that the drugs were not solely for Morris Fieldman's use. From Rome the volatile couple and their ménage of friends have flown by chartered jet to Venice where talk of hotel-room orgies, with participants of both persuasions involved, is scandalizing ears the length of the Grand Canal. Friends claim that ever mysterious Laura remains aloof from the bisexual swap-meets, but that it's breaking her heart. How long a marriage can stand up to stresses like that is the question everyone is asking . . .

It went on in that vein for several more paragraphs. You needed a cast-iron stomach and kitty-litter brains to read it.

I jammed the magazine back in the rack and stood there waiting to check out my groceries. So that was what had happened to her. It sounded like she was going down the tubes, some very elegantly lubricated tubes to be sure, but tubes all the same. You can do heroin in a luxury hotel with a view of the Grand Canal, or with the soiled, lost souls on Hollywood Boulevard. One way the gossip columnists write you up, the other way the county does the paperwork. They say it's a question of style. Maybe it is. But on a coroner's report a description of an overdose reads much the same for one junkie as another. Coroners don't give a damn about style.

The food in my shopping cart suddenly didn't look very good to me. I put it back on the shelves and left without buying anything. For nice bones, pretty silver-blue eyes, and a goodbye kiss at the airport, I was taking her awfully damn seriously. She'd written, in her letter, of playing that kiss back to herself like a piece of music. I'd conjured and ransacked the memory of that kiss quite a few times myself. But while I was daydreaming in Los Angeles, Sassari had pursued her and married her. From the story in the scandal sheet, of course, it was possible to say that I had missed out on some very dubious pleasures. Regardless of Laura's mystique nothing alleviated the heartbreak of a relationship with a junkie. You didn't escape the squalor and horror because your particular junkie was poignantly beautiful or in some way remarkable. That only made it that much harder. But I would rather have found out for myself.

I went to a bar that night where they hadn't seen me in years. It was my depression bar where I'd done all my serious drinking after my wife died. The bartender remembered me. He understood high tragedy, the sacramental kind of boozing the abandoned American male resorts to in a bar. We went through the ritual in respectful silence: He poured, I drank. He warned the other drinkers off me by a roll of his eyeballs. He was very proper, very formal like an undertaker who has mastered the etiquette of grief. I had given him a twenty-dollar bill when I came in, which he must have used to pay the taxi that took me home.

In the morning of course I had a blistering hangover and I told myself I was making a mountain out of a molehill. All this ersatz melancholy over Laura Cassidy was weak, puerile, essentially asinine. Hungover, I am a vicious name-caller. The hell with Laura Cassidy and her lousy husband, I thought. I should have gone to bed with her when I had the chance and taken Sassari's money as well.

ten

It was about seven o'clock on a stormy Sunday morning in late October. I was lying in bed listening to the wind blowing the branches of a tree across the roof. The house was groaning and rattling as if the foundations weren't going to hold it to the ground. It was not a very solidly built place – just a small guest-house thrown together without planning permission out of knotty pine and redwood slats. The couple who rented it to me owned the ranch house at the end of Bundy Drive. To avoid detection they had buried my shack under blankets of ivy and generally let the garden grow up around it. The gate into their property was wired to activate a tape recording of a German shepherd barking and snarling. They thought it was safer than keeping a real German shepherd because a live guard dog could always be given doped meat by a burglar. They were from Florida originally, Tampa Bay, where they had lived next door to a policeman. Ordinarily a Bundy Drive address would have been beyond my means but they let me have the guesthouse cheap. Having a private detective next door gave them a sense of security. I was suposed to be a human version of that tape recording of a barking German shepherd.

I would have drifted back to sleep but I heard the sound of a car climbing Bundy Drive, something high-spirited with a racing engine's growl. It passed my house, made a U at the end of the street; the driver gunned the engine once and turned it off. The wall I was leaning against backed onto the garage. I heard the whoosh of wheels as the car rolled to a stop, followed by the emergency brake being set. I waited for the sound of a car door opening but there was silence.

I got out of bed and padded into the kitchen and pinched the curtain back an inch. There was a white Aston-Martin DB-4 convertible filling the driveway. Laura was in the driver's seat using the rearview mirror to correct her makeup and arrange her hair.

She did it all very swiftly, with hurried movements, but with that unwavering concentration in her eyes which women assume when faced by a mirror. She was wearing a white terry cloth robe with a hood and broad, drooping sleeves that looked like something a girl might drape over her shoulders after a swim off a private yacht. I saw her stepping out of the car holding a bag of groceries, and caught a glimpse of her long, bronzed legs.

Was it resentment that made me stand in the kitchen letting the doorbell ring? I suppose it was. There was a lavish presumption and courage implicit in her showing up unannounced at seven o'clock on a Sunday morning. I might have been in bed with someone else. I might have been shacked up somewhere else. I suppose it annoyed me that I wasn't. I let the doorbell ring enough times for her to taste fully the knowledge that I wasn't home. Then I wrapped a towel around my waist and threw open the door.

I said something like 'Jesus' to convey my surprise at finding her of all people on my doorstep.

'Surprised?' She pecked my cheek and eased past me down the short passageway into the living room. She dropped her bag, checked to see no one was in the bedroom alcove, then turned and smiled at me. She just about carried off this razzle-dazzle impertinence, but not quite. There was a little too much nervous energy being expended for her confidence to be genuine.

'What's a married woman like you doing out on a morning like this?' I sat down at the table and nodded at her to take a chair. I was playing it very amused, as if there had never been anything between us but some light human comedy. She cut right through that.

'Do you think I'm a terrible person?' she asked.

'For getting married to *him*.'

'For getting married to *him*.'

I lit a cigarette and had Part One of my morning cough. 'Let's say you're kind of a mild pain in the ass for telling me all those lies.'

She would have preferred anger, I could see: being a mild pain in the ass didn't accord with her idea at all.

'I'm sorry. Would you like to know the truth?' she asked.

'I'm always a sucker for the truth.'

She stood up and smiled meditatively at me. She stroked my

cheek. There was a certain starry, abstracted look in her eyes. She bent down, took a bottle of champagne from the grocery bag and vanished into the kitchen. A moment later I heard a stifled pop and she came out, carrying the bottle and two glasses. She did the honours, pouring it out, sliding a glass to me, settling back in her chair.

'I knew you'd be here. I knew you'd be alone. I also knew it wouldn't be easy – to face you. I am not a mild pain in the ass. I wish I was only that. Cheers.'

'Cheers.'

She appeared in control now, like a student who has mastered a subject, learned it, and feels ready to deliver it aloud. She had clearly thought out what she was going to say to me, not because it wasn't genuine, but because it was difficult and in part humiliating for her to bring it out. There is a gadget called a PSE which measures subaudible microtremors in the human voice which occur when a person is wilfully lying. It is much superior to the traditional polygraph. Everyone has his own private PSE for navigating the ocean of half-truths and lies which make up so many human situations. I was listening to her with mine on, ready for something not to ring true.

'From the start I was never straight with you,' she said. 'That night on Harper the argument with Fieldman was my fault. Morris is not really a bad guy. He could have told Paul where I was but he didn't. We got very loaded that night on smack. He wanted to have sex. He started to touch me and I didn't stop it – I was wasted and if I closed my eyes and pretended he was someone else, it was all right. He made me come. Morris . . . not very romantic, not exactly an advertisement for my taste in men, but he did. Then, of course, he wanted me to do something to him – go down on him, to be perfectly graphic. I started to, and then I couldn't. I felt sick . . . lost, scared of how ugly it all seemed. I had to get out of there. I told him I had to go to the bathroom for a minute. I got dressed. I made up. I took my time, thinking he'd nod off, or lose interest if I waited long enough. When I came out, he hadn't lost interest at all. I thought, what the hell, one lousy blowjob, but then I thought, If I do this, I'll be lost for good. I won't know who I am. Anyway I ran out and he chased me. After that it was just bad luck. I didn't mean to scare him. If he hadn't been so scared, he wouldn't have tried to beat me up. When you popped out, I just babbled the first thing that came into my head because I thought you were a cop and there was heroin in his apartment.'

'I'm not a judge. You don't have to tell me all this.'

'There's more. I want to level with you. I was never asleep in your car, or when you put me to bed. I just pretended so you wouldn't make a pass at me. Not for the reason you think . . . it was because I liked you and I didn't want to go straight from Morris to you. It was too sleazy. I am a sleazy chick. Anyone who puts dope in her arm and balls Morris gets classified as a sleaze. So I was a sleaze who got a sudden attack of romantic delicacy. I liked you. I did look you up the next day. I even called your office and got that recorded message which of course flattened me because I thought you were working for Paul.' She took her first sip of champagne, mainly to wet her lips. It was me who was doing all the drinking. 'I know I gave you that line about this detective following me on my parents' orders. Well, that is an unfortunate habit of mine. I make up stories. I have no parents. Correction. I don't know who my parents are so I make up parents who are rich and spend all their time searching for me. Do you know what I'm talking about? It's very common. Standard practice for orphanage brats.' She twisted her lips into a self-contemptuous smile. 'How do you like it so far?'

'I like it.'

'I hate that bitch,' she said.

'Who?'

'Your redheaded friend. Miss Mouth.'

'I get sleazy, too.'

'I don't even want to hear about it.' She shrugged angrily. 'I came here to tell you the truth. You don't have to tell me anything. That night on Hollywood Boulevard – I was scoring some smack. When my connection saw you and then the cops, he took off. I said I wasn't using then but I was. I am clean now.' She rolled her sleeves up and showed me her arms. 'I haven't used heroin since the last time I saw you.'

'Who was Fieldman carrying the stuff for?' I asked.

'You know about that?' She looked puzzled.

'I read something in a magazine.'

'The cocaine was for us, the smack was his. Paul has totally screwed Morris. I'm helping him through a guy in Rome, a lawyer. I'll get Morris out.' She said it defiantly. 'Paul is such a bastard . . . he won't do anything.'

I watched her light a cigarette, draw on it, blow out the match. She studied me keenly, her mouth set firmly, trying to hold me with her eyes. She wasn't proud of what she'd done but she was vain about telling the truth. They say no one is as fanatical as a recent convert; she was being very serious about laying herself bare, and I suppose it subtly annoyed me: I wasn't interested in being her conscience, or her mentor. I found myself more concerned with the pale blue veins in her eyelids, her scent, the golden hue of her neck and breasts. The champagne had landed on an empty stomach but I kept drinking it. I'd been careful before with her and regretted it; this time I was determined to be rash.

'What's your husband think of all this?' I said. 'Does he know where you are?'

'My husband is asleep in the arms of some actress. There's a big party going on out at Malibu. I'm sure they're all too drunk or stoned to have even noticed I'm not there.'

'And you don't mind?'

'My marriage is not very long for this world. Whatever you read about it, it's a lot worse.' She was getting that intent expression on her face again, an imploring look, as if she needed all her concentration to keep herself focused on the truth. Again, what she said had the quality of a set piece: it could have been some painful insight she'd acquired in therapy. She was a woman who was thinking very hard about her life and apparently refusing to spare herself.

'I married Paul because he's a rich and famous writer. He's a cult. I wanted to be close to someone creative. I thought some of it might rub off on me. I married him for who he is in the world, not what he is. I suppose I was attracted to him because he's such a son of a bitch. He knows what he wants and nothing stops him from getting it. I thought that was strength when, in fact, it's just ugliness on a big scale. Anyway,' she shrugged, 'I've got just

64

what I deserved. I'm rich and useless and so bored it's all I can do not to cut my wrists. So there it is. Don't ask me why I tell you all this. For some reason I want you to know the truth about me.'

'I'm glad,' I said. 'I thought you just wanted your Picasso back.'

'It wasn't the damn Picasso I wanted back.'

It was the last thing she said before I kissed her. The next time we spoke, it was as lovers lying satiated in the tangled sheets. It had been an act without finesse or imaginative preliminaries. There had been too violent a chemistry between us to allow for technique or tenderness. It was a wild, crazy rut with an ending that went off like a concussion grenade, leaving us dazed and winded. My whole being felt stunned, as if I'd been flattened by a shock wave. And I knew suddenly that she had held out just such a promise of sexual thunder the first time I'd glimpsed her; it was this experience which I'd been nosing after all these months. It was a feline jungle lust, a savage, funky itch that had nothing to do with mind or love or respect. If it was violent in its intensity, there was nothing of rape in the act. She had answered me thrust for thrust out of her own animal impulses, neither wanting or giving any quarter.

'That was my fantasy,' she said after a long while. 'How I imagined it with you.'

I held her by the ears and kissed her. I didn't have anything to say. I wasn't really ready for language yet. We lay there while our sweat dried, our bodies touching. The sky was a surly, dark yellow through the window and you could hear the scream and crack of the chaparral bending under the wind. After a while she slipped out of bed and went to the bathroom and came back with something hidden behind her back. 'Can I corrupt you with some of this?' She held out a vial of cocaine with a small spoon attached to its top. 'Really, Thomas, Sherlock Holmes mainlined the stuff and he kept his act together.'

It was one of those moments where the mind shuffles a million thoughts and hesitations, balances and weighs them. Then you do something simple, just a casual gesture but it is like the first brushstroke on a canvas that will come to haunt you.

I dipped the spoon, piled it high, raised it up and snorted deeply. Then I repeated it with the other nostril. A cool, chemical pang suffused itself through my nose and the back of my throat. Well, this is foolish, I thought, it's confusing her world with mine, an abdication of sorts, but I had not much will left. There was a tingling hush in my ears and pretty soon I felt myself in possession of a remarkable clarity. I felt solid and light, aware of the cool, sweet subtlety of things. I was one cool fool all right.

'Do you like it?' She smiled wickedly.

'I like you.' I was still, in my heart, not altogether with it and half regretted that she should feel coke was necessary, as if it was a poor reflection on me. On the other hand I sensed that she wanted to bring me something and it would be churlish to deny her that satisfaction. She helped herself. It occurred to me that she had more than likely been using it all night.

'There is plenty I still don't know about you, isn't there?' I smiled. 'Sudden trips to Morocco, orphanage childhoods, picture-book marriages . . . you're not exactly the girl next door.'

She got interested in her jewellery, twirling her bracelet around her wrist. It was a hoop of solid platinum with one bluish-white diamond cut like an emerald and surrounded by baguette diamonds. The bracelet as a whole exceeded my annual income for the last two years; she was twisting over twenty-five thousand dollars around her wrist, unhappily.

'Morocco was a dope deal – I helped some people move some grass. I'm through with dealing now. I'm too rich.' She talked in a low key, with an ironical edge she always stuck out to make sure you knew nothing was serious. 'Money is the last big illusion, money and marriage. I didn't think they were going to solve my problems. It was more like trading the old ones in for a new set.' She laughed in irritation. 'You wouldn't believe the babes I hang out with. How hard they have to work for their kicks. These rich women who shoplift out of boredom, who ball the help, who get Rolfed, hypnotized, massaged, with a different analyst for every day of the week. They're so insulated from everything. They're like people in wheelchairs who have to have their muscles artificially exercised. It's a sick scene.' She helped herself to some more coke.

'How much of this stuff do you use a day?' I asked.

'I'm a chicken, Thomas. I don't really get into anything, not even a habit. I've always been like that. I've been in drug scenes where everyone fell apart and I walked away without a scratch. I'm a survivor.' She had a sweet, twisted smile on her lips, a Madonna smile of melancholy. 'I've tried to crash because I know I deserve to get punished, but it doesn't happen. The people around me get strung out, but I don't seem to go down.'

The cool buzz of the coke was receding, leaving behind a sense of jarred nerves and fatigue. It was meant to be an aphrodisiac but it had rarely worked that way for me. I took the vial and snorted up some more.

'What is this "deserve to get punished" business?' I asked.

'I'm a conspicuously useless person.' She shrugged. 'I consume a lot of luxuries and I don't give anything back. I think eventually useless people have to pay a price.'

'So why not do something useful?' I was surprised that she should hold such a stern concept of things. 'Getting a drug habit isn't going to square the debt.'

'I know how to put on makeup and dress well. I can move drugs. That's about it. And I don't care. I'm just someone who's going to follow the line of least resistance.'

She looked bronzed and bursting with indestructible vitality. She was physically immaculate, with glossy black hair and silver-blue eyes shining in her dark face. It was the coke that made her talk like that; it let you entertain certain insights into yourself but emotionally you didn't experience them. She could run herself down all day and so long as the coke lasted it would all be just talk, painless revelations. I preferred her with a soiled face, a lost soul on Hollywood Boulevard. There was something too elegant and slick about her present despair.

'You get a little too hip for me, Laura,' I said. 'I don't believe in that kind of guilt.'

'What do you mean?' Her eyes widened with fear.

'I mean don't you put that Malibu scene down so hard. I think you get a little more out of it than you like people to believe.'

'I've gotten more here in a morning than I've gotten there ever. Ever.'

'Then how do you make it?' I was not quite over my resentment and distrust of her. 'That *is* your scene.'

She gazed around and I recognized that pinched thoughtful expression on her face that I'd seen that night in Hollywood. It was a look of obsession, a self-absorbed grimace she wore when she was cataloguing all the things wrong with her.

'Maybe,' she said softly, 'those people are so warped and trivial, I can sometimes get a good feeling from watching the act. Maybe I'm not going to stay long. I'm a whore anyway. It makes sense to live in a whorehouse, wouldn't you say?' Her eyes had darkened and the skin around her mouth looked curiously frozen. 'Oh hell, can't you see that I'm *not* making it? I ran out. I just got in my car and split. I didn't even put on any clothes.'

'Just your diamonds,' I said.

'Damn you. I wanted to look nice.' She started crying. 'I wanted to give *you* something for once instead of always feeling like a pauper.'

I gripped her wrists and pressed her backwards into the pillows. 'You look nice. You look better than anyone else who was ever in this bed. If I thought about it, I'd tell you to take your toy and pedal it back to Malibu.'

'Don't . . .' Her mouth sought mine. She arched her back to press her breasts against my chest.

'I don't want your cocaine and champagne and diamonds. I don't want any of my life mixed up with his. Do you understand? I'm not a genius. I'm not rich. I've got this small life I lead, and it fits me. I don't want my peace of mind poisoned because I feel jealous about that asshole you married.'

'Don't think about it.' Her mouth closed on mine and I felt tears sliding down her cheeks and breathed in the erotic heat of her skin, her sex, and tasted the perfumed fatigue of her mouth. The critical, suspicious machinery of my mind turned over more slowly until I thought brains were for the birds. Who needed them. Eyes were okay. A guy could use them to watch her. Hands could caress her, hold her down, move her around. Hands were necessary. And every twenty minutes or so coke was necessary to freeze out the nervous fatigue that kept creeping up my back.

There were more drinks as the afternoon wore on but they were not such good crisp drinks as the champagne. There was more sex but not so much detail or perception to it. She finally fell asleep and I studied her, with my face very close to keep her in focus. Her lips were dilated and bruised, her cheeks glowing and raw from my stubble; her hair had curled in damp, black tendrils to her brow. There was a delirious, wildly fucked glow on her and she smelled like a distillation of everything rank and sweet we'd done.

eleven

She visited me on the next three Sundays in a row, always arriving early in the morning when the all-night party at Malibu was winding down. She brought food and champagne but never any drugs. She usually stayed until late afternoon. After that first marathon confession she never told me much about herself or how things were going with Sassari. It wasn't a subject which could be casually broached without touching on her future and the future was a subject we both avoided. She used to talk about Fieldman, because he was one of the few people we knew in common. As a result of her efforts he was due to be sprung from prison in Rome. She had a fiercely sentimental side which I hadn't even guessed at. Perhaps it was growing up in the fragmented world of an orphanage, but she made almost a fetish out of loyalty. In the conventional sense she had no morals; I could have stolen something or killed someone and it wouldn't have dented her feelings towards me. She would have defended me, without asking questions, with the savagery of a lioness protecting her cubs.

Most of our talk was about me, my past, my work. She never stopped asking questions. By the third Sunday I began to notice a pattern. The one area of my life which I didn't want to discuss, Vietnam, was what she always returned to. When I asked her why, she said she had a friend, a boy she had grown up with in the orphanage in New York. He'd been drafted and done a three-year tour of duty. On his return from Vietnam she'd seen him and hardly been able to recognize him. He talked slowly, with a kind of robotlike fixity. There was something lobotomized about him, and at the same time he seemed full of fear. It was not an unusual reaction, I said, if he'd been in combat. That was the strange thing, she said. She'd asked him about it and he claimed that he couldn't remember what he'd done there. He'd drawn a complete blank on the subject. It was as though those three years were missing from his life.

At that point I got interested.

'Where is this guy now?'

'God knows,' she said. 'I haven't see him in years. He was a New York friend.'

'A boyfriend?'

'Sort of. We were pretty young and he was too shy to go to bed. When he came back, we tried once but he was impotent. It always makes me wonder about him when you talk about Vietnam.'

I had a good idea of what had happened to her friend but I wasn't sure whether to tell her or not. In the end I decided to let it lie. I had had friends in the army who suffered from similar memory blanks. Whatever they had done in Vietnam, the army had not wanted them to remember. They were debriefed in military hospitals through hypnosis and drugs like sodium pentothal, their minds programmed with posthypnotic blocks designed to trigger off intense anxiety as soon as they started to recall any sensitive material. It was often done without the individual's knowledge; he was simply tampered with, turned into a partial zombie, erased like a tape. The veterans hospitals of America were filled with guys who'd worked for the government and couldn't tell you anything about it: blank human tapes.

I remember that conversation with Laura because it made her cry. She said they had destroyed his soul. She was in a blue mood anyway, and I thought this soldier was just a pretext for other woes in her life. Still, it was like a high point of sweetness in my feeling for her. If she was cynical enough to marry Sassari for all the wrong reasons, I thought, she was also tough enough to admit it to herself. I liked her very much. I suddenly saw her compassion as she wept spontaneously over this boy's ruined life.

I decided that next Sunday I was going to ask her to leave Sassari. I was suddenly no longer satisfied with what I had of her.

twelve

That Sunday she didn't turn up. I wanted to phone her but I was afraid it might cause her trouble at home. I had to wait for her to get in touch with me. She didn't.

I went to the office on Monday morning and sat around waiting for business. The phone rang every hour or so, but none of the jobs were worth it. Most of my work came through attorneys. The little guy who took out his Yellow Pages and started phoning private investigators on his own was usually just toying with an idea he had no intention of carrying out. He was a guy who had been turned down by the glossy, expensive agencies. By the time he reached the smaller investigators with the less fashionable addresses he was in a belligerent mood, angry that he had no money to buy help, annoyed at himself for not being serious in the first place. He was a guy who wanted to prove that his wife had a secret bank account with five hundred dollars in it that she had saved behind his back. He was an ex-Scientologist who wanted the electronic bugs removed from his ten-dollar-a-day hotel room because the buzzing in the wires gave him headaches. He was a guy who knew who really killed Robert Kennedy and wanted to sell me the secret. Most depressing of all, he was a guy who had to be a flake because flakes was almost all I ever got. If you come to me for help, I thought, there's something wrong with you.

I was thinking about that when I heard the jingle of the door opening into my anteroom. The average nutcase will spin his fantasy out over the phone; the really serious screwballs just show up to tell you their stories in person.

There was a soft knocking at the door.

'Thomas?' It was Laura.

She came into the room, with her face averted.

'Don't look at me,' she pleaded.

Of course I did look at her. Her right eye was bruised, her mouth swollen so much it was hard for her to speak. She had on a padded neck brace concealed by a grey chiffon scarf.

'I'm such a fool,' she said. 'I wrecked the Aston-Martin.'

I tried to get her to sit down but she said she only had a minute. Sassari was meeting her at the doctor's and she was running late.

'I'll come tonight,' she said. 'It doesn't matter about Paul – that's over. If I can't come tonight I'll phone you at home.'

I had a million questions to ask her, but she was adamant that she had to go.

'I may have to collect the Picasso,' she said. 'I'll explain later.' She kissed me and was gone.

I stood by my desk, trying not to think, trying to put the brakes on the paranoid machinery that serves me as a brain. I wanted to trust her. I didn't want to act like a private detective, but my intuition was ringing like a burglar alarm. I heard the elevator's worn gears and frayed cables rumbling faintly through the building's bricks and plaster as she descended to the street.

I took the emergency stairs four at a time and came out on the parking lot behind my building. I was about to slip around the corner to catch her coming out of the entrance onto Hollywood Boulevard when I saw her. She was hurrying down the side street, and the neck brace was in her hand. The white Aston-Martin pulled out of a parking space. She got in on the passenger side and took off. I didn't get much of a look at the driver but there was nothing wrong with her car or her neck.

So the remission was over. Things were again no longer what they seemed with Laura Cassidy Sassari.

The evening passed slowly at home. I listened to the cars ascending Bundy Drive, trying to pick out the Aston-Martin.

But then, I thought, she wouldn't drive the Aston-Martin, because according to her it was wrecked. Maybe she has two white Aston-Martins and she wasn't lying at all. Maybe the doctor told her to only wear her neck brace a few hours a day. Maybe she lies to you just like she must lie to her husband. Maybe she's got guys stashed around the city for every day of the week.

By midnight she still hadn't telephoned, so I went to bed. There was just the faintest memory of her perfume still on the sheets, and a few strands of black hair on the pillowcases. I thought of having a few drinks and taking a pill to help me sleep but I didn't do anything about it. I must have wanted to stay clear and alert. I ended up reading until four in the morning. My reading lamp was still on when the doorbell woke me. It was nine-thirty in the morning. I got out of bed, wrapped a tangled sheet around my waist, and opened the door.

A thin, hollow-cheeked man with flat, expressionless eyes was standing there. It was hard to tell his age; he had one of those boyish faces which at first glance make a man look younger than he really is. In unpressed, grey slacks and a shapeless corduroy jacket he looked like a teacher who'd been up all night marking term papers. He stood quite still, looking hard into my face, not saying anything for just long enough that it frightened me.

'Thomas Kyd?' His voice was soft, with an almost feminine lilt. 'Marcus, Captain of Detectives L.A.P.D.' The wallet appeared in his hand already open, revealing the polished glitter of his badge. He dangled it, pinched between thumb and forefinger like a wet negative in front of my eyes. He had delicate, small white hands that went with the boyish face and the adolescent timbre of his voice. I nodded in answer to his question. As he put his wallet away, I caught a glimpse of his shoulder rig and the oiled walnut grip of his weapon.

'What's the problem, officer?'

'I'd like to ask you some questions relating to Laura Sassari.'

I don't know why I let him in – it was probably fear, fear of all the things that could have gone wrong. Once inside I expected him to make a quick visual inventory of the place, but he just stood there in the darkened room looking at the closed curtains. I went over and drew them open.

'I'm just going to put some clothes on,' I said. 'Have a seat.'

I took a pair of jeans and an old work shirt into the bathroom and put them on. I splashed cold water into my face. My hairbrush on the shelf contained some of Laura's long black hairs. I pulled them out and flushed them down the john, knowing as I did it that it meant nothing.

When I came out, he was still standing in the same spot.

'Let me read you your rights,' he said. 'You have the right to remain silent, but anything you say may be taken down and used against you.'

'Why don't you sit down?'

He glanced at me sharply. He was thin, boyish, with a high voice; they were not qualities that helped a captain of detectives. A man had to be made of something unusually fierce and intelligent to make captain with such disadvantages.

He set himself on the edge of the worn suede armchair opposite the coffee table and took out a pad and pencil.

'You own a short-barrel Mauser, registration PH8429?'

'Yes.'

'Could I see it, please?'

I walked out to the kitchen. The gun was in a plastic bag filled with oil hanging in the broom closet. I brought it out and laid it on the coffee table. He never looked at it.

'What other weapons do you own?'

'I've got some spear guns in the garage.'

'You were in the army,' he said. 'You sure you haven't got any other firearms?'

'A gun is not the kind of thing I would forget.'

'What about knives? Got any switchblades? Bayonets? Ornamental daggers?'

'The only knives I own are for cutting food.'

I studied his face but his expression was inflexible; it showed no humour, no irritation, no trace of personal feeling. It was such a well-trained face, you could almost admire it as you would admire a tool, or for that matter, a weapon.

'When was the last time you saw or spoke to Laura Sassari?'

'I'd like to talk to a lawyer before I answer that.'

'Any particular reason?' He looked up from his notebook.

'You tell me.'

He ignored my remark. 'Where were you between the hours of ten o'clock last night and four this morning?'

'I was here. Alone.'

'Did you receive any telephone calls? Is there anyone who could verify that?'

'My cat.'

Again he ignored what I'd said which, as he surely intended, only increased my anxiety. He was like a shrink: he refused to be pulled into a personal relationship. He had a knack of creating an atmosphere where your own words resounded with an unintended significance.

'Do you want some coffee?' I said.

'I'm nearly finished, Mr Kyd.' He lifted his face from the pad and leaned on me with the dead weight of his eyes.

The phone rang. I made a pained expression and picked it up. 'Yes?'

'It's Laura. Are you alone?'

'No, I already get the *Times* delivered,' I said.

'I'll call back.' She hung up.

I put the phone down and noticed the misty print of my hand on the black plastic handle. Marcus stood up.

'Any objection to me holding on to this?' He lifted the gun from the table.

'Take it.' I shrugged.

He stuffed the gun in its plastic envelope into his side pocket. 'We got your name from some people, Mr Kyd. According to them, you were or are one of Laura Sassari's lovers. We'd like to talk to her.'

'Is that all? All this talk about guns and knives. I thought it was serious.'

'I'd ask you some more questions, Mr Kyd, but you wouldn't answer them and I've got other people I need to question. Don't leave Los Angeles.'

'Listen.' I smiled. 'You tell me what this is all about maybe I can help you out. I'm ready to cooperate. I just like to know what's going on.'

'This is a murder investigation,' he said evenly. 'You can read it in the papers.' He turned and walked to the door, opened it, and stepped out. He lifted his hand and shaded his eyes against the glare. Then he looked back at me.

'I guess you can't read about it,' he said. 'It doesn't look like they delivered your paper this morning.'

I watched him walk down the garden path, unlatch the gate, and climb into a waiting brown Dodge Matador with his partner at the wheel. They took off fast like cops always do, as if the radio dispatchers just ordered them to a homicide in progress. They take off the same way when they're going around the block for coffee. High school kids in late model Chevys with lowered front ends and big Mag racing tyres also take off like that but I don't know who copied it from who.

I shut the door and stood there for a moment and tried to count how many times that icy little boy wonder of a cop had got the better of me. I was leaning against the door, teeth clenched, panting softly. My shirt was starting to stick to my skin. Why hadn't I thought of something other than not wanting the *Times* delivered to my door? Something which he couldn't have caught me out on? And he hadn't even smirked when he made that crack about the paper not coming today. No, he was superior to that. He just tossed it off: a pearl for the swine, the wise guys, the Kyds who overslept and answered the doors in sheets.

I made a pot of coffee and drank it without tasting it, looking at the overgrown back yard through the open sliding door without seeing it. There was nothing to do but wait. I sat there for the best part of an hour, chain-smoking, trying to hold my panic down.

The phone finally rang.

'It's me,' she said.

'Where are you?'

'You know that Paul is dead.' She spoke very deliberately like someone spelling out a difficult name to an operator. 'He was killed last night. I'm in a lot of trouble, Thomas.'

'I'm waiting.'

'There was a party last night, a big party. Paul was doing his usual number, coming on to everyone, making sure everyone got off. A lot of dope. A lot of swapping around. Paul was trying to set up this three-way between us and some girl. Some smacked-out TV actress. This girl was so loaded . . . it doesn't matter. Paul's been trying to get me into that stuff. I can't do it. I made a scene. I threw a glass at him and I said all kinds of things. I said I'd kill him if he tried to touch me. Everyone . . . heard me. I went up to our bedroom to call you and there were four people in our bed, people I didn't even know. They tried to get me to join in. I was hysterical. I suppose I said a lot of hysterical things. It was so sick. I locked myself in the bathroom for a long time. When I came out, I went into Paul's study to phone you. Paul was in there.' Her voice finally broke. I could hear her wheezing, struggling for breath. 'There was a knife in his chest and he'd cut his hands trying to pull it out. I tried to help him. I tried to pull it out. I couldn't pull it out. He just looked at me. I don't think he knew who I was. And then so much blood came out of his mouth that he choked. One of the guests came into the room. I don't know his name. He saw me with my hands on the knife and the blood all over me and he just backed out. He started screaming – he thought I was killing Paul.'

'Where are you?'

She wept in sudden uncontrollable anguish. It was so loud I had to hold the receiver away from my ear.

'Running doesn't sound like the greatest idea.' I tried to sound steady.

'Thomas.' She sniffed. 'I tried to be straight with you. But there are things I never told you. The police are going to find out. I'm just not . . . I always wanted you to think well of me. I've been in trouble, bad trouble.'

'Do you have a record?'

'Yes, a record. There's a record.'

'Come on, Laura!' I had to fight not to shout.

'I have possession convictions for hard drugs. I was arrested a lot when I was younger. I was a model then. It was the only work I could find after Juvenile Hall. And I got into dealing through this guy. I had all this money from modelling and I just started using it. It's like . . . it starts out so small and suddenly it's so big, there is so much money involved, people are trying to kill each other over it.'

'Yes.'

'Look, there's a warrant out on me in New York for something that happened a year ago. They want me as a material witness to testify against this friend of mine. He killed a dope dealer. He had no choice. The guy was trying to rip him off.'

'You saw it?'

'I was in the car outside. I'm an accessory unless I rat on my friend. They know about me. I tried to get out of that life. I came out to the Coast. I changed my name to Cassidy. I got married.'

'You're crazy to run from this.'

'Thomas, who'll believe me? They'll bring up my past record. They'll get that guy to testify he saw me.'

'Where are you?'

'I don't know. I'm in Westwood.'

'We'll get an attorney and you can surrender and you'll be out on bail within twenty-four hours. Use your head.'

'I'm not going back to jail for something I didn't do,' she said. 'I'm going to ask you something. If your answer is no, just say no, and pretend I never said anything.'

'Ask.'

'In that portfolio I left in your attic there's a passport. If you could leave your house for a while, someone could pick it up. That way you're not involved. I would say the Picasso is yours but it's always been yours.'

'To hell with damn Picasso. There was a cop here asking questions when you called. How did they know to come to me?'

'I'm sorry. I told people you'd helped me. Peaches probably told the police.'

'Who's helping you, Laura? You've got to trust me.'

'It's someone sticking his neck out – I promised not to give his name.'

The first gust of hysteria was over and I could feel her defences hardening. I was getting nowhere trying to convince her over the phone: I had to see her in person. If necessary I'd bring her in myself.

'Some time after eight come to the Westwood Mortuary. There's a wall on the north side. It looks like a wall of safety-deposit boxes. In the middle there's a plaque with a bouquet of roses in a brass container. The passport will be rolled up in the flowers.'

'You don't have to do this,' she said.

'It doesn't look like I'm going to be seeing you again. I don't know why I'm doing it. You're the worst fuck-up I've ever seen.'

'I didn't kill Paul,' she said. 'You've got to believe me. He beat me up. The other day I said I'd been in an accident – I didn't want you to know he'd hurt me. He did a terrible thing but I didn't want him killed.'

'The passport'll be there, but it's the last thing I ever do for you.'

'I love you, Thomas.'

'Goodbye, Laura, and good luck.' I hung the phone up.

Her passport was tucked down inside one of the plastic folds in the portfolio. It was made out to an Eva Louise Bomberg, born in New York in 1953. Hair blond, eyes blue, height five feet seven inches, weight one hundred and eighteen pounds. The photograph showed a younger Laura with curly bleached-blond hair and a great deal of eye makeup. Had she already dyed her hair blond to fit this photo, or had she waited to see if I'd bring it to her? There was a space where the bearer was meant to write down the name of the person to be notified in case of death or accident but it was empty. Cassidy, Sassari, and now Bomberg. I wondered if that space was blank on all her passports.

I had a feeling if I thought about what I was going to do, I'd change my mind. The name of the game was accessory to murder. Even if the police couldn't make it stick, the charge alone was instant death to someone in my profession. If I was caught with the passport in my possession, I'd just have to claim she'd left it in my car. It would be like those handguns which defendants up on dime murder charges always claim they found lying in the gutter in perfect working order.

It was nearly seven o'clock. Bundy Drive was quiet except for the hiss of sprinklers and the distant, fluttery beat of a helicopter heading towards the San Fernando Valley. I kept a close watch rolling down the canyon to Sunset but no one picked me up. I turned east on Sunset and followed it to the Bel-Air gate but I still couldn't spot anyone. The empty, curving streets of Bel-Air are ideal for flushing a tail. I drove randomly, at varying speeds, through the deserted, residential maze. No one seemed to be following me. Overhead nothing seemed to be going on except a classical bedroom-pink sunset observed by some burning clouds.

I cruised around Bel-Air for another twenty minutes. It was nearly half past seven. The rush hour was over; Sunset was relatively free of traffic. I made my way to Westwood with the slow, conscientious care of a man taking his first driving test.

thirteen

The landscaped green plot of the Westwood Mortuary lies hidden behind the insurance and oil company skyscrapers fronting Wilshire Boulevard. It's a small, quiet park with a few benches and trees. It's virtually unknown to the thousands of moviegoers filling Westwood Village every night. The older graves are mainly flat stone plaques which lie like giant playing cards in the grass. On the north side are three low, pale buildings, the Sanctuaries of Love, Peace, and Remembrance, each with a stained-glass ceiling and walls containing variously sized vaults and urns. In one of them a glass bookcase has been cut into the wall and a man's ashes are kept in a brass urn shaped like a book. The name of the deceased and his dates are scored on the cover like title and author. A French poet once said the whole world will one day end in a book. Anyway, this guy did. To the side of these sanctuaries there is a low wall of what look like post office boxes. Every day a florist delivers a bouquet of a dozen fresh red roses to one of the brass boxes.

At a quarter to eight I entered the grounds and let myself into the Sanctuary of Remembrance. It was not quite dark inside;

the pale night sky shone through the stained-glass ceiling. I could hear the traffic on nearby Wilshire. I stood just inside the entrance and studied the expanse of lawn, the illuminated caretaker's lodge, the cars parked along the far loop of the circular drive.

I slipped out of my shoes and padded silently over to the wall, feeling in the dark for the brass container in which the flowers were set. I curled the passport and slipped it into the brass loop. I returned to the sanctuary and set myself to wait.

I had told her the passport would be there from eight onward. I sat down on the cold stone floor just inside the entrance looking out at the wall. It was too dark to see much, but I counted on hearing anyone who approached the spot. The night wore on. The traffic, which had died down once the movies started, picked up again when they let out at ten-thirty. Around twelve-thirty there was another flurry as the late shows ended and then the streets were quiet.

I was cold, weary. I wanted a cigarette; my bladder was bursting. Hardly any light came through the stained-glass ceiling. By four in the morning I'd given up hope but I stayed on anyway. I was stretched out flat on my stomach on the cold stone floor with my chin in my hands in a mortuary waiting for a girl I'd seen driving a naked man around Hollywood. I was playing dangerously with my career, my freedom. I was thirty-six years old and I was a fool.

The birds started singing in the cemetery around five. The light turned from dark blue to blue-grey and slowly the trees revealed their outlines. A mist lay over the lawn; on the far side an automatic sprinkler came on with a soft hissing.

In a few minutes it would be light. Somewhere a Japanese gardener had already set out from home on his way to tend this small park with its lawn and flower beds. I got to my feet and dusted off my clothes. I was washed-out, stiff, as if I'd been lying submerged in a cold swamp all night.

I opened the iron gate to the sanctuary and let it bang on its hinge. As I was walking across to the wall, my footsteps resounded loudly in my ears like footfalls in an empty, tiled swimming pool. I didn't care; it was a pleasure to make a little noise.

I pulled the roses in their cellophane wrapping out of the container. They were the small, dark red variety, the petals closed, touched with dew drops as neatly formed as tiny balls of mercury. They were expensive and they smelled like the essence of everything rare and sweet but there was no passport curled around their stems.

I stared at the brass plaque and at the roses in my hand and at the wall. I turned around and looked in various directions. I felt like an ape in one of those intelligence tests puzzling over the chair which it must place on the table to reach the banana. I checked everything again but there was still no passport.

The wall was about seven feet high. I stepped back from it and took a running jump. I got my hands over the top but felt too weak to pull myself up. I finally managed it by using a near-by wheelbarrow filled with bags of fertilizer. The top of the wall extended back about six feet and dropped ten feet into some bushes on the other side. At either end there were spots where a person could have easily scaled it from outside the cemetery. I lay myself flat on the wall and reached my arm over the edge. I was a fraction over six feet; by straining I could just reach where the passport had been.

I heard a cough and froze, hanging upside down over the wall. A moment went by and I smelled tobacco smoke and then fear went off in me like a strobe. There was someone standing in the shadows of the Sanctuary of Peace, smoking a cigarette and watching me.

'That's how she did it,' I recognized the soft, adolescent lilt of Captain Marcus's voice. He came out of the shadows, hands in his pockets, the cigarette clamped between his teeth like a cigar. He looked awful: like he'd been sitting up all night in a cemetery. He grinned through his fatigue; it was if an under-taker had twisted up the corners of his lips in one of those con-fectionary simpers they paste on corpses. He bent down and re-trieved the roses and placed them back in the brass container. He read the name plate: MARILYN MONROE 1926-1962. He made a low rasping sound in the back of his throat and hurled his cigarette away.

'Get down from there.'

I did as I was told. I didn't even care when my foot split the plastic bag of fertilizer in the wheelbarrow and I got it all over my shoe. Whatever dignity I had left wasn't worth defending.

'You're a real hero,' he said. 'You are really some kind of a hero.'

I could think of no answer.

'I'm filing a report on this, Kyd. You aren't ever going to practice in this state again. I just hope your playmate doesn't get hurt when we catch her, because it'll be your fault. I'm not even going to take you in. I'm just going to let you carry on playing your games so I can really ream your ass.'

'You don't even know what I'm doing here, Captain.'

'Sure I do. You're the boy who's going to come through for her when the chips are down. You should have left it to Hollywood. What was it? Dope? A passport? Whatever it was, she screwed you. We could have had her last night. We could have staked the place out, but you're too self-important for that. You're too hip to go to the cops. You think you're defending some kind of princess against a dragon. That bitch *works* for the dragon.'

'Maybe you're wrong.'

'I'm not wrong. Killing her husband was just where she was heading. She was a hype, she pushed dope, she's wanted on an accessory-to-murder charge in New York under the name of Thompson. That's who you're helping, pal.'

'I was trying to bring her in,' I said. 'What the hell do you think I waited around for?'

'A guy like you, who knows? Maybe murdering her husband was your idea. It doesn't worry me a lot. I was watching you up on that wall. You're just bound to end up in the joint one way or another over this deal.'

'It wasn't her, anyway,' I said. 'She couldn't have reached the flowers from the top of the wall.'

He smiled contemptuously at me. 'Good thinking. You going to tell me who it was? Or what you left? Or what she told you over the phone? You got anything helpful at all?

What could I tell him? The second I opened my mouth I became an accessory to murder. Maybe I should have cooperated then and there, told him she had another passport under a name they didn't know about. What was the difference? The only reason I'd brought the passport was in order to catch her. I'd tried to fool her and she'd outwitted me and left me holding the bag. Why not rat on her forthwith? What held me back? Memories of making love to her? A hangover of mingled guilt and loyalty? It was all that, but the main thing was an impression of her as someone incapable of committing violent murder. If there was violence in her, it was self-directed on the order of putting a needle in her arm and imprisoning herself in a destructive marriage.

'You want to go the hard way,' he said. 'When we catch her, she's going to trade testimony. There's a couple of hooks she's going to slide off of and we'll hang you on them. She'll testify against that guy in New York, and she'll tell us how you helped her. We'll be grateful. Busting you on an accessory beef will round things out nicely. That's the hard way. Or you can tell me what you were doing here, and I'll ignore anything that incriminates you.'

It was a fair offer, better than I could have expected. He read my answer in my face.

'Go on, get out of here,' he said.

When I was about twenty yards away, he shouted:

'And stay out of it!'

Sure, I thought, stay out of it, but how? It was like advising the air to stay out of your lungs.

fourteen

The murder of Paul Sassari and his wife's disappearance competed that morning with the assassination of a federal judge, mass killings of Asians in Kenya, and the death of the Los Angeles Rams's star quarterback in a car crash. That was just the major competition; there was a vast oil slick at large off the

Oregon coast, famine in northern India, and gang warfare raging in Philadelphia. There was also a chilling item about a sixty-nine-year-old Encino grandmother who'd poisoned her son, her daughter-in-law, and five grandchildren with an arsenic-laced turkey dinner because they wanted to put her in a retirement home. She wasn't ready to retire yet, she told the police.

The Sassari story made the front page, bottom right-hand corner, ran six lines and then got shunted to page fourteen where it ran for several columns between the Akron and Levitz advertisements. From the way the party was described, you'd think forty harmless show-business types had assembled for an innocent evening of Scrabble and charades. There was no mention of the naked foursome in the master bedroom; nothing about the cocaine, the barbiturate fog, the heroin. The story left out the atmospheric details, and without them it wasn't possible to picture the obese and powerful being courted by the beautiful and hungry, or the ringmaster, Paul Sassari, trying to coax his hysterical wife into bed with a smacked-out starlet. There had been too many famous names at the party, too many stars and studio big shots. Scandal could sell movies but this one was bad for the industry.

The police had leaked certain sensitive pieces of information to the press. Laura was not presented as Sassari's wife so much as an impostor. She was not the former Laura Cassidy; she was Mary Thompson, wanted in New York in connection with another murder. I was wanted, too. 'Police are seeking Thomas Kyd, a Los Angeles-based private investigator, for information on Miss Thompson's whereabouts.'

It was not as bad as it could have been; they might have said Thomas Kyd was having ecstatic carnal relations with the suspect for the past month.

When I got home, I checked with my answering service: I had had calls from four newspapers to my home number and a few early calls at my office, all asking to be phoned back. I didn't know any of their names but I tried them all. They were as I'd expected, curiosity seekers who'd been alerted by the mention of my name in the newspaper.

'I don't know what's wrong with the police,' the last one told me. '*I* found you.'

'You did, indeed.'

'That's all really,' he said cheerfully. 'I just wanted to know if you were there.' He hung the phone up.

It had seemed like a call from an innocent nutcase and maybe it was. They were probably all meaningless calls. Still, when the last guy had said, 'I just wanted to know if you were there,' it made me suspicious. Laura might choose to find out if I'd returned from the cemetery by having someone call me.

I forced myself to eat some breakfast and then showered and changed into fresh clothes. It was pointless to wait around for Laura to call and explain because she wasn't playing it that way. She didn't trust me. She had probably never trusted me. Her whole relationship with me had been a series of unveilings and disappearing acts: something happened and I interpreted it a certain way and then at a later date I discovered I was wrong. The illusion was then replaced by the truth; history got rewritten, but that truth in time turned back into another illusion. I kept peeling her back and thinking I'd reached the last layer, the last veil, but I was really further away than I'd ever been. I remembered how my early reaction to her had been dominated by a desire not to know. My intuition had warned me off her. Now she was no longer playing dangerously with just her life; we had become linked like Siamese twins to a point where her actions were rebounding on my flesh. What if that haunting, lovely face of hers was a masterwork of treachery? What if Marcus was right and she was a killer? Then many things would be finished for me apart from my career; the springs of self-respect and conscience would be poisoned. I could have refused to help her and gone to the police but I hadn't. Now I could just hope for her innocence.

And there was the Picasso, too. That was mine now, she'd said. I wondered if, like so much else about her, that too was not what it seemed. It was all she'd left; it would be a masterly stroke if she had bought my loyalty with a counterfeit.

There was an antique gun sale on at Sotheby Parke-Bernet, and the busy receptionist told me I would have to make an appointment if I wanted to see anyone in any of their departments. I said that was too bad. I had this Picasso drawing I wanted to sell. I didn't suppose it was worth much. It was of a bullfight, but the figures in it were all these ugly three-eyed women who didn't even look like real people. Picasso must have been drinking when he drew it, I said. It was just something I'd inherited. The truth was, I needed a new transmission on my pickup truck and I thought maybe I could get something for it.

There are doors which nothing but the appearance of stupidity will open. The receptionist stared at me as if I'd just pulled a live turtle out of my mouth. She stammered something about having misunderstood me and in her confusion stubbed her cigarette out in the well of her typewriter.

'It doesn't matter.' She waved it away. 'You want to see Miss Wykham-Tenent, the head of the European Painting Department.'

She phoned through, smiling raptly at me, never taking her eyes off me. I guess there's something about a sucker that touches the world's heartstrings. She was only the receptionist. She wasn't going to make a dime off me but liked the idea. She just loved it in principle. I put my hands in my pockets, tilted my head back and stared around with the air of a country boy awed by his first visit to a museum of art. I let my mouth hang open a little.

She held a whispered conversation and then put the phone down and came out from behind her desk.

'Right this way, sir.' She swished down a corridor, looking back at me over her shoulder with her shiny eyes and shrewdly pursed smile. 'No, that's the men's room, sir,' she said. 'You want this door.'

'Got you.' I nodded.

'Good luck.' She leered encouragingly as she ushered me into an office. 'And have a nice day.'

Suddenly I was having one. Miss Wykham-Tenent was coming towards me from behind her desk, her fine, white hand rising to take mine, involving me in her perfume, lingering nicely close as she sat me down. She was English, in her late twenties, with long charming legs and light grey eyes. They worked hard, those eyes. They were all over my face and hands and clothes inquisitively and openly taking me in. We sat there on opposite sides of the desk looking each other over, making eye contact, and flaring our nostrils like two evenly matched dogs who might yet end up going for each other.

'I don't think there's anything wrong with *your* transmission,' she finally said. 'I seem to know you. Do I know you?'

'I don't know. I'm sure it's impossible.'

'Oh.' She fitted a small cigar into a blunt, yellow jade holder and lit it from a box of kitchen matches on her desk. 'Why?'

'I would remember.'

'Charming of you to say so.' She watched me with her forefinger pressed thoughtfully against the side of her nose. 'Who are you, Mr Kyd? You don't seem quite the person the receptionist described.'

'I'm a private investigator.'

I didn't need to tell her, but it was interesting to see her face change. She had the common reaction which is something like an oyster reacting to a squirt of lemon juice. I might as well have said, 'I've got tertiary syphilis.'

'I'm not here as a private investigator.' I smiled.

'Good.'

'I just like to tell people. It's the kind of thing if they find out later they tend to feel they've been deceived, so I just try to pop it in as quickly as possible.'

She was still not quite recovered; whatever thoughts had sprung to mind at being confronted with a private detective were still with her.

'Not a child molester, not an axe-murderer, just a private detective on his day off.'

'Of course.' She got herself back into focus. 'There's this beastly man who's suing us. I accidentally spilled coffee over his Rowlandson print and he's been very unpleasant about it. I thought you were from him. I could lose my job over it.'

'That's tough.'

'Well, it is really. I've got an ex-husband who's always trying to prove I earn a huge amount of money so he can slither out of paying the child support. I thought you might be from him, too. Shall we have a look at what you've brought?'

I laid the portfolio on her desk and opened it to the drawing.

She leaned her face forward as I did it and for an instant I was so close I could sense the heat of her skin. It was as smooth as soap with a touch of a red glow under the cheekbones. She had the complexion of a Celt: very white with a wine-red blush put there by a thousand years of Irish mist. She studied the drawing carefully and then closed the portfolio.

'It's an original,' she said.

'Any idea what it's worth?'

'The last time we auctioned it off, it fetched six thousand dollars.' She gave me a cool, rather sad look. 'Do you actually own this drawing, Mr Kyd?'

'I'm told I do.'

'Would you be willing to tell me whom you got it from?'

'It was given to me by a woman called Laura Cassidy.'

She sat back in her chair and gazed at me, perplexed, dubious, with more than a little curiosity. 'Correct me if I'm wrong, but is this Laura Cassidy the lady who the police are looking for?'

'That's the one.'

'And you're that private investigator . . .'

'I've already spoken to the police,' I said. 'That item about me was out of date before they printed it. I was given the drawing as a gift. I'm just curious to know what it's worth and whether it's hers to give away.'

'Imagine just giving you a Picasso.' She dipped her light grey eyes and something seductive in her voice hardened into mockery. 'You must have been terribly close to her.'

'I knew her before she married Sassari.'

'Do you believe she actually murdered her husband?'

'I can't believe it,' I said. 'But I don't know why I'm telling you.'

'I'm a bit mad. That's probably why. People tell me all kinds of things. I think they imagine I'm rather too scatterbrained to understand properly.'

She was about as scatterbrained as a NASA computer.

'Would you like to know the details of its sale?' she asked.

I told her that was exactly what I'd like to know.

'We sold it for a French dealer and it was bought by Peaches Romaine.' She clicked her jade cigarette holder against her teeth. 'But you see, I've seen it since then. It was brought in June by a man for appraisal. He was in a terrible rush and wanted us to advance him money on it because our next sale wasn't until midsummer.'

'What was this man's name?'

'If this is your day off, I'd hate to see you when you're working.' Something about her communicated the message that I would have to give something more of myself if I wanted the information. She was on the verge of telling me to go.

'I had an affair with Laura Cassidy. My interest in this drawing is about that affair, really. Someone gives you something and you want to know if they had the right to do it. I want to know how on the level she was. About certain things she wasn't entirely honest.'

That line of approach appealed to her more. A man in love is naturally interesting to a woman: I had offered her the possibility of perhaps undermining that love with some piece of information which only she held.

'His name was . . .' She skipped through her desk diary. 'Raymond Kepler. It was quite legitimate. He had a bill of transfer from Peaches Romaine. I remember him quite well. I thought he was English. He spoke like an Englishman, rather dry and very outrageous and I suspect quite pissed. He's an American, actually, but he was educated in England. Do you know him?'

'I met him once.'

'Perhaps he gave it to your Laura Cassidy.'

It seemed like an expensive gift for someone who'd been described as Sassari's secretary. If he was in such a rush to raise money on it, he wouldn't give it away, nor did I see Laura as the type to have a spare six grand to invest in a work of art.

'We didn't advance him any money on it,' she said. 'I wanted to – he made me laugh – but I was outvoted.'

'I'll make some inquiries. Could I leave this with you?'

She gave me a form to sign proving I'd left it in their keeping for appraisal and a receipt. Then she slid her business card over the desk. It had her full name, Augusta Wykham-Tenent, on it.

'If you decide to sell, I hope you go through us,' she said. 'I rather get the impression this business is masses more involved than it seems but I do wish you luck. I must say, you must have done something rather wonderful for her to give you such a valuable gift. I'm rather curious about that part.'

'In what way?'

'But it's fascinating, surely.' She'd come around from behind her desk to walk me to the door. She seemed to be standing awfully close to me, with her face lifted, and her eyes dipped at half-mast. Suddenly she reached out and ran her hands down the sides of my chest. 'No gun?' She sighed thoughtfully. 'I thought all you sleuths carried them.'

'Try again,' I said.

'Really? Have you got one?' She narrowed her eyes; they held a cold speculative glow of excitement. For some reason I was reminded of the playacting that went into childhood games with girls: the official role of doctor one adopted to get them to take their pants off. 'I don't believe you.' She started to pat me down again and I caught her in my arms. I tried to kiss her mouth but she turned her face away, her body stiffening.

'You must be mad,' she said. 'I don't even know you. This is insane.'

I wasn't violent but I was persistent and I ended up kissing her. She wasn't passionate so much as affectionate; it was a tender, teenager's kiss. After about thirty seconds she disengaged and firmly pushed me out of the door.

'You've got lipstick all over you,' she said. 'Goodbye now . . . goodbye . . .'

I found the men's room and washed her lipstick off my neck and lips, but I couldn't get it off my collar. I couldn't get the dreamy, glazed look off my face either.

fifteen

The lamp on my office desk lit a rich fire in the dissolving golden depths of the Scotch. I turned the glass slowly around in my hands, watching the changing play of light in the liquor and ice. It was a hundred-watt bulb and twelve-year-old Scotch and the visual effect was as fancy as sunlight filtering through a stained-glass cathedral window. I should have been home in bed instead of waiting in my office, but the hours had passed and I'd hardly moved from my desk. There was something out there in the city that wasn't done with me. The sounds of night traffic on Hollywood beat at the office windows while a red flush of neon filled and emptied the walls at two-second intervals. Now and then sirens wailed off in the distance; ambulances and police cars contributed their chorus to the soundtrack of the city. With the red neon washing the walls and the raw, baying panic of the sirens, the office felt like a waiting room in hell.

I got tired of looking into my glass of Scotch so I poured it down my throat and slowly built another one.

When the phone rang an hour later, I had still not touched my second drink.

'Is that Thom-uus Kee-id?' It was a phony voice; it sounded like he had a sock over the receiver and nose-clips on. As an extra touch he was talking in an imitation hick accent.

'This is Kyd.'

'Joe DiMaggio here.' He snickered. 'You know, the old ball player who sends those roses to Marilyn.'

'Hi, Joe.'

'You're a fink, Kyd. You don't fool me. I just wanted to let you know that you don't fool me.'

'Who is this?'

'Joe DiMaggio, I told you.'

'You just struck out, Joe.' I hung up carefully.

In a minute the phone rang again. I opened my desk drawer, pulled out my recording attachment and connected it. I wanted this character for posterity.

'Yes?' I answered.

'Hanging up on me isn't going to help you.'

'I can see that, Joe. But sometimes people like you only have one dime.'

'You're the problem,' he said. 'You're not part of the solution.'

It was no good trying to have a straight conversation with him. He was playing it as a lunatic, jamming me with non sequiturs, mystery clues, private jokes.

'What was Marilyn like, Joe?' I asked. 'Was she as good as they said?'

'I'm not Joe DiMaggio,' he growled. 'You can call me Joe, but it isn't my real name.'

'All you people from outer space use false names. I know.'

'Wrong,' he said. 'I'm from *inner*space. That's how I knew you were hiding there. You and your cop friend. You want to know something?'

'Sure.'

'I'm not Joe DiMaggio. I'm really Clark Kent. I'm in a phone booth right now changing into my Superman duds. That's how I saw you in the dark, sucker – I've got X-ray vision.' He gave me a short, obscene raspberry and banged the phone down.

I read the time and date into the machine and switched it off. I nibbled at my drink and then played the tape back. Whoever he was, he had been at the cemetery and he knew Laura. His craziness sounded as assumed as his heavily disguised voice. His motives for calling me were another matter, but there was a definite competitive edge to his remarks; he had wanted me to know that he'd got the better of me. But what was the problem of which I was not the solution? I didn't fool him but presumably I fooled someone: Laura? Had she been standing there while he was on the phone?

Joe DiMaggio didn't have any trouble getting in touch with me. Why didn't she call me?

I opened the windows as wide as they would go to air out the office. I thought of the tongue-lashing Marcus had given me at the cemetery and wondered if, after all, his contempt wasn't justified. He believed absolutely in Laura's guilt. What did I believe? What could I believe after the phone call from Joe DiMaggio? I didn't even know if Laura was still in the city. The passport might have already done its work; Eva Bomberg might be recovering from jet lag in a hotel room on the other side of the world, congratulating herself on a successfully accomplished murder.

I locked up the office and went home but I barely slept that night. In that bed I had been caressed by hands that might yet prove to have killed a man. It was a thought to touch off the keenest kind of terror, for I'd helped her and was still helping her by my silence.

sixteen

I called my service after breakfast the next morning. The newspapers were still trying to get hold of me and there was another list of people who wanted me to return their calls. Perhaps among the dozen or so names there was one that would turn out to have some legitimate business, but only one interested me: Dix Landau, Sassari's literary agent. He was to be reached at the Malibu number.

A man answered on the second ring and growled, 'Sassari residence. Can I help you?'

'This is Thomas Kyd. I'm returning Mr Landau's call.'

There was a pause and the voice dropped in volume.

'I got to talk to you. This is Fieldman.'

'How are you, Fieldman? I thought you were still in Rome.'

'Yeah, well I'm not, am I? I'm in Malibu, California, USA, home of the stars. It's important I talk to you, understand?'

'Sounds like a conversation to me.'

'Private talk.'

Landau picked up another extension and told Fieldman to hang up.

'Can you come out here right away?' he said. 'I think you could help us on something – it's important.'

'Certainly.'

'There are all kinds of reporters outside the house. For God's sake don't talk to them, or tell them who you are.'

'I wouldn't do that.'

'I just want to warn you not to,' he said testily. 'Please hurry.'

It was childish of me, but his anxiety gave me pleasure. I had a vague confidence that when things went badly for Landau they were somehow starting to tilt more in my favour.

It was overcast along the Pacific Coast Highway. The ocean was still and glassy, just barely going through the motions of breaking on the shore of the deserted beach. I pulled off on the shoulder of the road about fifty yards from Sassari's house, crossed the highway, and began checking house numbers. Up ahead of me several media wagons were parked outside the Sassari driveway, with photographers and technicians leaning on them.

'Good afternoon.' I approached a photographer. 'I'm from the Board of Architectural Examiners. Could you tell me where number eighty-nine hundred is?'

'You're standing in front of it. Something wrong with the place?'

I looked at the house: the low-pitched roof projecting enormously at the eaves and gables, the cutesy, scalloped shutters, the carved balcony where you expected to see Julie Andrews belting out 'The Sound of Music'. Instead of the Bavarian Alps it was backdropped by the vast, windless expanse of the Pacific Ocean.

'What's wrong with the house?' the photographer insisted.

'Termites,' I said stiffly.

'You know whose place this is?'

'That movie-writer guy. I don't care about that.'

'We want to know who's in there. We're looking for a story.'

'I'm just here for termite inspection. They told me to check the foundations and that's all they told me.' I tried to look stubborn and stupid which for some reason has always been easy for me. The photographer turned away in disgust and told the others.

'He's a goddamn termite inspector. We'll try and get a shot when they open the door.'

I walked over the arched wooden bridge and glanced down into the still waters below. Some goldfish cruised back and forth along the glittering white gravel bed, pale bloated creatures with warts and protuberant eyes. The bottom was littered with debris from the party: green splinters from a broken champagne bottle, a paper cup, a pair of shattered sunglasses, a disposable cigarette lighter. The objects looked picturesque, as if they'd been consciously arranged to provide some colour and amusement for the fish.

The door opened before I could ring the buzzer and Fieldman let me into the hallway. He had lost weight in prison, lost his suntan, lost his gold jewellery, and lost his hairpiece. One of his front teeth was missing. It suited him better; he looked more human without the glossy matinee-idol props.

'I got to have a word with you,' he said. 'After you talk to Landau.'

'Okay.'

'That day you came out here. I had to give you a hard time. No hard feelings?'

'Forget it.'

We shook hands. Without the extra weight his eyes looked larger; the broken tooth added to the impression he gave of being a crafty old hustler.

'I fought Golden Gloves,' he said. 'I could have murdered you but I knew the score. You saved my ass that day.'

He was the only person I had in common with Laura and for a moment I felt partial to him.

'I didn't know you'd arrived.' Landau appeared at the end of the hall and frowned pointedly at Fieldman. 'We're in the kitchen.'

As I squeezed by Fieldman, I told him to wait for me by my car down the road.

The air in the kitchen was blue with cigarette smoke and soured by the smell of burned coffee.

A woman in her late twenties was sitting at the table, head in hand, with a pile of wadded-up Kleenex and a mug of coffee steaming in front of her. No makeup, lots of springy, brown curls, an unusual woman with a nice, soft, decadent feel about her. She had a white, dreamy face as round as a coin and faintly slanted brown eyes marked by a Mongolian fold. She had been crying and from the look she gave me, it was clear she had plenty more tears in reserve.

'This is Anne Kepler.' The agent introduced us with an irritated wave of his hand. 'Raymond's wife. Anne is my personal assistant.'

'I'm glad you've come,' she said in a small voice. Her hand crept to her chest and checked that her blouse was buttoned. It was a brown silk blouse, cut very tight, with small, shiny black buttons. Laura had been wearing it the night I met her on Harper. Had Laura given it to her, or had Kepler's wife already started looting Laura's wardrobe? It was a glamorous article of clothing and didn't go with Mrs Kepler's long peasant dress.

'Before I tell you a thing,' Landau began forcefully, 'I have to know you'll remain absolutely silent about it.'

To show him how good I was at keeping quiet I didn't say a thing.

'I've come to you because I'm going to have to trust you. That's all there is to it.'

The prospect of trusting someone clearly ran counter to all Landau's instincts. There was a nervous distaste evident in all his movements; he was performing a pantomine of an anxious man, moving about the room, rubbing his hands, changing the position of chairs.

'I'm a private investigator,' I said. 'Keeping quiet is my business, Mr Landau.'

'I know that.' He stared at me, suspecting mockery. Something about his behaviour suggested to me that he was putting on a show for Anne Kepler. He seemed determined to put me in my place in front of her. 'And what are your fees?'

'It depends on the job. A hundred dollars a day and expenses usually covers it. Expenses are gas, phone calls, meals, parking tickets. By meals I mean take-out food. Why don't you tell me what it's about first? It might be something a different kind of agency could handle better.' I threw the modesty in just in case it showed that I was interested enough to pay him the hundred bucks a day to work on the case.

'You don't sound very eager for the work,' he said.

'I don't know what the work is yet.'

As he studied me, I felt the slightest sign of eagerness on my part or ingratiation would have decided him against me. It was as if he knew he could only trust someone who didn't even particularly want the job.

'For God's sake, tell him,' Anne Kepler hissed.

Landau winced around the eyes; there was something in her voice which he reacted to like the threat of a physical blow. He gave a sick smile, shut his eyes briefly like a man about to take a plunge.

'All right,' he said. 'Mrs Kepler's husband is missing. He hasn't been seen or heard of since about two o'clock Sunday morning. He was at the party and as far as we know, he left about an hour after the police came. He'd been drinking pretty heavily, but we didn't take much notice because, well . . .'

'Because he's always like that.' Anne Kepler gave me a pained smile. 'Dix is being polite, Mr Kyd. My husband is an alcoholic. I'm told that it's better to use that word. To face it directly. All right, Raymond is an alcoholic. He's also a very fine and sensitive and kind person. He's more than an alcoholic and that's why he's run away.'

'Could you be a little more specific? I know this is painful.'

I noticed Landau was looking bored and impatient. She glanced at him and said:

'Paul and Raymond and I were all at UCLA together. We graduated the same year. Raymond has never done as well as Paul. He was angry with Paul the night of the party because Paul refused to give him money. My husband gambles. He has terrible debts. When Paul was killed, I think Raymond overreacted. He felt guilty. He'd been furious with Paul and suddenly Paul was dead. I know how Raymond's mind works. He blames everything on himself.'

'That may all be so,' Landau broke in, 'but there's more to it. There's a script missing. Paul's script. Raymond took the script, the early drafts, the notes, the wastepaper, the whole damn thing. This isn't any old script. This is the root of a seven- maybe eight-million-dollar picture. We've got nothing but a four-page outline registered at the Screenwriters Guild. We've got investors lined up. We've got stars committed. I mean if he loses this thing, it's a calamity.'

'Why would Raymond take off with the script?' I said.

'Now *that* is what I'd like to know,' the agent said. 'It's only three-quarters finished. Raymond is a natural choice to help finish it. Paul discussed a lot of his ideas with Raymond. Damn it, you'd think he'd jump at the chance.'

'Who owns the script?'

'Paul does. We have deals pending the completion of this screenplay. *Big* deals. But when your writer is murdered and his script is stolen you can kiss your deals goodbye.'

'How do you know it was Raymond who took the script?'

'He'd been typing it up in Paul's study on Saturday morning.' Landau reddened a little under Mrs Kepler's scrutiny. 'Since he disappeared and the script did too, I assumed that Raymond took it.'

'When was the last time you saw the script?'

'Late Saturday morning. It was all laid out. I saw the filing cards and the boxes with the discarded pages and the script itself.'

'I presume that as soon as Paul was discovered, that study was full of people.'

'Yes. I was one of the first. Of course the study had been cleaned up. The script had been put away in the desk. I only looked then because a detective asked me if anything was missing.'

'So the police know the script is gone?'

'No, of course not. I didn't tell the police, because the police would have told the papers, and I didn't know who'd taken the damn thing.'

'And I presume you're not interested in pressing charges against Raymond?'

'All we want is the damn script,' he said. 'And Raymond, of course. We're naturally worried about Raymond.'

'How do you know that Laura didn't take it?'

'I don't. But it seems unlikely. She was in hysterics. She went out the window and jumped off the roof. I don't see her doing that with her arms filled with manuscript pages.' He said it bitterly. She had killed the goose that laid the golden eggs. 'Of course,' he went on, 'there's Fieldman, who seems to be under the illusion that Paul owed him a considerable sum of money for the

99

prison sentence he served in Rome. I wouldn't put anything past Fieldman except that if he had the script, he would have already offered to sell it back.'

'Was it just an illusion that Paul owed him something?'

'Anything that isn't down on paper is an illusion in my book.' Landau snorted. 'If he thinks he's going to get anything out of me as Paul's agent, or out of Peaches, he's out to lunch.'

'Right. We'll leave Fieldman out of it.' I nodded sympathetically. 'It's Raymond we want to find and the script.'

'I don't know how you're going to do it,' Landau said hopelessly. 'We've exhausted every possibility.'

'Would you say your husband is the kind of man to go on a binge when he's upset, or would he hole up somewhere and think about it?'

'I don't know.' She groped for the Kleenex box. 'I *know* him and I don't know where he is. I don't see how a perfect stranger will be able to locate him.'

'He gets off on horses, college games, pro ball, right?'

'Yes.'

'When he can't pay his bookmaker, he tries to hit people for cash?'

'It's a disease,' she said. 'He can't help himself.'

'Take it easy, Mrs Kepler. If he's gambling, we'll find him. Does he go out to bars to watch the games?'

'Yes.'

'You know which bars? You know any of his bookies?'

'I know some of the bars he goes to, because when I empty his pockets to hang up his clothes I find cocktail napkins and matches. One place is called The Blue Bird in West Hollywood. And there's another called Daddy's Girl in Venice. I heard him on the phone once asking to talk to Baltimore Red, and another time to someone called Fruitcake.'

'What about a shy?'

'I don't know what that is.' She looked helplessly at Landau.

'A shylock. A loan shark. Someone who loans out money above the legal interest rate on short term.'

She gazed blankly at me.

'I don't know your financial condition, but compulsive gambling runs into big money. Chances are there've been times when he had to use a shy.'

'Is this the best way to go about finding him?' Landau said. 'Raymond isn't an underworld figure. I hope you appreciate that.'

'Bookies and shylocks keep tabs on their clients, Mr Landau. If Raymond isn't where he's supposed to be and he owes people money, those people are going to be looking for him. So my instinct is to check those bars and run down his bookies. They'll talk to me. They want him for the same reason you do. He's got something of theirs.'

There wasn't much he could say to that. While he was making me out a cheque, Mrs Kepler wrote down the information I'd asked for and gave me a photograph of Raymond, Sassari, and herself taken in the UCLA sculpture garden. There was an older man in the picture. A small dark European-looking man in a Panama hat. I asked Mrs Kepler who he was.

'That was one of our professors.' She stared at the photograph. 'The promising class of sixty-nine and look where it ended up.'

'You all studied under him?'

'Professor Bustamente, yes.'

Landau glanced impatiently at the photograph. 'Bustamente's got nothing to do with this. He'd be the last person to know where Raymond is.'

'Oh, why's that?' I asked.

'It's a very long, boring story.' Landau scowled. 'Damn it, don't you have another picture, Anne?'

'That's all right, Mrs Kepler.' I pocketed the snapshot. 'This is good enough.' I turned to Landau. 'Could you just tell me one thing that I don't understand. If Raymond took the script, it must have been *before* Sassari was murdered. Presumably he couldn't have known that was going to happen. So what could he hope to gain by taking it? The very worst thing he could do would be to destroy it. But so what? Presumably Paul could re-write it. How could he have known Laura was going to kill Paul that night?'

'Of course not.' Landau looked confused.

'Of course not what?'

'Of course he didn't know Laura would do that. What are you trying to say?'

'I'm just trying to construct a possible motivation for taking an uncompleted screenplay. In Raymond's case it doesn't make sense.'

'Damn it, neither Anne nor I understand this,' Landau said angrily. 'It may be that Laura took the script.'

'Why should she do that?'

'Revenge. I don't know.'

'She got her revenge, though.'

'You've got all the answers,' he said frostily. 'I hope you can do the one thing we've hired you to do.'

I looked at him steadily. 'Give me a break,' I said. 'You're asking me to find a missing person without telling me why he's missing. Okay. You don't know. I do a lot of missing person work and I know that when people run away, it's because they're under some intolerable pressure. I also know that they tend to do certain characteristic things. They go back to people and places which meant something to them in the past. They try to retrace their steps. They contact old flames, look up childhood friends, revisit spots where they were happy, or where their lives changed. I've found a lot of older men sitting in the playgrounds of schools they attended as kids, or in a bar they hadn't been to since they were married. That's why I asked about Professor Bustamente. Apart from Baltimore Red and Fruitcake, it's the only name I've got.'

'Maybe I'm overexcited,' Landau conceded. 'But I can assure you, Bustamente is the last person in the world who'd know where Raymond is, or care.'

'I guess you've both had a damn rough time.' I shook my head. 'I still can't believe Laura could do a thing like that.'

'Terrible thing.' Landau nodded vehemently. 'I'm a good friend of Vern Mazo, the guy who caught her . . . doing it. I can tell you, he's been in a state of shock ever since.'

I paused at the door. 'By the way, what's the script called?'

'*Shoot the Singer*,' he said. 'It's about an American soldier in Vietnam in one of the assassination squads. His Vietnamese girlfriend is killed and he goes looking for the killers and slowly, piece by piece, he reconstructs the crime. In the end he discovers that it was he who killed her. It's going to be a real indictment of the war.'

'Was Sassari in Vietnam?' I asked.

'Of course not.' Landau was horrified. 'He was against it. Were you there?'

'Up to here in shit and blood,' I said.

'I can imagine.' He looked at me uneasily. 'Yes, I feel somehow that Paul would have wanted us to do everything possible to make his movie. In its way it's a very radical, courageous movie.'

I wanted to ask him where all the radical courage had been during the war but I knew the answer: the closest Hollywood got to the subject was John Wayne zapping the Cong in his green beret. But time heals all wounds; it was as if the statute of limitations had run out on the crimes of Vietnam; the subject was finally dead enough to be good box office. The war could be safely resurrected, its horrors dusted off and dramatically structured for public consumption. America could get a final thrill out of that violently staged nightmare, with the added bonus of some painless moral indignation. One way or another, I thought, they will get you. The irony wasn't lost on me; it was burning me up like some corrosive in my blood. In a roundabout way I was now working for Paul Sassari and Landau. By finding the script, I would help them mine that ugliest of wars for its entertainment value. And I would do it, too. It would be the final betrayal of those poisonous visions which haunted me still. There was a way to make a buck in these times without betraying yourself, but it was a trick I'd never mastered.

'A terrible war.' Landau nodded earnestly.

'I'm sure it'll make a great movie.' I put away my notepad and told Mrs Kepler in my best bedside manner that she was not to worry because chances were, Raymond would surface of his own accord.

'And not a word to the police,' Landau cautioned me. 'That's why we're hiring you.'

I left then because I knew if I didn't leave, his gift for the obvious would have me ripping my hair out.

seventeen

When I got back to my car, I found Fieldman dozing in the passenger seat. I got in behind the wheel and nudged him. He didn't wake up with a start; he sort of flowed back into consciousness with a lazy smile on his lips and something fixedly radiant about his eyes.

'I must have dozed off,' he said. 'It's jet lag.'

'Beat it.'

'What's the matter?' He was outraged. 'What did I do?'

I leaned across him and opened his side door.

'Out.'

'What's happening, man?'

'You are stoned, man, that's what's happening.'

'What are you talking about?'

'You want to have a conversation with me and the first thing you tell me is a lie.'

'A little taste. I had a little taste. You don't know what it's been like for me.'

'Don't jive me, Fieldman. You fixed. You can hardly keep your eyes open.'

'All right.' He rubbed his face with his hands. 'I'm loaded.'

'That's better.' I smiled. 'See how easy I am to please? The simplest things make me happy. Someone doesn't lie to me and I'm ready to weep for joy.'

'To hell with you,' he muttered. 'How do you think I feel? You think it's been easy for me? I kicked cold turkey in the wop jail. It was so bad I had fits. I knocked my own goddamn tooth out. For what? So that sawed-off guinea motherfucker could go free?'

'Sassari's dead.'

'That is too bad because I can't kill him.' He looked at me, his head very faintly nodding, his features tranquillized. It was bizarre to hear such venom coming out of a placid face. 'You don't think I'd have killed him?' he asked. 'You don't know Morris Fieldman. *Nobody* does that to me.'

'I know. You're so tough you ended up taking the rap for him.

You're such a heavy customer, you came back and started hanging around again like old times.'

'I was going to get him,' he growled. 'Don't worry about that. I was going to get my bread if I had to squeeze it out of him.'

I let him ramble on in that vein for a while longer: he had been duped, exploited, lied to, and betrayed. He had suffered greatly; even his drug habit was Sassari's fault. And now he was owed something for his pains. They owed him, whoever they were. He was full of bravado and dark threats about the revenge he would exact. It was an obsession: his self-respect demanded compensation.

'They sentenced me to ten years, man!' he wailed 'Ten long years!'

'You served a couple of months.'

'That's not the point. Sassari was going to let me do the whole ten for his dope.'

'Your dope, too.'

'Man, he was going to sell me out. It was Laura who sprung me.'

'Who cares? You knew what Sassari was. You must have seen him double-cross plenty of people in your time. You didn't give a damn about them. Where do you get off feeling so sorry for yourself now?'

'You don't know what that family did to me,' he said. 'I worked six years for Peaches. I've been the best friend that bitch ever had. I kept her son out of trouble. I tried calling Peaches collect from Rome. She wouldn't accept the call! Can you believe that? And Paul. You know what that rancid, evil bastard told me when I got back? He says maybe he can find some stunt work for me. *Maybe!* He's not sure though, because people are funny about hiring a guy with a record. No apologies, no explanation. I'm supposed to beg him for a job. No, sir. I don't beg. My begging days are over because, in the end, there are things which can't be forgiven. Oh, man,' he said gloomily, 'if you knew what a royal screwing I got.'

I didn't say anything. I'd wanted to get him angry so he'd talk, but so far he'd stuck furiously to the subject of his persecution. 'I suppose,' – he got his eyelids open enough to give me a slow, calculating glance – 'you're working for Landau now. He'd like his precious script back.'

'Why, do you have it?'

'Who? Little old me?' He shrugged and stared with a sullen slack expression at the passing traffic. 'No, I haven't got it. If I'd been smart, I would have it. But I've got something which ought to be just as good.'

'Sure you do. You're just bursting with valuable information.'

'That's right,' he said reflectively. 'Too bad you're working for Landau, or I could cut you in on it.'

'I can smell losers, Fieldman. You haven't got a damn thing.'

'Oh yeah? I know a few things about the great and gifted Paul Sassari that his mother would like to keep about as secret as her real age. I know that, too. She's fifty-six.'

'Thanks for the big tip. The door's open. Just lean to the right and you'll fall out.'

'You're no better than the rest of them,' he said grimly to himself. 'You think I'm full of shit. That's all right. We'll see who comes out of this on top. You think Raymond took that script, you don't know anything about human nature. He hasn't got the guts to even take what's his.'

'Why did Peaches give that Picasso drawing to Raymond?'

'Wouldn't you like to know.' He smiled knowingly to himself. 'Why did Peaches endow the UCLA theatre arts programme?' he said tauntingly.

'How did Laura end up with the drawing?'

'Oh, that.' He yawned. 'Laura was always a soft touch. She probably bought it from him as a favour because he was in a jam. He's a drag, Raymond. His whole life is one long jam.'

'Thanks for the help, Fieldman.' I started my car. 'Let me return the favour. You keep shooting up and making threats to blackmail people, someone's going to do something about you.'

'Who?' he demanded. 'I got a legitimate beef.'

'Whoever killed Sassari.'

'What are you talking about?' He was scared. 'Laura did it.'

I leered at him, saying nothing, with the faintest trace of scorn.

'When you're ready to tell me something.' I said, 'I might let you in on a little secret about that. But I doubt it. You know, she used to talk about you a lot, Fieldman. She went to considerable pains to free you from jail. She told me you were one of the best friends she had. You were a guy, she told me, who saw beneath the surface of things. It's funny that you can't see any further than the cops.'

It's hard to play on a junkie's sense of shame; the drug insulates him from almost all anxiety. He's like a rich man who cannot understand the poor. But in a superficial way my remark made him uncomfortable.

'Hey, man, I'm grateful,' he said.

'You have a very obscure way of showing it.'

'Well, you got to let me think about it. I need some time. You really think Laura didn't do it?'

'If I thought she killed Sassari, I wouldn't be talking to you.'

'I don't know,' he muttered. 'I'll have to see how things go.'

'What things?'

He threw me a soft, unfocused glance, rubbing his lips with his fingertips.

'Fieldman,' I said, 'you got to help me – for Laura's sake.'

He ducked his head and slowly eased out of the car. He closed the door and stepped back, glancing towards the house.

'We'll see.' He wouldn't meet my eyes. 'You know, once in a while, it's like . . .' He shrugged profoundly. 'You got to think about yourself first. I'm broke. I got no clothes, I look like hell, I got a habit. You don't know what you're asking me.'

'Okay.'

'It's my last chance.' He touched his balding forehead where the hairpiece used to lie. 'I got to get something for myself out of this.'

There as no use trying to get anything more out of him. I told him to phone me if he had a change of mind. He stayed in my rearview mirror for several hundred yards, a lone figure by the side of the road. It didn't matter that he hadn't told me much. I was just pleased that he had a story to tell me. Like Landau and Anne Kepler he was guilty of not telling the entire truth and that filled me with hope. The guiltier they all were, the more chance that Laura might be innocent.

eighteen

Old clapboard houses, weed-infested lawns, broken fences, pavements thick with shattered bottles, and dog litter. The ocean breeze mingling with the sweet rotten stench of garbage and neglect. Venice was Welfare-and-Food-Stamp Town. It was weight lifters and nude gay sunbathers and stagnant canals. A resort built originally for summer use, it was now inhabited all year around by poor Mexicans, elderly Jews, blacks, surfers, junkies, poets, religious freaks, purse snatchers, health-food faddists, rapists, conceptual artists, and tarheads. It was Malibu after the Fall, where the sixties had gone to die, the black sheep of the southern California beach towns.

Daddy's Girl was located ten blocks from the beach on a tree-less street running parallel to some rusty train tracks that had once carried the Red Cars in a system connecting points as distant as Newport Beach, Pasadena, Hollywood, Beverly Hills, and the San Fernando Valley. That was back in the Dark Ages of Los Angeles, before the freeways, when the city was domed by clear, sparkling blue skies and had the most extensive public transportation system in the world.

From the look of it Daddy's Girl had been around then. It occupied a single-storey, red-brick building with high, barred windows and double doors padded in red Naugahyde and dotted with brass studs. It was flanked by a men's shop called Fancy Pants specializing in leather and rubber clothing accessories. The rest of the block was taken up with a family grocery store, a health-food restaurant, and two liquor stores.

I parked opposite the bar, rolled up the windows, and locked all the doors. There were three Mexicans blocking the pavement in front of the liquor store, and two of them were trying to summon the coordination to have a fight. It is not easy to get up on your toes and jab on reds and muscatel. They exchanged a few limp, roundhouse blows, tottered into a clinch, and fell over while the third one shouted encouragement. A wino sitting on a fireplug watched without much interest and the pedestrians going by paid it no attention at all. No one was paying me to look at it either. I crossed the street, threaded my way through the broken glass and refuse, and stepped into the dark cool interior of Daddy's.

It was not much but it beat the street. There was a long bar padded in lime-green vinyl with matching barstools, a dozen empty lime-green vinyl booths, a low ceiling of stained, sound-proof tiles, walls papered in imitation oak panelling, two pay phones, and a lot of photographs of fighters and horses. The click of cues hitting balls and men talking came from the rear, where all three tables were in use.

I took a stool at the deserted bar and ordered a Beefeater's up with four olives. The bartender was young, freckle-faced, with a long, flat, Irish mug, unhealthy green eyes, and a cold, dead-pan mouth. He didn't have a left arm any more. It took him a little longer to mix the drink.

I left the change from a twenty on the bar and divided my attention between the drink and a show called *Bugs and His Buddies* on the colour TV. When I was finished, I ordered a refill.

Halfway through my second drink a city construction worker asked the bartender for change and made a call from the pay phone near the door.

He said: 'This is Mr Clarke to speak to Lonesome. I'm at Daddy's.' He hung up and took a seat a few stools down from me. He gave me a perfunctory looking over, asked the bartender a question with his eyes, and ordered a draft. They talked about the virtues of double-barrelled carburettors for a solid five minutes, briefly surveyed the world of steel-belted radial tyres, and were just launching into an in-depth analysis of different fuel-injection systems when the phone rang. The hard hat let it ring five times and picked it up.

'Clarke here,' he said. 'What's New York?' He made a few calculations on a matchbook cover. 'I like Los Angeles ten times. What d'ya mean? I told you they got this new system. They pay us every two weeks. Sure, you're top of the list. Fuck my wife. My wife don't have nothing to say about it. Friday, I'm telling you, Friday. Okay, *five* times.' He hung the phone up hard and went back to the pool tables.

As far as I could tell, it was a simple conventional book being operated. It was known as a callback system, with all communications going through a third party, probably a housewife willing to operate an answering service out of her home. A bettor like the construction worker would call, ask for Lonesome and leave a number. Every fifteen minutes or so Lonesome would call in for any messages from the service. Whoever ran the service would not have the bookie's number or probably even know who he was. The construction worker had liked Los Angeles ten times which meant fifty dollars on the Lakers over the New York Knicks at whatever the line happened to be. It was not a large bet but even then the bookie had refused to extend him more than half of it on credit. It sounded like the guy's wife had made it hard for him to pay the bookie in the past. Maybe the guy was a lot of fifty-dollar bets behind and his pay-cheque for the next three months belonged to the bookie. Gambling is like any other addiction. The small-time gambler starts out like the guy who joy-pops heroin on weekends and swears he's never going to get a habit. Of course there are exceptions. The multi-billion-dollar drug and gambling industries encourage everyone to believe in exceptions. They like a lot of exception. All their steady customers are former exceptions.

'What's yours?' I asked the bartender.

He gave himself a shot of bar Scotch, lifted it to his lips, and smiled coolly over the rim. I lifted my glass. We both drank. He had bloodshot eyes ringed with wan puffed skin: drinker's eyes. He couldn't have been more than twenty-five but he was already there. In another five years it would show in the nose and cheeks. He had that pale, thin, Celtic skin that shows up the broken blood vessels. With the missing arm and his general style I made him for a veteran. His father wasn't a doctor or a lawyer. He was from the bottom rung of the social ladder and that's all they ever sent to Vietnam. I could dig it. I'd got close to looking like him for a while and I'd come back with both my arms.

'You aren't in Robbery,' he said flatly. 'I know everyone in Robbery.'

'Then I'm not in Robbery.'

'You're police.'

'You asking or telling?'

'I'm just trying to stay awake. It's slow work. A guy plays guessing games to pass the time.'

'I'm a private detective,' I said. 'A dumb racket. I find dogs and husbands. It sticks out a mile, huh?'

'I don't know. We get a lot of cops in here off-duty. But you ain't a cop, huh . . .'

'I told you what I was.' I looked him in the eyes. 'Didn't I tell you?'

'Easy, man. I'm just talking.'

'Give me another.' I pushed the glass over. 'And don't pay any attention to me. I've been on my feet since seven this morning looking for a guy.'

'Divorce case?'

'The guy's run away and his wife wants him back. Who understands women? This flake bets his lungs on anything that moves. He's got tapioca for brains and a drinking problem and she's ready to pay to get him back.'

'How would someone go about finding a guy like that?' The bartender laid a bowl of peanuts on the bar, tossed one in the air and caught it in his mouth.

'Simple. You ask his wife where he drinks and what his bookie's name is and then you go there and wait around until someone asks you what you're doing there.'

'As simple as all that, huh.' He fingered his empty shirt-sleeve. 'This one of the bars this guy frequents?'

'Naw, I just thought I'd drop by and watch some cartoons.'

'You're pretty sharp. Were you in the army?'

'That's right.'

'Yeah, how'd Charlie treat you?' He smiled at me.

'Not so hot,' I said.

'Charlie took a giant shit on me. I'm the only one-armed bartender in town. I always knew I was going to grow up and be something special.' He poured himself another shot of bar Scotch. 'Has your guy got a name?'

'Raymond Kepler. You want to see his picture?'

'Naw, I don't want to see his picture.' He walked quickly to the end of the bar, ducked under the hatch and went to talk it over with three blacks playing pool.

111

They looked me over and I looked back and I knew I'd seen one of them before. He was a very tall, coffee-coloured dude with smooth features and slanted eyes. A dandy's hairline moustache decorated his upper lip. He was dressed in the kind of fine, sedate clothes you associate with an English county life dominated by horses: a tweed hacking jacket, cavalry twill trousers, pale grey shirt and striped blue cravat. His shoes were highly polished jodhpur boots. He was dressed all wrong to hang out at a local Venice dive like Daddy's Girl. When this sport wanted amusement, he went where they helped you into your chair and inquired if the oysters were sufficiently chilled and did just about everything short of chewing the food for you.

The bartender came over and said, 'Mr Lucien thinks he might be able to help you out with your problem.'

'Would that be the great Mojo Lucien?'

'That's him.' The bartender grinned.

Across the room, his face radiant under the pool-table lights, Mojo Lucien bowed faintly to me and made a slight gesture indicating one of the back booths. I'd seen him last in the late sixties playing basketball for the UCLA Bruins. In those days Mojo'd worn Fidel Castro fatigues and sported a beard and out-size Afro. He was too small for the pros but as a college player he'd thrilled every crowd that ever saw him. He was the kind of substitute you put in the game when you were down ten points with five minutes left on the clock. He couldn't rebound or de-fend and wasn't a team player, but he had moves galore and he could hit the jumper from any angle on the court. If he was hot, he could wreck you in a couple of minutes. But he had no stamina. He was strictly someone you threw in to get you ten quick points. People said he was high-strung, temperamental, because every five games or so he couldn't hit the backboard. That was the only explanation for his bad nights, until a bookie called Jack the Beard hit a gambler too hard trying to collect on a bet and needed something big to give the police to drop the charge of manslaughter. Jack the Beard gave them Mojo Lucien who had been shaving points and controlling the UCLA spread since his sophomore year and was by then a very well-off senior. He had never been high-strung or temperamental except when someone paid him. I knew Mojo but I doubted if he'd remember.

I carried my drink over and joined him in a booth facing the men's room. I told him my name was Thomas Kyd and I guessed the bartender had told him what I was doing there.

'Tha's too bad about Raymond's old lady,' he said. 'That dude is thinking wrong these days, you know, the way he's doing is dangerous to his health. Hey, the man owes me his shirt. Where's his fucking shirt?' His slanted eyes swept the room and fixed back on me. 'I'm talking to you, man.'

'How much credit did you give him?'

'Wha's your name again? *Kyd? Kiddo?* Where you get off asking me questions like that? I don't think you got all your shit in one bag. You know who I am, mother-fucker?'

'Sure, you were a big noise on the Folsom Prison basketball team.'

The two other blacks slid into the booth and let their jackets hang open so I could see the revolvers in their waist bands.

'Hey, you hear how Kiddo talkin' 'bout the man?' He shook his head in sad disgust. 'Wha's a matter, sucker? You lose money on poor old Mojo?'

'What's with the heavy artillery?' I said. 'Did something I say scare you?'

'I jes' love this dude to death. He so cute and sassy. Yeah, white boy. I'm feelin' jumpy around you. How come you know so much about me coming around here looking for Raymond and asking all these off-brand questions? You some kind of cop?'

'Raymond's gone. His wife wants to know where he is. I told you I was a private detective up front. If there's bullshit in the air it isn't coming from my side of the booth.'

'The man's right!' Mojo slapped the table, nodding rapidly at the other two. 'That's right.' He moved his eyes from them to me. 'Raymond owes me five large. I'm hearing the dude's been getting down with other parties, you know, in Hollywood, and like this is very distressing to us. You tell his wife from me. I'm gonna collect. You understand? Maybe first I'm gonna put his TV set through the window and put my foot in his face but I'm gonna collect. Five large, tha's a lot of credit for that dude. That dude take a hike on me, I'm gonna have to sell a lot of my shoes to make it good with my man. You tell that to his wife.'

'I'll tell her.' I finished my drink and pushed it away.

'Yeah, tell her. I want cash, dig? I don't want him coming to me with no bullshit drawings, you know. Hey man, it's a hard life. I got to collect my bread. I got to do it now. I got a hunch Raymond's all washed up what with his main man getting knocked over like that.'

'Sassari?' I said. 'You know who he is?'

'Dig this white boy.' Mojo's face went smooth. 'Wha's wrong with you, Kiddo? Ain't you heard how the coloured folks learned how to read the newspapers? They lettin' some of us even watch the six o'clock news on TV these days.'

'I thought it was just another rumour.'

It was a dumb thing to say, characteristically dumb. I see an opening, I automatically respond: a dumb, combative reflex from childhood. Mojo's hand snaked out and grabbed my collar while the guy next to me leaned his weight against me and took hold of my ear. A second later I felt his gun barrel jab hard into my ribs. He must have liked doing it because he did it again twice as hard. I would have gasped but Mojo's knuckles were pressing into my Adam's apple.

'I got me an idea to see if you can swallow a pool cue,' Mojo whispered.

'He got two, Mojo. He don't need his ear. Let's take him in the back room and do an operation.'

'How you like that, white boy?' Mojo hissed.

'How do you like that nice patrolman who just walked in the door,' I croaked.

Mojo's face split into a beautiful smile as he patted my collar back into shape. 'My man! You're right.' He watched to see if I was going to do anything but the smile never left his face. 'You so lucky, white boy, I'm starting to like you, you know that?'

'Beating up on Raymond isn't going to get you your five grand.'

'That was just talk.' Mojo shrugged. 'Hey, it's cool. I ain't looking to shit on my friend Raymond.'

'You're looking to do anything you can to get your money. So am I. I like Raymond the way he is. I don't get paid if I bring him back in bits and pieces. Raymond's good for the money. He's got well-paid writing work the second he decides to come home. Look at it this way. If you hurt Raymond, then I've got to go to the cops, and that's hassle for you. The cops down here leave you alone, but your protection doesn't cover cutting off people's ears. If I go to the cops, then you start trying to hurt me. That way everyone loses because then I'm going to be looking to hurt you. Losing doesn't interest me. Going up against you doesn't interest me either.'

'I hear you.' He shrugged. 'The word is moderation.'

We all turned to watch as the patrolman waved goodbye to the bartender and walked out the door.

'What's the word now?' I said.

'Everything gon' be cool. Reason has prevailed. You find Raymond, you tell him I'm waiting for my bread. If I find him first, I'm going to take his ass back home. That way he can start making the bucks to piece off the man.'

'Okay.' I got up to go. 'Stay with it and you'll get your money.'

'You a familiar lookin' dude, you know that? Where might I have seen you before?'

'I thought you'd never ask.'

'I know you?' he demanded. 'Who the fuck are you?'

'You remember scoring fifty-seven points against Hollywood High?'

'Check it out. That was my big night.' His face got happy thinking about it. 'No one could do nothing with me that night. I run that Hollywood guard right off the court. You saw that? I was something, huh? Yeah. See, I could do it. I *always* could do it. The papers used to say I was flash, you know, just a street player? But that's just how I did it for the man. What the pros do, man, I was always hip to that. I didn't need no fucking University of California, you dig. Fifty-seven points! They said I had no stamina. Shit, I put the idea into their heads. It wasn't no good if I played the whole game. I had to come in at the end when the score was close to put the finishing touches on it.'

He was beaming enthusiastically, reliving his memories while the other two were gazing blankly off into space, having heard it all before.

'Fifty-seven points,' he mused. 'And then I got into a fight with the Hollywood guard in the fourth period. Some little white boy, you know, got physical with me. That sucker must have been crazy. You remember that, huh?'

115

'I remember it.'

'It was a loose ball and we both went for it. That was one crazy dude. Like we were ahead by thirty points and this mother-fucker is giving me a hard time.' He batted his eyelids, his mouth turning down modestly. 'You must have seen me deck him? I had my ring on. I only hit him one punch, you know, in the forehead. Shit, I never saw a guy drop like that. Course they threw me out.'

'No, they carried you out,' I said.

Mojo smiled at me with a wary, empty look in his eyes and then it dawned on him. 'Lookathat.' He snickered. 'You got the mark still on your forehead. You the worst chump I ever scored on.' His coffee-coloured face glowed with pleasure. 'You all hear what the man said?' He turned to the others. 'Me and this dude went to fist city. Oh man, was you fun to play against. Like going one-in-one with a fire hydrant. You got them good honky flat feet and that's why you ended up a cop. Sheiiiiit! You a bad dude with your fists. What that bitch of Raymond's paying you to come around mess with the bloods?'

'A hundred a day and expenses.'

'What you been doing to get yore ass in such a rinky-dink undaprivileged type situation? You-all married or something?'

I told him I was divorced.

'This here's Baltimore Red.' Mojo gestured expansively as if he was introducing me to royalty. 'And that dude next to him is Moth on account he likes the bright lights.'

Baltimore Red and Moth nodded at me without interest, and I nodded back.

Mojo's spirits had improved: 'Baltimore and me run the book at Folsom for the bloods. You thought Baltimore was jiving you when he talk about cutting off your ear. The dude's bad, man. How many ears you cut in Nam, Baltimore?'

Baltimore shrugged heavily and mumbled something about never having kept count.

Mojo beamed at me like a proud father whose little boy has just said something clever. 'Listen, Kyd, now that we so friendly and all, lay some words on me. Where Raymond get the green to bet the way he does? The cat got an old ride. He got threads on I wouldn't use to check the oil of my El Dorado. Where he comin' up with the bread to play with me?'

'I don't know. Maybe he wins somewhere else.'

'The dude don't *win*,' Mojo scoffed. 'Never. Me and Raymond been getting down since college days. I get me a new ride every year just off what I make from Raymond. And that's just the action he gives to me.'

Mojo closed his hands into fists and shook them near his ears as if he was listening to the rattle of dice. 'I'm thinking, Kyd, how Raymond's wife paying you this sad amount of green and you such an evil dude with your hands. What say you work for me? Baltimore and Moth both fine collectors but sometime the white folks like dealing with their own. My main man's Italian, you know what I mean, the top man and he don't want me using the bloods all the time.'

'Thanks, but no thanks.' I stood up, and this time Moth and Baltimore moved quickly to let me out of the booth. 'I haven't got the stomach for the work. I was in Nam. I've seen guys cut ears off stiffs. It never did anything for me except make me sick.' I smiled into Baltimore's watchful ill-humoured face. 'That's strictly an animal act you got there, friend. That shit belongs in a cage.'

'Who me?' Baltimore turned indignantly to friend Moth. 'Is he talkin' 'bout *me?*'

'The man gotta go now.' Mojo stared up into my face. 'I be hearin' from you real soon, Mistah Private Detective.'

I gave Baltimore a wide berth and headed for the door. The bar had filled up with men getting off work and there were lines of people waiting to use both phones. The two off-duty detectives in a corner booth drinking beer were engrossed in reading the sports page and weren't in the slightest interested in the action around the pay phones.

nineteen

I drove back to Hollywood but Raymond's other hangout, The Blue Bird, was dark on Monday nights.

There were no messages on my service when I returned to my office. I spread out my notes and the photograph on the desk and stared at them as if they meant something. Daddy's Girl and The Blue Bird were accounted for; I knew who Baltimore Red was, and he wasn't any help unless you wanted to end up looking like Van Gogh. That left a bookie called Fruitcake and I didn't think he was listed in the Yellow Pages.

I phoned Anne Kepler at her home number. She wasn't holding up too well. Her voice was small and choked and my news didn't contribute to her state of mind. I asked her if she had been able to think of any other bars or bookmakers patronized by her husband. Was it possible Raymond was staying with a friend and the friend had been persuaded to keep it a secret? Could he have gone to stay with a relative? She answered negative on all my questions.

'Why would this Professor Bustamente not care what happened to Raymond,' I asked.

'They had an argument. Raymond would never talk about it. That was seven years ago, don't you understand? I know we haven't given you much information but I can't think of anything else.'

I fired the next question at her quickly: 'Did Raymond take that script, Mrs Kepler? Isn't that sort of out of character for him?'

'Of course he didn't.' Her voice had lowered to a whisper. 'He'd never do anything to hurt anyone.'

'Is Mr Landau there?' I asked.

'Yes, all right,' she answered in a normal voice.

'Listen, Mrs Kepler. If we haven't heard from Raymond by tomorrow, I think you ought to go to the police. The script doesn't have to be mentioned. You just file a missing person report.'

'I'll have to ask Dix,' she said weakly.

'It's your husband that's missing, Mrs Kepler.'

'But I haven't got any money,' she wailed. 'I haven't got anything. Raymond took the car. I couldn't even afford to hire you for a day . . .' From the sounds she was making, I could imagine her contorted, tear-stained face, and I thought, living with Raymond, she had probably had a lot of practice crying. 'They're going to turn the phone off tomorrow and Raymond won't be able to call.' She sobbed. 'We're two months behind on the rent.'

'He'll call.' I tried to sound convinced. 'And let Landau worry about the money.' I cut it short then, because she wasn't making any sense and the sound of her sobbing rattled me. Putting the phone down, I wondered what it was about guys like Raymond that inspired such emotion in women. Why did he rate a bright, pretty loyal wife and two children? Why didn't she find someone who wasn't a constant emotional drain? There's a certain kind of woman who gravitates towards crackups; the more problems a guy's got, the more she likes him. She'd graduated from the same class as Raymond but ended up with two kids and a job as a secretary while her husband supported bookies all over town. She wasn't complaining either. She wanted him back. And she had a sad, round, pretty face and a slender figure and a kind of batty, myopic charm.

There was no reason to look in the Los Angeles White Pages for a professor called Bustamente but it was the only thing I could think of doing apart from putting an ad in the newspapers. It was that or hit the office bottle and I was a little sick of the office bottle.

Like so many of my hunches, it paid off. There was a Bustamente. Indeed, there were so many Bustamentes listed I didn't why I didn't meet one every day. I copied down the numbers of six of them chosen at random and began dialling. I talked to a Fausto, a Juventino, a Raoul, a Maria, a Sam, and a Fidel, all Bustamentes, who had never heard of a relation being a professor in the UCLA Theatre Arts Department.

I was out in the cold. I could feel it but I kept dialling anyway. I spoke to an airline pilot I knew in Palos Verdes whose daughter was a UCLA graduate the same age as Kepler. The daughter was now living up north in Alameda County. She was in the middle of serving dinner when I reached her. She'd been a foreign language major and had never heard of Bustamente but she had a girlfriend in New York who used to go with a teaching assistant in the Theatre Arts Department. I called the girlfriend in New York. It had been five years since she'd spoken to the teaching assistant, and all she could give me was an old Long Beach number. From her tone it was clear the teaching assistant was the last man in the world she wanted to think about. The Long Beach number turned out to belong to the teaching assistant's mother, who gave me a Florida number for her son. I woke him up. He told me that Bustamente had left UCLA before his time but someone called Greg Thackeray in Los Angeles might know where he was.

Thackeray turned out to be a former student of Bustamente's. The professor was now teaching at the American Academy of Dramatic Arts in Pasadena. There was a Pasadena listing for him. I called that number, my seventeenth call, and spoke to his wife long enough to find out that Bustamente was directing an evening rehearsal at the Globe Theatre on Kings Road in West Hollywood.

I telephoned the theatre and spoke to the stage manager, who promised to get Bustamente to call me as soon as there was a break in the rehearsal.

I said: 'Tell him it concerns Raymond Kepler, and it's urgent.'

The stage manager didn't think Bustamente would be free for at least an hour.

He was wrong. Within minutes Bustamente returned my call.

'This is Peter Bustamente,' he said guardedly. 'Can I help you?'

'You don't know me, Professor,' I said. 'My name is Thomas Kyd. I'm a private investigator working for Raymond Kepler's wife.'

'Yes?'

'I presume you read in the papers about Paul Sassari's death?'

'In the papers, yes.'

'Raymond disappeared two day ago. I understand from Mrs Kepler that he was a former pupil of yours.'

'He was, yes.'

'Okay, the point of it is that Raymond is going through some kind of emotional crisis, and I just thought he might try and get in touch with someone who'd been important to him in the past.'

'No, I haven't spoken to him since nineteen sixty-nine.'

'Well, sorry to have disturbed you. Raymond's a missing person. Some pretty dangerous people are trying to locate him and I'm just trying to get there first.'

'What did you say your name was again, please?'

'Thomas Kyd.'

'K-Y-D?' He spelled it out.

'That's right.'

'I do not find this a very amusing joke,' he said angrily.

'There's no joke. You can check me under INVESTIGATORS in the Yellow Pages.'

'Perhaps it's a genuine coincidence. I am directing a play here, *The Spanish Tragedy*. It was written by an Elizabethan playwright called Thomas Kyd.'

'That is just what they called me when I was born,' I said. 'I was named after my father.'

'May I ask how you got my number?' He had thawed down from freezing to polite coldness.

'It took a lot of phone calls. I finally got it from an ex-student of yours called Thackeray.'

'I see. I don't suppose you're at liberty to tell me what trouble Raymond is in.'

'I'm not quite sure of *all* the trouble he's in, but he owes money to professional gamblers. I think his health depends on me finding him before they do.'

'Agh!' He scoffed sadly. 'He is still gambling. A strange character, that boy. A kind, gifted person and then a weakling, a moral coward. There are really two Raymond Keplers.'

'If there was anything you could tell me . . .' I paused. 'Though maybe the bad feeling's still too strong.'

'There was never bad feeling on my part,' he replied sharply. 'My quarrel was with Sassari, his so-called friend. Raymond was a victim. I forgave Raymond long ago. It is Raymond who can't forgive himself.'

'Why do you say that?'

'These are old stories, Mr Kyd. I do not gossip about people.'

'I've broken a professional confidence just talking to you. When a piece of information may save a life, it's more than gossip, Professor. Something happened in sixty-nine. It could be connected to some of the destructive things that have happened this week. Have you ever seen a gambler after a collector's gone to work on him?'

'No, of course not.' He was on the defensive.

'It takes one swing with a baseball bat to turn a knee into a jigsaw puzzle and there is no way to put it back together again. I spoke to some bookmakers this afternoon who were talking about cutting Raymond's ears off. You don't live in that kind of world. But it's closing in fast on Raymond. I'd like to know what went wrong in sixty-nine. Knowing that may just save Raymond's life.'

'Like your namesake, you have a gift for melodrama,' he said. 'However, I wouldn't like to feel I'd contributed to hurting Raymond. Let me put it this way. I am from Italy. I was educated at the University of Rome and took my doctorate at Oxford. In European universities when a student fails, he receives a failing mark. In American universities sometimes one is pressured to give a passing mark to a mediocrity. A question of politics. He may be the son of a powerful alumnus, or an athlete who must remain eligible so the university can continue to fill its stadiums. I do not do such things. I was made to understand that Sassari's mother intended to offer the school an endowment which would not be forthcoming if he failed my course. Do I make myself clear?'

'I think so.'

'You think so?' he said vehemently. 'There is in my world also this equivalent of gangster's breaking kneecaps. One can lame an academic professionally for life. I resisted their pressure. Raymond made a difficult position impossible for me by secretly helping Sassari with his work. I protested and was dismissed by the university, needless to say, without references. A man in my profession without references ends up in small drama schools in Pasadena.' He made a kind of spitting, hissing noise in his throat. 'I get sick recalling such ugliness, such insolence from

Hollywood trash. Imagine the greed and vulgarity of Sassari and his mother. It is not enough for them to be rich and famous. No, their narcissism is insatiable. They would also like to *buy* academic honours.' His voice, which had steadily risen in volume, degenerated into bronchial coughing. He finally said, 'No, it is no good thinking about it anymore. Such a thing could poison a man for life. I have never regretted what I did. It is Raymond who let himself be ruined, whose conscience punishes him. He was a very sensitive, talented boy, you know. He had serious promise.'

'We could be talking about two different people. The Kepler I know is an alcoholic gambler who types Sassari's scripts.'

'It's precisely the Raymond Keplers of the world who are most susceptible,' he said. 'They have no resistance. When I met Raymond, he was a healthy, honest young man with serious ideas about film. He was quite an innocent. Such a type succumbs to the Sassaris of this world the way your American Indians died of the common cold. There is no place for them in Hollywood.'

'I only saw him once, Professor. I don't know what he was like as a student but I know he was gambling heavily. He may have been gambling before he ever met Sassari.'

'No, they met in my class. Raymond was no gambler. He was a scholarship boy. He'd been educated in England. Sassari corrupted him. He cultivated his weaknesses. You think corruption is an old-fashioned word, perhaps?'

I said nothing. The truth was he had me under his spell a little. He made Kepler sound like a Lord Jim character: a man irrevocably ruined by one act of moral cowardice. Still, other thoughts, other possibilities nagged at me: all I had was Bustamente's side of it.

'I am sorry about Raymond,' he continued. 'I do not feel so sorry for Sassari. That is a harsh thing to say, but there it is. I must get back to my actors, Mr Kyd. Goodbye.'

I looked at the list of telephone numbers I'd scrawled over three notebook pages. I wouldn't be able to put them on my expense sheet since my client specifically told me to steer clear of Bustamente. Still, I'd obtained some new information on what held Raymond Kepler to Paul Sassari. Or maybe not. The well-educated are the best liars of all. Bustamente might have given me a highly distorted picture of the events that had led to his dismissal.

I sat listening to the slow, shuffling steps of the janitor passing outside, checking the door handles of the locked offices, followed soon after by the slap and whoosh of his mop swabbing down the linoleum. It was nearly eight o'clock, and I wasn't thinking clearly any more. I had a headache, and my stomach felt as empty as the deserted building.

I'd put on my jacket, snapped off the office lights, and started to close the anteroom door when the phone started ringing. I hesitated. I thought of the prime rib I'd planned on washing down with a bottle of wine. It kept ringing. It rang too many times. On about the tenth ring I picked it up.

'He phoned me.' Anne Kepler's voice burst through the receiver. 'He's all right. Raymond's all right.'

'I'm glad, Mrs Kepler. What about the script?'

'He doesn't have it.'

Landau took the phone from her.

'I think you better go get him, Kyd. He sounded pretty drunk, like he'd been drunk for days. Bring him home and . . . ah . . . look around. Don't let him leave anything behind.'

'Like the script?'

'We'll discuss it later,' the agent said tersely. 'He's in bungalow three, the Ocean View Motel, thirteen fifty-six Pico Boulevard. He called about twenty minutes ago.'

twenty

The Ocean View Motel was eleven blocks from the ocean in Santa Monica and all it had for a view was a look across a busy street at a bowling alley. A white picket fence enclosed the front lawn of the bungalow office, which was actually a weathered, two-storey house similar to the other two-storey houses on the street except for a little red VACANCY sign winking in its bay window. In the middle of the front lawn there was an abandoned white plastic sofa, a baby carriage without wheels, and a partially melted television set. The path was littered with handbills and old newspapers which had been delivered but never opened.

I wondered why the missing people I traced never did their drinking in the Polo Lounge or holed up at the Beverly Wilshire Hotel. Knowing Kepler's taste in bars, I should have guessed he'd choose a flophouse like the Ocean View.

Except for a moth-encrusted porch light all the windows in the bungalow were dark. A hole had been cut in the porch screen-door and its ragged edges were matted with dog hair. It was a large hole used by a large dog and by the time I'd opened the screen door, I could hear it starting up inside. Barking dogs aren't a problem; they're barking. When a dog means business, it doesn't bark at all; it emits that low growl through clamped jaws and snarling lips and by the time you hear it you should have already been up a tree. The dog inside was the real article. None of your warning *woof-woof*. He was clawing the door and hurling himself against it hard enough to shake it in its frame.

'Whaddaya want?' A woman's voice screamed from an upstairs window. 'Who's that down there?' It was the kind of voice you hear coming from the cheap seats at wrestling matches when the beer has done its work and it's time to start throwing bottles at the referee.

I stepped off the porch and peered up and got a look at her face in the moonlight. She had wild, spiky orange hair. Her eyes weren't on good terms with each other. The best thing I could think to say about her was that there wasn't much you could teach her about snarling.

'I'm looking for a party in number three.'

'In back.' She screamed, 'I'll kill that dog. Shut that dog up.'

'Thanks.'

'So help me God, I'm gonna kill it.' She vanished from the window and I heard her muffled shouting, 'I *will* kill it.'

I walked around the bungalow and the dog followed my progress, moving from window to window, snapping its jaws against the glass. It had a lean white face and pointed ears and formidable jaws. The woman appeared for a second in the window, got her arm around the dog's throat and toppled out of sight. I heard a noise of scuffling and whimpering and then there was a squeal of animal pain cut short by a cracking thud. I felt it. I winced in sympathy. She'd brained the dog with something that was harder than its skull. The snarling had stopped.

I waited on the gravel path behind the bungalow, but the woman didn't seem interested in me. She went back upstairs and a moment later I heard canned laughter and voices coming from a television set. I didn't want to see what the woman looked like, or how she lived inside her house. I didn't want to know if she'd actually beaten her dog to death. I just hoped she had no children.

The path petered out after a couple of yards and I was knee-deep in damp, luxuriant weeds. Directly ahead were four white clapboard cabins, each with a miniature porch and TV aerial. No lights were on in any of them. Rising out of the weeds on the left was a charred coatrack and the burned hulk of an upright piano, its ivory keys and brass pedals blackened with soot. The whole instrument was festooned with what looked like huge whisps of dried shaving cream, the remains of fire-extinguishing foam. In the breeze the whisps of foam stirred and fluttered over the piano like ghostly limbs. There was lots of moonlight and maybe the entire scene, the piano abandoned in the weeds, the fluttering tendrils of foam, had some uneerie beauty, but it acutely depressed me. The Ocean View was the kind of run-down rooming house establishment that I hated because I could see myself at sixty living in one. Drinking alone in my room. Separated from other lonely old people by a wall of plywood not thick enough to cut down the sound of my neighbour's TV. Sixty-year-old private detectives don't get a lot of work, and if they're independents they have to make it through their last years without a pension. Maybe I could meet a rich client and marry her and avoid the nightmare scenario I saw for the autumn of my life.

That's what was going through my mind as I rapped my knuckles on the door of cabin number three. It swung open on its hinges.

'Kepler?' I reached my hand in, groped for a switch, and then something grabbed my wrist and yanked me forward into the darkness. In the time it took me to scream I was hit on the neck and shoulder and then the blows reached my head, and I stopped screaming.

twenty-one

The woman with spiky, orange hair was playing the burning piano but for some reason her hands moved so swiftly and cleverly, they eluded the crackling flames. I could not understand how it was done, nor how her hands could be white and beautiful while her face was so brutal and stupefied. Just the sight of the flames scorched my face like a forest fire. Beside the piano the white dog lay stretched out in the green weeds like an Ingres nude on a velvet sofa. Its belly was a delicate salmon-pink but the tongue lolling out of its mouth was black as carbon. I understood what had happened. The point of the charred coatrack had been driven into my ear and the intense heat of my thoughts had set it on fire. Every note the woman played fanned the flames higher. Raymond loomed over me and his mouth moved without making a sound. His face did annoying things like blow up in size and then shrink and then wheel in a circle like a carousel turning in a funny mirror. But it wasn't funny.

I told him not to be afraid of the dog because it was only sleeping. I didn't want to let on it was dead. I was no fool. I knew the dead white dog was the only one I could trust.

I came to sitting on the floor with my back against the foot of the bed. There was a stranger slumped opposite me, a man with sickly white skin and blood coming out of the side of his head. One side of his face was swollen out of shape.

The cabin door opened and the stranger disappeared. Raymond Kepler came in with a glass of water and closed the door behind him. I'd been looking at myself in the mirror on the back of the cabin door.

He kneeled next to me and put the glass of water to my lips. I stared at him like a vegetable. He had curly auburn hair and deeply intent brown eyes with a sad, hunted look about them. It was a thoughful, stubborn face, with a look of pinched sensitivity around the nose. He hadn't shaved for several days; there was a sweet reek of bourbon coming off him and a sour smell of dried sweat. It was as if the crack on the head had given me new powers of smell. Even as he kneeled beside me, I got a whiff of something coming loose inside him, some dank terror opening his pores. His hand trembled as he held the glass to my lips; it made a clicking sound against my teeth.

'Is my other ear bleeding?' I asked him. My voice sounded as if I hadn't used it since I was a child.

'I don't believe you were hit on that side.' He said it with a careful clipped precision. 'Would you care for some more water?'

Vaguely I recalled he had been educated in England. It seemed very queer, the way he was talking to me: the cool, polished words, casually drawled, did not fit the unshaven face and trembling hands.

'Did I bleed from my nose or eyes?' I insisted.

'I believe it was just your right ear.'

I could see several bloody hand towels lying in the corner. He had a little on his hands and on the cuffs of his shirt.

'I still could have a fracture,' I said, 'but I don't think I'd be making sense. Am I making sense?'

'You're doing very well.' Something like mockery very faintly touched his face.

'Help me up.'

'If you'll stay there a moment.' He rose to his feet. 'I'll go call an ambulance.'

'Come on.' I stared up at him. 'Give me a hand.'

'Don't be a fool.' He stepped back, a scowl of annoyance and impatience on his face. 'You're damn lucky to be alive.'

'Did I bleed from my eyes or nose?'

'You already asked me that.'

'Sorry I'm such a bore.' I leered foolishly at him and started to get to my feet. There was no dizziness, the walls refrained from spinning; my senses were perfectly clear. When I was halfway up, though, it suddenly felt like a hot plate had been applied to the side of my head. Kepler caught me, but I weighed more than him. We ended up on the floor in a heap. It didn't matter. The pain in my head was on full throttle; you could have bounced me off the walls and I wouldn't have felt any different. We got ourselves extricated, and as I turned I caught sight of the back wall of the room. Someone had written across it in pale red lipstick. RAYMOND K. WILL PAY. The letters were a foot high, block capitals stylized like Chicano slum graffiti.

We lay there for a moment, winded, covered in blood. The thump of our bodies hitting the floor had set the bare bulb in the ceiling faintly swaying.

'Have you got a drink?'

He started to crawl and then thought better of it and stood up and walked with excessive deliberation to the dresser. He removed a pint of bourbon from a brown paper bag. He started to look for a glass, but I told him to just give me the bottle. He wasn't having much joy with his motor control; his face had a dazed, cheerless look and I realized he was making a superhuman effort to conceal the fact he was plastered. He turned around and tried to get me into focus, keeping his hand on the dresser for support. He didn't want to let go of the dresser. I must have looked very far away to him on the other side of the room. I watched him trying to figure out how he was going to negotiate the distance without falling flat on his face. It was interesting; he was obviously a fellow with certain standards; he had his dignity to keep up. Drinking himself comatose on cheap bourbon in a shabby motel room was one thing, but appearing drunk was another matter. He had the Englishman's obsession with correct form. In the end he decided speed was his only hope. He walked very swiftly towards me. It was only five steps but by the third he was starting to lean sideways and he only made it by landing on the bed.

I poured as much of the bourbon down my throat as I could stomach, paused, and forced down a little more. He was sitting on the edge of the bed, trying to keep his back straight, but swaying the smallest amount. His head would start to topple forward and he would snap it back so forcefully that he would have to lean forward again to keep his balance. It was taking all his concentration just to deal with the gravity problem.

'Where the hell were you?' I asked him.

'The liquor store.' He paused, seemed to savour what he had just said. 'I stepped out to the old liquor store.'

'Didn't your wife tell you I was coming here?'

'Ahh, now I see.' He crinkled his eyes and smiled to himself. 'She told you I was here. I should have guessed it was the wife.' He beckoned politely for the bottle but I didn't give it to him. 'I wouldn't mind a drink,' he said with a disarming smile.

'You're quite a boy, Kepler. I walk into your room and someone beats me to a pulp and writes RAYMOND K. WILL PAY on the wall and all you've got to say about it is, "I wouldn't mind a drink."'

He wasn't in the slightest bit offended. 'This whole town could be hit by a tidal wave and I still wouldn't mind a drink. It's my character, you see – you are talking to a man with a flawed character.'

'In that case,' I tipped the bottle upside down and let the bourbon out on the rug, 'you'd better try your character out on that.'

He didn't flinch, or scowl. He merely raised his eyebrows slightly. '*Very* good,' he said appreciatively. 'Well done. Don't just refuse me a drink. Empty the bloody lot on the carpet. Done with flair, old boy, excellent gesture.' He said it all with a polite deadness of manner as if he was complimenting me on my golf swing. 'But then,' he mused, 'you're a great one for gestures, aren't you? I remember you standing up to Fieldman that day in Malibu. You wouldn't tell Paul where Laura had gone. He tempted you with money, threatened you but you stuck fast. Admirable stuff! Wish I'd done it myself. And Landau, too. I'm sure he waved his chequebook in your face and got no for an answer.' He was speaking faster, his sarcasm more charged with feeling. 'And then with Laura herself we all heard how you'd helped her, what a prince you were, helping her again and again and never demanding your pound of flesh. Remarkable behaviour, really. Only it didn't make a damn bit of difference in the end. It was all kindness down the drain. But perhaps that

was the beauty of it – its utter uselessness . . .' There was a ve-
hemence in his voice now which he could barely control. 'And
here you are again . . .' He rocked himself very slightly to and
fro on the bed. '. . .Trying to help my dear little wife recover her
erring husband. I suppose I ought to be touched. I really ought
to take my hat off to you. You really are rather tediously noble.'
His eyes widened and for an instant they shone with a fine
sparkle of hate. 'I wonder why you bother, Kyd? Why do you
bother?'

He had a captive audience; I felt too shocked and sick to
answer.

'Why help all these people who don't want to be helped?' he
asked softly. 'Why not use your head while you still have one?
We are, none of us, worth helping. Take it from the horse's
mouth, chum. There's a San Andreas fault running through all
our lives, and we're all going to break apart just like this city.
We're in hell. You can't just have a little look around hell, old
boy. You can't pay hell a visit like a tourist and expect to go
home with some interesting snapshots. Damn it, man!' He
raised his voice. 'You've got no business being here. I've got
enough on my conscience without seeing you get hurt. You
haven't got the first clue what's going on, not a clue. I'm sorry
you caught what was obviously intended for me, but for God's
sake stay out of it. There,' he sighed, 'I'm finished.'

'Nice speech,' I said. 'Who's your friend with the pink lipstick?'

'Do give up. I'm not answering any questions.'

'It wasn't Mojo,' I said. 'It must have been someone else.'

'Mojo?' It was more annoyance than surprise. 'What an in-
dustrious fellow you are. No, it wasn't Mojo.'

'I suppose the script isn't here, and you don't know anything
about that either.'

'The script.' He gave a little shrug of distaste. 'How typical
of Landau to think I took it. He's a stupid, wretched man with no
more imagination than a pocket calculator. I suppose, in a horrible way, it's funny him thinking that. And now please let's
have no more questions. I don't intend to make a drunken confession to you, though I do think you might understand. You

seem to have a certain genius for lost causes and useless gestures. Believe me,' he added rather sourly, 'you're not the only one.'

'That's what Bustamente told me.' I watched him closely. 'He said you used to be a regular little Don Quixote.'

The mention of the name cut through his alcoholic torpor. It dazed him and then he smiled bitterly, as if he was amused that anything could still pain him.

'Bustamente.' He rubbed his mouth stiffly with a clenched fist. 'Is he still around? Poor old Bustamente. He must have told you the tale of the tragic Rise and Fall of Raymond Kepler. It's one of his set pieces like the Role of the Victim in Twentieth-Century Fiction. How is Bustamente?'

'He fell out of favour back in sixty-nine and it's been downhill since then.'

'Didn't we all?' Kepler scoffed. 'He's another fellow who got a shock when he found out how expensive principles were. You really have been busy nosing into my private life. I don't think I care for it, but it probably doesn't matter. Your opinion of me won't alter a thing.'

I got a cigarette lit and said: 'Why don't you get your things packed and we can get going.'

'I envy you,' he said. 'Seriously. Things are simpler for you.'

'Between feeling sorry for yourself and condescending to me, Kepler, you haven't got the room for envy.'

'You're a hard man and of course,' he gave me one of his ironically poisoned smiles, 'you're dead right.' He almost said something more but decided against it.

I lay back against the side of the bed while he lurched around the room filling a Safeway bag with his few effects. A concussion does not do a great deal for anyone's reasoning powers. Like Fieldman he was full of innuendos and very stingy with facts; he was also, for all the liquor raging in his blood, not even close to revealing anything. Something was eating him up inside but he was committed to not mentioning it. He hadn't even bothered to explain himself or any of his actions. Instead he'd given me a drunken meditation on various individuals. It had been a startling performance, cynical, savage, charged with self-hatred. The impression it left behind, however, was curiously unreal, as if he was straining to be something he wasn't.

When he was finished packing, he stuck three ten-dollar bills under the empty bourbon bottle on the dresser. He gave the room a last glance: the bloody hand towels, the stained carpet, the lipstick-smeared wall. 'I came, I saw, I made a bloody mess of it – as usual.'

We made a charming pair walking out of the Ocean View Motel. Kepler was weaving and I limped along hunched over like Quasimodo with a hangover. One of Nature's mercies is that when pain reaches a critical point you're meant to faint. I wondered just how much agony had to come from my head and shoulder to qualify. The world was full of sensitive souls who would have passed out at the sight of me. I didn't faint. Instead I had a lengthy, incoherent argument on the pavement with Kepler about whose car we were going to take, who was in better shape to drive, and where we were going. He wanted to drive me in his car to a hospital. I had several things to my advantage: Raymond couldn't remember where his car was parked, he'd lost his car keys, and once we got under way, he passed out.

twenty-two

He lived in the Wilshire district in an older neighbourhood that had bloomed and then declined and was now having a revival. None of the houses was a showpiece but each was unique enough to distinguish it from its neighbours. The lawns and flowerbeds were well tended; generous numbers of palms and magnolias had been planted along the spotless pavements. The Kepler house was situated in the middle of the block, a single-storey building that wasn't quite sure if it was a miniature castle or an enlarged English cottage. There was a nice rounded sweep to the black-tiled roof; the windowledges and arched entrances were inlaid with mosaic tile. In most of the windows round and square stained-glass panels added a touch of ornamental richness. In the forties, when it was built, it would have been a typical home for an office worker. Time, which passes so swiftly in Los Angeles, had already given it the look of an antique.

I parked and nudged Kepler awake. He came to very determined to fight the alcohol in his blood, talking with a forced cheerfulness.

'You must come in,' he said. 'This calls for celebration.'

'It's past my bedtime.'

'Nonsense. I insist. A nightcap with the little woman and her prodigal husband safely returned from the fleshpots of Santa Monica. I'm getting a second wind, old fellow. I absolutely insist you come in and have a drink with me.'

I didn't say anything in reply. I could feel his eyes on me. After a moment, he said, 'How you must despise me.'

'It's a job, Kepler. I'm a connoisseur of deadbeats and you're nowhere close to the bottom.'

'How depressing.' He sighed. 'And I thought I'd plumbed the depths.'

'You could have stayed missing. You're the one who phoned your wife.'

'Old habits die hard. I suppose I've made myself an object of great suspicion.' He said it with a kind of defensive facetiousness. 'Paul is murdered and the script disappears and so do I. Doesn't that strike you as strange? I suppose you think I have something to do with killing him.'

'I wouldn't know. Up to now you look to me like someone who kills himself every day a little bit at a time. That's how most people do it. They take a lifetime.'

'That sounds *very* boring.'

'Unless you're going to tell me something about what happened tonight, I think you ought to go inside. I think your wife's waiting.'

'Can't wait to get rid of me, can you?' He smiled. 'Many others share the sentiment.'

'You don't need me to hold your hand going in there, and if you need it, it wouldn't help.'

He opened the car door and got out and I handed him his

Safeway bag from the backseat. He had the look of a man who's in a indefensible position but still wants to make a speech. The urge to justify himself struggled in his face with something else that weighed him down. And the other thing won out, hardening his features into a stoic grimace.

'Thank you,' he mumbled. 'I . . . thank you.' He turned and walked very quickly across the lawn and nearly stumbled over a submerged sprinkler. When I saw the door open and his wife rushing out with her arms open, I pulled away from the curb and drove off.

twenty-three

By the time I left UCLA Emergency Ward I was so wasted on painkillers I could hardly keep my eyes open at traffic stops. There were twenty-three stitches holding my ear together and another eleven in my scalp all concealed under a large, padded dressing. They'd had to shave the side of my head to treat the wounds so I looked grotesquely plucked and lopsided. The medical bills and the cost of my ruined suit were going to tripe my fee. In the movies guys get tapped on the head with gun butts and drop like sacks of cement. When they wake up they rub their skulls and squint a little to show the audience it hurts. An hour later they're acting like they never had a sick day in their lives. In real life you get your skull shaved and they paint it purple and sew it up. The headache from a violent concussion doesn't go away; it can linger for weeks like the after-effect of a car accident. It's usually still there long after the stitches come out.

But then sometimes you get slugged on the head and when you come to, your eyes no longer react to anything. You can no longer control your bowels and bladder. You don't have enough co-ordination to spit. It was fortunate, according to the doctor, that I'd been hit on the ear, which had cushioned the blows. Whoever it was hadn't intended to kill me because it would have been simple to finish the job while I was unconscious. But only the chance position of my head in the dark had·kept me out of the vegetable kingdom. As far as I was concerned, the difference between him and a murderer was as thin as the varnish on a night stick.

Some time in the night the phone woke me up. I mumbled hello. A muffled, nasal voice said.

'Thomas Kyd?'

'Speaking. Who's this?'

I heard the click of the receiver being put down. Someone had wanted to know if I was home. Sure, I'm home. What's left of me is home. I took more painkillers, disconnected the phone, and dropped into blackness.

It was worse in the morning. I had to take more painkillers and then lie in bed and wait for them to take effect. After a while I crawled out to the kitchen and drank almost a quart of milk and half a loaf of bread. The concussion had impaired my senses; the bread and milk tasted of copper. When I lit a cigarette it felt like I was inhaling vacuum cleaner dust.

Opening the front door to collect my newspaper, I had to shield my eyes against the sunshine that was pouring into the canyon. Across the shimmering tarmac road the eucalyptus trees crackled in the sharp breeze and the birds screamed out at the morning. It all looked so bright and alive I didn't know how a human being could survive in it.

I made a pot of strong coffee and sweetened it with brandy and let it burn down into me over the morning paper. Sassari's death had gone from the front page news to almost the back pages, where it shared space with reports on minor congressional bills and the news that a four-star general of eighty-three was in fair condition following brain surgery. WITNESS DENIES TESTI-MONY ran the headline:

Vern Mazo, sole witness to the knife slaying of screenwriter Paul Sassari, testified to a coroner's jury that before signing it, he had not been permitted to read over his statement to the police. 'Half of it,' said the well-known fashion photographer, 'I never said, and half of what I did say, they didn't include.' Mazo

136

electrified the court by the frankness of his replies and on several points flatly contradicted his signed statement. 'Mrs Sassari was kneeling over her husband,' said Mazo, 'crying for help when I came into the room. I never even saw a knife. All I saw was blood. She was crying for help when I opened the door. That's why I opened the door.' Asked why he ran from the study, Mazo replied, 'I'm allergic to blood and I didn't know the Sassaris. She was screaming "help." I started screaming "help," too.'

Mazo's initial statement included a description of Mrs Sassari repeatedly stabbing her husband in the chest. A coroner's department representative testified that Sassari died of a single stab wound to the heart, all other tissue and cartilage damage being caused by subsequent efforts to dislodge the murder weapon. The coroner's jury moved to postpone a verdict until it hears further testimony later in the week.

It wasn't a big break but it was something. Discrepancies were emerging, flaws in the police procedure which might bode well for Laura. I couldn't summon much enthusiasm for any of it.

I went back to bed and slept a few hours, but it wasn't any good. I woke up freezing and drenched in cold sweat and saw that blood had seeped through the dressing to stain the pillow-case. I got up, swallowed more painkillers, turned the heat on full blast, wrapped my head in a towel, and lay on the couch.

The pain had settled down to a dull throbbing. If I kept still, I could live with it. It was the depression it carried in its wake that frightened me. Perhaps it's what a woman suffers after being raped. They say a rape victim often goes through a long period when the memory of her violation poisons the act of making love. The experience of violence has sickened her; the result is a sense of horror of all men. It was how I was feeling. I didn't lie there muttering to myself and vowing revenge, but my rage was making me ill just the same. Being unexpressible, the anger diffused itself over everything and everyone, including myself. I knew it wasn't doing me any good taking it like that, which only made me angrier. The crime of beating a man nearly to death doesn't lie in the pain you inflict; it's that you've created a *beaten* man. Even if I got the chance to pound on his head, it wouldn't remove the memory or make me whole as I'd been before he beat me. I would have to act like a savage animal to get my own back and then his victory would be complete. I'd be right down there with him. For the moment it was a risk I felt more than willing to take.

At some time during the afternoon I must have put the phone back on the hook because it woke me up in the night. I lay there in the dark, conscious of my bursting bladder and empty stomach. The phone sounded incredibly shrill and loud. If it had been next to the couch, I would have lifted the receiver and put it down again to cut the connection. But it was on the table across the room. It kept ringing. Finally I dragged myself over and lifted the receiver to my good ear.

'I've thought about it,' Fieldman said. 'You better come over here – I'm ready to talk.' There was a grim, melodramatic tone in his voice. He was taking himself very seriously.

'Couldn't you tell me over the phone?'

'I've got something to show you.'

'Couldn't you bring it over here?'

'I don't have a car,' he said impatiently. 'I'm staying at a friend's place who's out of town. Landau told me I couldn't stay at Malibu any more. Wasn't that nice of him? He told me Peaches didn't want me in the house.'

I made some sympathetic grunting noises. 'Take a cab over here,' I said.

'No!' he shouted. 'If I'm going to talk, I'll talk where *I* want. Do you realize I haven't even got money for cab fare? Do you realize that? Forty-three years old and I had to hitchhike from Malibu into town. I wouldn't treat a dog the way they've treated me. Not even a crummy couple of grand, not even a couple of hundred, not even cab fare – just out in the cold. They think I'm afraid to talk. A little kindness was all I asked, a little common decency, but no, that's too much for them . . .'

'Fieldman, have you got the script there?'

'I told you I didn't take the script.'

There was a pause. I could hear him breathing heavily.

'Listen,' he snarled. 'I tried to *sell* my information. I'm offering to *give* it to you. I don't have to justify it over the goddamn telephone.'

'I'm just asking you what it is.' I snapped on the table light and looked at my watch: it was only nine o'clock in the evening. I felt like I'd been asleep for days.

'It's one of Raymond's diaries,' he said reproachfully.

'How'd you get hold of that?'

'I'll tell you. I was snooping around Paul's study. I was looking for money. Sometimes he kept cash in books. Look, are you coming over here or not?'

'What am I supposed to do with his diary?'

'I just thought since you were such a big friend of Laura's it might interest you. Peaches and Landau won't give me anything for it. But if it's too much trouble to drive to Hollywood, forget it.'

'I didn't say I wasn't coming. I've been sick.'

'Okay, you got flu or something. You're washing your hair tonight. You want to see his diary or not?' He was shouting again.

'Give me the address, Fieldman.'

I scrawled it with a ball point on the back of my hand.

'You're going to have to pay me something for it,' he added.

'I thought you were giving it to me.'

'I've changed my mind – I've got proof here about the whole business. Paul, Raymond, the script. I used to suspect Raymond was the guy who really wrote Paul's material and I was right. But this time it's worse than that.' He lowered his voice. 'I'm telling you, these people are bad. I'm talking about greed, man, real evil.'

He started to tell me how vicious Hollywood was and I told him to save it because it was such a terrible story I had to hear it in person.

twenty-four

The pavements of Hollywood Boulevard thronged with every variety of nightlife. There were fat ladies in print dresses with nylon stocking bunched up around their knees; bowed, elderly people on street corners trying to summon the courage to brave the traffic; old broken-down queens; young hustlers with ravaged, restless faces; scornful, tight-mouthed whores; ageing strong men; dwarfs; livid-faced drunks; and sullen, princely black pimps in Greta Garbo hats and flowing foxes and minks. There were businessmen in town for conventions, and tourists and teenagers who'd driven from all over Los Angeles to participate in the evening traffic jam.

I watched them through my windscreen as they moved through the changing neon light thrown out by the bars, amusement arcades, and junk-food stands. I was so stoned on painkillers, I was close to rear-ending the car in front of me. My vision was just blurred enough that it was hard to read the street signs. The action on the street came to me muted, like a soft-focus advertisement, romantically blurred, with the colours running into each other. That's how you want to view that part of East Hollywood: no sharp edges, no harsh details, just keep your eyes moving and barely focused and don't linger over anything, because around there, if you ever stop and see what you're really looking at, you get depressed and start hoping for the earthquake that they're always predicting is going to drop the city into the cleansing waters of the Pacific.

I turned off Hollywood and found the address half a block down a residential side street. It was a yellow brick apartment building crisscrossed with rusty fire escape landings and a dimly lit lobby that smelled of paint fumes that were still not powerful enough to mask the odour of rot. The elevator was about the size of a fat man's coffin. The inside had been painted yellow but the fresh paint was already scarred up like a service station rest room.

I stepped out on the third floor and followed the narrow corridor around a turn and past an open door with a party going on inside. The guests were all young men. Most of them had on short-sleeved T-shirts and tight jeans rolled up over boots and short cropped, very carefully tended hair. At a superficial glance they looked like a gathering of extremely clean, beautifully groomed truck drivers and garage mechanics. There was a definite blue-collar feel about them. In my suit and tie and with a bloody bandage holding in what was left of my brains, I made a certain impression on them. They are a wary, cautious breed, even in the heart of their own territory, and their conversation took a nose dive as I passed the door.

The apartment number Fieldman had given me was the last before the window at the end of the corridor. The window was open and I could see two men standing on the fire escape outside looking towards the Hollywood sign. They didn't see me. I pushed the buzzer but heard no buzz so I knocked forcefully.

I knocked several times. Someone from the party down the hall came out and watched me while he took his time lighting a cigarette. I felt about as inconspicuous as a man with reindeer antlers growing out of his forehead. I knocked again.

'He's there,' the fellow at the end of the corridor said. 'He had a visitor a little while ago. He hasn't gone out.'

I tried the door handle, but it was locked.

'Are you sure? He just asked me to come over.'

'Oh, I'm sure.' The fellow moved a few steps closer. He was big and blond with a handsome, rugged face and a smooth, baritone voice. He was the strong, clean-cut type of man who plays cowboys in cigarette commercials and is macho enough not to care how much tar he inhales so long as it tastes good. He was an imitation of an imitation. He was what passed for the male article in a previous decade.

'He's so uptight,' he said. 'You can't miss him.'

'I hope he's all right,' I said.

'I'm the manager. We can check.' He approached down the hall, talking more easily now. 'It's Rudy's apartment. This guy Fieldman is just staying there. I promised Rudy I'd keep an eye on things. We get all kinds of stuff in this place. It's a regular soap opera. We get stuff here they don't even have in insane asylums.' He was looking at everything but my scalped, bandaged head. He tried several keys and finally got the door open and we looked into a vestibule dimly lit by a guttering candle set on a low deal table. Other people from the party had filtered down the hall out of curiosity.

I called Fieldman's name very loudly three times but there was no reply. The candle had melted into a pool of liquid wax and was dripping over the edge of the table.

'You're the landlord,' I said. 'You'd better go in first.'

'Why do you want *me* to go in first?' There was a flicker of hysteria in his smooth baritone.

'You're the landlord.'

'I'm sorry, I'm not the landlord, I'm the manager. And he's your friend.'

'He's not my friend. He's just someone I know.'

'Are you a cop?' He stepped back a little.

'Forget it.' I walked into the vestibule and shouted Fieldman's name again. There was a warm, used quality to the air, you could sense people had been breathing it recently. A faint stink of gunpowder hung suspended in the atmosphere. I really didn't want to stay there. The side of my head was on fire and I felt the slightest blow would finish me off. In a sudden panic I said, 'Did you see Fieldman's guest leave?'

'Yeah,' the manager said. 'What's the matter?'

'I smell gunpowder.'

'What gunpowder?' He turned to the men behind him. 'He smells gunpowder.'

The word *gunpowder* got repeated a lot by the crowd behind me.

'Look,' I said. 'I'm just going to step in there and look around, okay? Keep your friends outside. Don't touch the door handle.' I took out a hankie and wiped my hands and smiled at him. 'It's cool, okay. You come with me. I just don't want to do anything wrong. We look but don't touch.'

'Who are you?'

'I'm a private detective.' I took his arm firmly and drew him forward. There was a lot of white showing around his eyeballs. The panic coming off of him calmed me. I kept a strong grip on his arm and moved him along with me. He didn't resist. The vestibule opened on the right into a small living room furnished in bamboo couches and polished glass and a profusion of spot-lighted plants. There was an empty bottle of tequila and a small plate of lime rinds crusted in salt on one of the glass tables. The kitchen was empty and spotless except for an ice tray lying in a pool of water on the counter. That left the bedroom which was at the end of a corridor lit by a Japanese lantern. It was an attrac-tive bedroom with a four-poster bed and silver-and-black Art Deco lamps on the glass bedside tables. There were some framed German expressionist prints on the dove-grey walls and a large antique wooden pig on rockers next to an exerciser bicycle. Fieldman was on his knees in the far corner of the room, jammed forward into the angle made by the walls. A white silk dressing gown was drawn tight across his broad shoulders and the centre of the back of his head was dark, darker than his hair. His hands were tied behind his back with the dressing-gown cord. I walked over and put my finger on his neck and felt for a pulse. The skin on the stunt man's neck was cold and stubbled and he had no more pulse than the *Venus de Milo*.

The walls, the back of his dressing gown, the carpet all bore tiny flecks and traces of brains and blood. When I turned around the manager was staring at me with his mouth open. He didn't have a suntan any more. His eyes blinked, not spasmodically, but with an almost mathematical regularity, as if they were res-ponding to a strobe light.

'Hey,' I said.

He squeezed his eyes shut and shook his head but he opened them, the blinking started again. Faced with death, it's not un-usual for a part of the body to go privately mad. Some people lick their lips compulsively, chatter their teeth, hyperventilate. This guy was a blinker.

I walked over to him and rested my hand on his shoulder.

'Now we go out and call the police from your apartment,' I said. 'We didn't touch anything, right?'

He nodded dumbly. ·

'The cops may give you a rough time. I mean, they're going to take one look at you boys, and they're going to give you a rough time.'

'I understand that.'

'But I don't want your friends to leave.'

'They won't leave.' His eyes finally stopped blinking and immediately tears gushed out of them. 'They'll think it's exciting.'

'Sure, that's the way people are.'

'Did you know him?' He kept his face averted from the dead man. His expression was perfectly wooden, but tears continued to pour down his cheeks. He looked humiliated.

'A little. He was a guy with a lot of problems. I don't think he was a bad guy. He had a run of bad breaks and he played each one of them wrong. He got backed into a corner.'

The ghoulish pun was unintentional, but all the same I felt the skin on my face tightening into a smile. I couldn't wipe it off. I could feel the air on my teeth and gums, my lips wolfishly drawn back in a snarl.

'Boy, are you funny.' He wiped the tears from his eyes.

'Don't let it worry you.' I steered him towards the door. 'Just get it right for the cops.'

On my way out I ran my eyes over the rest of the apartment but I couldn't see the diary out in the open. I couldn't afford to be seen searching for anything. I stationed the manager on the door and used the phone in his apartment. First I called Marcus. I made it brief and told him if he wanted a piece of it, he'd better make it fast because Hollywood Division Homicide would want to own it. He said he'd phone Hollywood Division himself. He had a friend there in Homicide. He said not to touch anything and not to let anyone go. After that I phoned Landau but got his service. There was no answer in Malibu. I finally reached him at the Keplers'. He said he'd been trying to reach me all day, but my phone had been off the hook. He wanted to inquire how I was. I told him just how I was.

'In a few minutes the police are going to be here,' I said. 'They're going to want to know who I was working for when I got this knock on the head. If they're at all alert, they're going to check this phone and see that Fieldman was calling you and Peaches and the Keplers today. Raymond's diary may well be in the apartment.'

'Why do you have to mention the diary, if it's not there?'

'Am I still working for you?' I said. 'Personally I don't know what I'm doing. Someone just blew Morris Fieldman's brains all over the bedroom.'

'I appreciate that. Absolutely,' he said.

'According to Fieldman, a lot of that script is Kepler's work.'

'Possibly, in parts, yes. It's not as simple as that. These things are – ambiguous.'

'That's a swell word, Mr Landau, but it's not in a policeman's vocabulary. You better lighten up on the ambiguity. I nearly got killed last night. A hundred dollars a day buys a lot of me, but it doesn't cover murder. If they throw me in the can tonight, I want lawyers on the job tonight and I want out tonight.'

'You can count on it,' he said crisply. 'Just try and keep Kepler and Paul out of it – the publicity could kill us.'

'Before I hang up. Do you have any idea what's going on?'

'Put it this way. Certain things I don't look into. There have been irregularities perhaps, relating to some of Paul's properties – nothing illegal. If I wanted to, I could make an educated guess but I'm not interested in doing so. But Fieldman I don't know anything about. He must have been involved with the wrong people.'

'Sure – the wrong people. He must have suffocated on the ambiguity they give out. Hear that noise in the background, Mr Landau – that's a police siren. You better get on the phone to some lawyers.'

twenty-five

Captain Marcus didn't arrive with Hollywood Division. The fingerprint and photo units and a cop called Loomis went into the apartment while a Lieutenant Detective Litvinoff herded the rest of us into the manager's place and closed the door.

Litvinoff had the angry deadness in his eyes you find on so

many big-city cops. He had the thin, clamped lips, the menacing, uninflected monotone, the aura of barely controlled disgust spoiling for a fight that grows on them like mould on bread. He'd seen it all too many times. All that was left alive in his face was contempt and the habit of power. And the contempt was as much for himself as anyone else. You could see it in the way he wore his clothes, in his unhealthy, poorly shaven face, in the cigarette burns in his jacket. He was about fifty. A quarter of a century of seeing the worst side of human nature was backed up in his eyes like poisonous radioactive waste.

You want to know what the people in a city are like: look at the faces of its police force, the ones who eat it and breathe it night and day in every corner of the city.

'You the guy who found the body?' Litvinoff asked.

'Yeah, with the manager.'

'Loomis'll talk to you. Someone hit you in the head, huh? Too bad. Next time you'll wear a crash helmet. Sit over there next to the guy with the earring. Looks like a nice party you were having. You must have all left your wives home. Just settle down, boys. Let's get it nice and quiet, and I'll ask you some questions.'

I sat on the edge of a sofa and listened, doing my best to avoid Litvinoff's gaze. After about five minutes his face was mottled with an angry flush and his eyes had become violently glazed. He reminded me of a cat watching birds in a cage, glancing from one to the other, mesmerized by all their twittering activity. Four of the guests had seen Fieldman's visitor arrive and two had noticed him leave, but they couldn't agree on his clothes, his height, or his hair colour. The composite description would have made a suspect out of a good half of the American male population. He was somewhere between five feet six and six feet, wearing either a pale raincoat, or a white turtleneck sweater, with or without a moustache, with either blond or dark hair, with or without lightly tinted glasses, aged between twenty-five and forty. Someone described him as handsome in a kind of dumb, heavy-set way and someone else said he wasn't cute at all. He was perfectly ordinary looking.

No one had heard a gunshot, but the music had been on loud. Several people remembered in retrospect hearing a car backfire, but as many of them denied hearing any such thing. As the questions were repeated, everyone became a little more fanciful and obscure and ultimately unsure of what he'd seen. The man who'd said the visitor was cute seemed the most definite and consistent in his descriptions. He claimed he could recognize the visitor if he saw him again.

'Oh, you could not,' the person sitting next to him said.

It degenerated after that. Litvinoff had his hands full. He obviously passionately hated homosexuals. He would have gladly shot the legs out from under any of them. There was an answer that might have accounted for the discrepancies in the description. The visitor might have entered the building wearing a raincoat and tinted spectacles with a blond wig and false moustache and simply removed them on his way out. It was the sort of suggestion which years of hard experience had taught me to keep to myself.

When the manager returned to his apartment, a young patrolman called my name and walked me down the corridor to the end apartment.

A cop in his fifties, with curly grey hair and a floridly handsome face, introduced himself as Captain Loomis. He had wild, black eyebrows and small but extremely striking blue eyes. His hair was more modishly styled than you'd expect on a cop and his clothes didn't come from a mail-order catalogue. He was dressed out of a Beverly Hills men's shop in a tailored, grey suede sports jacket and cream-coloured flannel slacks. His fingernails were polished. A whiff of cologne came off his smoothly shaven face. You felt it didn't worry him too much if people took him for an actor who played policemen on television. Marcus had arrived while I'd been next door. Slumped on the couch in his wrinkled, blue serge suit and tired dusty shoes, he had the air of an underling come to beg a favour. I looked at him, but he didn't return my glance.

'You must have fell out of bed.' Loomis gave me an icy smirk and winked; his fingertips jabbed my shoulder in greeting. He did it the way he would kick his tyres to check the air pressure. His hand climbed up my back and rested with a possessive weight on my neck. It was his routine for establishing ownership.

'Sit there.' He nudged me towards an armchair facing Marcus and moved off a few yards. I lowered myself into the chair and crossed my legs and tried to get some air into the bottom of my lungs.

Out of instinct, or according to conscious practice, they had duplicated the seating arrangement used in certain kinds of job interviews, and by psychiatricts working in pairs. While one talked to me, the other could watch my reactions; I could only keep one of them in view at a time. I was pretty sure it was instinct; they were hunters of men and I was feeling very much like game.

'Comfortable? You want a cigarette?' Loomis leaned forward, hands on his thighs, in the manner of a grown-up talking to a child. He could turn on a kind of bogus Irish charm, put a musical warmth into his voice, crinkle his eyes.

'I'm fine.' I forced my hands to open with apparent calm on the arms of the chair. I took slow deep breaths.

'You're fine, but you look like Frankenstein. Tell us about that.' He reached out and very delicately pinched a corner of the bandage on my head, smiling encouragement. Cats just before they kill something are meant to smile; it's involuntary. They can't help it. Neither could Loomis. He let go of the bandage and stood up straight. 'Tell us.'

'I was looking for a runaway husband last night,' I said. 'I located him in a motel in Santa Monica. He wasn't there when I arrived. Someone else was. I never saw it coming and I don't know who did it, or what he did it with. The husband didn't know anything either. I got him home and went to the hospital. I've been in bed ever since until this guy Fieldman called me. Fieldman was a . . .'

'We know who Fieldman was.' Loomis patted himself on the back of the neck; it made a steady slapping sound and he kept it up while I talked, studying my face. So far he was running true to form, working with the standard material of intimidation.

'Fieldman told me he had some big angle on the Sassari murder but he wouldn't discuss it over the phone. When I got here, he was dead.'

'How'd you know Fieldman in the first place?'

I told him about the incident on Harper in some detail, lingering over it because it was safe ground. At one point I turned around in my chair to get a look at Marcus. He was poised on the edge of the couch, watching me with his flat eyes. He had the extreme stillness of an animal settling itself before a jump.

'Okay,' Loomis said. 'That's how you met Fieldman. He was riding around Hollywood in the nude. A little improbable, but we'll let it pass. What then?'

'A couple of months later Sassari tried to hire me to find his wife. She wasn't his wife then. Fieldman was at the house. I never heard anything about him since then except what I read in the newspapers until he phoned me.'

The phone on the glass table in front of me rang and Loomis snatched it up. He said 'yup' into the receiver about six times and banged it down.

'How come,' Loomis said, 'you aren't worried?'

'Well, I'm worried about plenty of things. Which one in particular are you surprised I'm not worried about?'

'Maybe that I'm going to bounce your head off the wall a bit.'

'Try the cemetery.' Marcus spoke at last.

'Tell us what you were doing at the cemetery,' Loomis chimed in on cue.

'I don't know what I was doing there. It doesn't really matter because it wasn't anything you can hold me on.'

'We ought to have this guy lecturing at the fucking academy – he really knows law.' He brought his head down close to mine and whispered, 'You know, I don't mind you. A lot of cops hate investigators. I have no such prejudices. You're just a working man to me. I respect you for it. I respect you as a human being. Do you understand what I'm saying?'

'I do.'

'Then please,' he stood up again, 'don't play games with me. I'm asking you nicely. I know you're a sharp character, Kyd. You got the inside track on all kinds of things which we, humble policemen, don't know about. So enlighten us. Who was this runaway husband? What motel was he staying at? Who hired you to find him?'

'I'm sorry but I'd be breaking a confidence to my client.' I tried to sound sorry. Hell, I was sorry. I would have liked nothing better than to tell him.

'I see.' He nodded. 'You got this great job as a private investigator to the stars. If you talk to us, you're worried it'll get in the papers and ruin your reputation. Is that it?'

'That sort of thing.'

'Well, it's tough.' He sighed in distress. 'That's a nasty thing you got on your head. If I had a thing like that I'd be nervous as hell I was going to trip on a rug and hit it against the wall. Wouldn't you, Marcus?' He unbuttoned his suede jacket and hitched up his trousers. 'I mean I'd be a lot more worried about breaking my head than breaking a confidence. What I'm really trying to say is that I'm going to hit you right in the fucking mouth if you don't talk.'

'Hitting the handicapped would be about your speed.'

He swung his open hand at my face, just grazing the tip of my nose. I was too slow to duck and there was nowhere to go anyway so I just sat there. He did it again with the back of his hand and I felt the air whistle past my face.

'I wish my mother was here,' I muttered. 'She could whip your ass for me.'

I saw his open hand coming again, this time right for the bandaged side. I closed my eyes and bit down hard on my teeth, waiting for the explosion of pain but nothing happened. When I opened my eyes, Loomis's face was a few inches from mine.

'Why, I bet you need a change of underwear, son,' he said in a compassionate voice. 'Go on, say something. Say anything and I'll turn your fucking brainpan around.'

I didn't say anything. There was a bitter, metallic taste in my mouth. He stepped back and lit a cigarette and dragged deeply on it. He was breathing heavily. If that was his big play, it hadn't won him any esteem or information, but he seemed far from finished. The desire to strike me down was working in him like lust; his face was distended, his neck pumped out around his collar.

'You gonna let this yo-yo play games?' he said. 'I'm not.'

There was no sound in the room except Loomis's harsh constricted breathing.

'I'm talking to you, Marcus.'

'No you're not, Loomis.' The ghost of a shrug rippled across Marcus's face and shoulders; his voice communicated the most subtle and arid contempt. 'What you're doing is standing on your own dick.'

Loomis got a suffering look around his nose and eyes. He smiled quickly to himself, his nostrils quivering. His colour was suddenly not so good now, not so rich. Whatever blow Marcus had dealt him, whatever power he was invoking by the insult had touched Loomis where he lived. If it was a rehearsed routine they were acting out for my benefit, it was better than anything I'd ever seen. I had expected the classical hard-soft attack: Loomis playing it bloodthirsty with Marcus following it up as the sympathetic party. They were equal in rank. Any pinch to be had theoretically belonged to Loomis. It was not what was going on tonight.

'Don't talk to me about no more fucking favours, Marcus. You're clean out of favours as of right now.'

It was the first time I'd seen Marcus smile, properly smile. It was as if he was remembering something with grim pleasure and a kind of mordant amusement at how awful life could be.

'You know that's not so,' he said quietly.

Loomis took the cigarette out of his mouth and flicked it with his thumb and middle finger at my face. I batted it down with my forearm, showering sparks over my legs.

Then he was gone.

Marcus remained on the couch, hunched forward, staring dejectedly at the carpet. He had the gift of stretching out a pause until it grated on your nerves. Whether he slowed time down or speeded it up, it always seemed to be working for him.

'You shouldn't mouth off,' he said. 'That's the kind of cop could have you killed a half hour after you walk out of here.'

'Anyone can have anyone killed in this country. He doesn't impress me that much.'

'Okay, okay.' There was an uncharacteristic edge of impatience in his voice.

'It's too bad you only got this one Gestapo routine,' I said. 'Your idea of a conversation is sticking your thumb in someone's windpipe and asking him a question.'

Marcus slouched over to the window and stood looking out at the vast, pale vibration of light and exhaust fumes glowing over Hollywood Boulevard.

'Is that really how you met Sassari's wife – driving Fieldman in the raw?'

'That's the truth.'

'She didn't kill Sassari?'

'I don't know,' I said. 'She never struck me as the type to stab a guy to death.'

Marcus turned from the window and walked over to the living room entrance and glanced down the hall. You could hear a murmur of voices and catch a flicker of silver light from the bedroom where they were still photographing.

'I never saw one like that before,' he said. 'I had a stepmother used to do that to me when I was a kid. Make me kneel facing the corner when I'd done something wrong. When I walked in there and saw him it reminded me of her. Whoever killed him is something of a fancy guy. He ties him up, positions him, executes him. That takes time . . . it means a certain amount of talking. He didn't just want to kill Fieldman. He's trying to tell us something about Fieldman. It's theatrical.' He jingled the change in his pocket. 'Who knows? It might be a grudge-killing, or even a professional job. The guy might be one of those artistic types who likes to sign his work.'

'I don't know.' I thought he was being too nice.

'I should have taken you in that day I came to your house,' he said. 'It would have saved you a lot of trouble. I should have collared you at the cemetery, too. This time you leave me no choice. Get on your feet.'

'What's the charge?'

'Accessory to murder, withholding evidence, aiding and abetting a fugitive. None of them will stand up too long, but it'll be enough to get your licence revoked.'

'Thanks.' I stood up. 'Can I make a call?'

'You can use the pay phone at the station. It's out of order.' He snapped the handcuffs off the back of his belt and told me to remove my jacket. He put them on behind my back and then threw my jacket over my shoulders so nothing showed.

Going down in the small elevator we were jammed close together. A policeman can threaten and yell at you for hours, paint the most frightening picture of the years you're going to spend in prison and none of it touches you like those first moments of having your hands bound. He was perfectly considerate; he held the doors open for me. Coming down the steps, we were approached by some journalists. The police cars on the street had attracted a small crowd. Marcus didn't hold on to my arm, or in any way communicate to them that I was his prisoner, and they took me for a cop.

'No comment,' he said. 'It's not really our case.'

'What's it about?'

'Ask Loomis – it's his baby.' We walked through the crowd away from Hollywood Boulevard. We passed Marcus's parked car and kept going to the end of the block and then turned left onto a quiet, residential street. He set a very slow pace, sauntering along the pavement and stopping now and then like a man taking his dog out for a walk. I might as well not have been there; he ignored me completely. After we'd gone several blocks like that, he headed south towards Cedars of Lebanon Hospital.

'You were pretty good in there with Loomis,' he chuckled. 'Pretty good. I thought you were just a pain in the ass but it's worse than that.'

'Where are we going?'

'I'm trying to make up my mind. About a hundred yards back I was going to punch you in the guts, but the impulse passed. You're some kind of war hero – I looked you up. I don't know what those decorations mean. Loomis didn't dent you. I suppose you're another hard case.' He spoke casually, a man ruminating at his leisure. 'You don't respond to civilized pressure. Loomis doesn't work. Losing your livelihood doesn't affect you. So what am I left with?'

'Where are we going?'

'You like malt whiskey?'

'Yeah, I like malt whiskey.' I stopped.

'Glenfiddich . . . Laphroaig . . . Islay Mist.' He said the words like a kid naming the lineup of his favourite baseball team. 'Let's go . . .'

153

twenty-six

We were in a crowded, unremarkable bar on Fountain Avenue, drinking Islay Mist courtesy of the owner. The owner was a personal friend of his, according to Marcus. He looked to me like a guy who gave away free drinks because he was scared to death of the policeman. I was begining to understand how he felt. For some reason being handcuffed had affected me less than having the bracelets removed. I very badly did not want to have them put back on again to the point now of being willing to leak some information to Marcus. Whether he had guessed this would happen I couldn't say, but it was starting to dawn on me that the policeman had depths of cunning beyond my scope.

He took his whiskey with a small splash of water and polished it off with a kind of childish haste. He drained two doubles like a kid guzzling lemonade and immediately signalled for more, remarking that I drank like an old woman. His eyes were clear, the skin around them fresh and unspoiled. He was a man who perhaps got high once in a while though he was not a habitual drinker. But he was vain about his drinking the way an adolescent can be and it interested me: it was the first sign of weakness I'd detected in him. Meeting a cop off duty can be like meetin a movie star; you're disappointed at how ordinary they are.

'Loomis took a dislike to you,' he said over his third drink. 'You should always tell a cop something even if it's not true.'

'Loomis is a cynic,' I said apropos of nothing. 'I bet you he gets his clothes free.'

'Loomis is a fairy. I worked vice with him years ago. He belongs to me – for life. That's the only reason you got out of there in one piece.'

I removed my wallet and took Landau's cheque out and handed it to Marcus.

'That's who I'm working for. Raymond Kepler disappeared the night of the party in Malibu. His wife works for Landau. They hired me to find Kepler.'

'Go on.'

'Kepler's a gambler. A lousy gambler. He's got a lot of bad

debts and a big drinking problem. I talked to a bookie in Venice who was looking to collect on a five-thousand-dollar tab. But the bookie wasn't that worried. Kepler's been in the hole before. Someone always bails him out. This one guy was my only lead, and I got nowhere. That night Mrs Kepler phoned me and said she'd heard from her husband and would I go get him. He was meant to be drunk at a place called the Ocean View Motel. Kepler wasn't in his room when I got there, but someone else was. I got clobbered in the dark. When I came to, Kepler was back in the room. Very drunk, and totally uncommunicative. Someone had written RAYMOND K. WILL PAY on the wall of the room.'

'The bookie might have followed you.' Marcus signalled for more drinks.

'Whoever hit me was already there.'

'Kepler could have hit you. He could have written that thing on the wall himself.'

'It's a possibility.'

'Where does Fieldman fit into this?'

'The day I went out to Malibu, Fieldman was there, looking to get pieced off. He said Sassari owed him back wages and something for that drug bust in Rome. He'd been pestering Landau for money. I talked to him. He wouldn't tell me anything, just kept hinting that he had something that could blow the whole case wide open. And that's it . . . up to tonight.'

Marcus pushed himself back from the table and squinted at me dubiously. An unhealthy glow mottled his forehead.

'You're giving me a short count. You're giving me nothing.'

It was going to be all right, I thought. He would have to squeeze me for the next few bits of information, work hard for them.

'It's not up to me to justify all this stuff,' I said. 'I never said it made sense.'

'What were you doing at the cemetery?'

'I'll tell you, but I won't sign anything.'

'Go ahead.'

'I was delivering a passport to Laura. It was wrapped in a sealed brown envelope. I never opened it because I didn't want to know the name. She'd left it at my house in a portfolio a long time ago. I never even knew there was a passport inside it until she asked me for it. The passport was just bait. I was trying to get to her to convince her to surrender.'

'If that was true,' he said, 'you wouldn't have brought the real passport.'

'I didn't see it that way. Bringing the real one would have proved she could trust me.'

'What name was the passport under? I know you looked at it.'

'Well, you're wrong. But I'll tell you something else. The next night I got a call from a guy who said he was Joe DiMaggio . . .'

Marcus glared at me.

'I taped the call,' I said. 'You can have the tape. This guy was obviously the one who lifted the passport, or knew who did it. He disguised his voice. He was calling to let me know that he knew you and I'd been waiting there. He said he had X-ray vision, that's how he saw us in the dark.'

'Joe DiMaggio, huh?'

'No, by then he said he was Clark Kent.'

'I don't believe you'd be making all this up. But if you're pulling my chain . . .'

'He must have had a nightscope,' I said.

'What?'

'I just thought of it. That's how he saw us in the dark. They use them on cameras for shooting wildlife at night, or for jungle fighting.'

'Is that right?' He brought his face over the table until I could smell the fatigue and liquor on his breath.

'It's possible. Another thing I thought of – maybe the guy who killed Fieldman changed his clothes or was wearing a wig or something. It might account for the discrepancy . . .'

'Spare me.' He lifted his hand. 'The big mystery isn't Fieldman, or the joker at the cemetery – it's you. What's your angle?' He grinned belligerently. 'What's in it for you?'

'I've got four hundred dollars, a broken head, and a cop itching to drop the boom on me. Do I look like a guy with an angle?'

He didn't appear to hear me. He gazed truculently at the empty glass in his hand, stared at my untouched drink, and then switched them around. He bared his teeth in an incomprehensible grimace, lifted the glass in a toast, and drained it off.

'The Sassari woman pay you?'

'No.'

'That was your first big mistake. You're funny, you know that? A funny fucker. You belong somewhere else. You belong maybe in the thirteenth century. Do you get my meaning?'

'Not particularly.'

'You don't, huh? Sitting there with your busted head, and your four hundred lousy bucks, and your memories of this fancy flake of a broad who is still taking you to the cleaners. Galahad. I didn't even know they made guys like you any more. Noble bachelors. I thought they went out with high-button shoes. I thought they disappeared when gunpowder was invented. I thought everyone had agreed they were just faggots anyway.'

'You ought to drink more often,' I said. 'It does something for your personality.'

'The point is, stud . . .' He jabbed the air with his finger. '. . . The point it, everyone seems to make a fool out of you. Everywhere you step, there's a banana peel.'

'I'm not doing that bad.' I shrugged.

'No? One, that chick cons you into a grandstand play with her passport that leaves you holding the bag. Two, you try to find a guy and someone does a fandango on your gourd. Three, you walk right into a corpse and some very uptight policemen. What's next, Kyd?'

'I'm thinking of taking a vacation.'

'Don't even think about it.' He lurched up from the table and slowly cast his eyes around the room. 'Tomorrow I question Kepler and Landau. There's a big bad smell coming off this case and I just hope it's not coming from you.'

'I hope you don't get busted for drunk driving.'

'Don't worry about me. You ought to look in the mirror.' He grinned down at me. 'You ought to get a look at your eyes. You got the unluckiest-looking eyes I've ever seen. Know what I think? I think that chick's a killer, and one way or another you're going down with her.'

I thanked him for the observation and watched him negotiate

his way along the bar towards the door. I waited a few minutes, breathing in the noise and smoky air, slumped in my chair, and then I walked to the back of the bar and called Landau.

I gave it to him in that dead, uninflected monotone which I always pick up from being around cops. I told him I'd managed to keep the missing script and diary out of it, but that the police now wanted to question Kepler.

'He's going to have to explain a few things,' I said.

'You're damned right,' Landau agreed. 'I'll look forward to hearing his explanations. I haven't heard any yet.'

'For what it's worth, I think whoever killed Fieldman has Raymond's diary. It wasn't found in the apartment. What is it worth, Mr Landau?'

'Not having seen it, I couldn't tell you. I certainly wasn't interested in buying it.' He paused and cleared his throat. 'I don't think I care for your implications, Kyd. I have a responsibility to Paul Sassari and to his mother and to certain business interests. I'm trying to recover a script. I also have personal loyalty to Anne Kepler. I wish you would stop acting as if I'm concealing something from you, or as if I'm well informed about what's happening. I'm not. I'm just struggling to keep my head above water.'

He was lying to me. I'd lied to Marcus. Marcus had lied to the coroner's jury. It was starting to feel like a game of musical chairs, only every time the music stopped, someone went to hell.

'If you were approached by someone who had the script, would you be willing to pay to get it back?'

'Of course, though it would depend on the price,' he said. 'Why, is that a possibility?'

'The way this case is going, I wouldn't be surprised if a mermaid walked out of the Pacific Ocean with the script between her teeth.'

'Be serious.'

'I have this overwhelming urge to laugh insanely but I'm conquering the impulse. One more question. If you never recover the script, what then?'

'Initially I thought Raymond might be able to remember enough of it to produce a rough draft. The way he's behaving now, I doubt it. And frankly, with people being killed, my main concern is protection. To tell the truth, I'm glad the police are getting involved.'

'That's good. They are very eager for involvement.'

'But of course I'm still hopeful,' he added. 'I don't want to announce the script is gone until I'm absolutely sure there's no way of getting it back.'

'Yeah, well it would help my position with the police if you gave me a little warning before you announced that. I just spent the last two hours perjuring myself blue in the face so they wouldn't find out about it.'

'Naturally, Kyd. That goes without saying. And don't think I don't appreciate your efforts. Is your . . . uh . . . injury better now?'

'It only bothers me when I breathe,' I said.

'Glad to hear it. Fine. I'll talk to you tomorrow.'

I hung the phone up and followed the last of the diehard drinkers out of the bar. The night air was like a cold, wet kiss from someone with gas fumes on her breath. I retraced my way back to Fieldman's apartment where my car was parked. The windscreen was misted over and the vinyl upholstery and plastic steering wheel were cold to the touch. I thought of Fieldman's cold stubbled neck where I'd dug for a pulse. To die on your knees in a corner with your hands tied; there was a terrible abnegation about it. It was how the VC used to execute collaborators, line them up on their knees in front of the villagers and go down the row with a handgun. We were more wasteful of our ammunition when it came to that kind of thing, just emptying clips into the unfriendlies. I thought of all the Jews who'd got it kneeling before open trenches. Or the mob, who also knew how to make a point in the way they executed, shooting an informer in the mouth to illustrate the penalty of talkativeness. Maybe Marcus was right and there was some message in the style of Fieldman's death. Some derision, as if the stunt man had not been deserving of respect. He had been a bad boy; bad boys traditionally got put in the corner.

The killer might have had no such motive in mind. I could only guess and by then my guessing was heavy with fatigue and pessimism. Three men, Sassari, Kepler, and Fieldman, had been either murdered or attacked in the space of a few days. I didn't even know what they had in common. Laura's role in it, if she had one, was so unknown to me, I didn't even know where to start speculating on it.

It would have been nice if Laura had telephoned and explained her part. It would have been a great help if Kepler had told me what he was doing at the Ocean View Motel that night. I would have liked Landau, my supposed client, to level with me. But then, no doubt, the police felt the same way about me. They would have liked to know about the missing screenplay and diary, the treachery that Fieldman had hinted at before he was killed. Laura's passport under the name of Eva Bomberg could be knowledge of vital importance to them. But nothing like that was happening. If there had ever been a clear right and wrong in the case, it was now masked. Something akin to vertigo struck my conscience when I thought of what I was doing, and not doing. Was there any decent ground left to make a stand? I could see nothing but a confusion of individuals manoeuvring against each other and I was one of them. I had lied to protect Laura and now I was lying to protect myself, breathing the same soiled, murky atmosphere as the others. And for whom? For Laura Cassidy? For Laura Sassari? For Mary Dana Thompson? For Eva Bomberg?

I started the car and let the engine idle. I thought of what Kep_ ler had said about not being able to pay hell a visit like a tourist. You could not see it, or search through it for someone without being there yourself. In some way, without knowing when or where, I had joined Laura and lost my bearings. Skindivers call it the 'whirly bends'; you're under water and suddenly you lose all sense of up or down. You strike out in panic, but it's impossible to tell which way the surface lies. Light seems to beckon from all directions and turn black as you struggle towards it. It's caused by a trickle of overly cold water seeping into the inner ear, disrupting the seat of balance.

I put the car in gear and steered it out into the deserted street. I could see all right and I had my sense of balance but some cold, deadening fear lay on my conscience. The policeman had said I had unlucky eyes. Maybe what he had really noticed was the guilt I was starting to trail around, the suspicion that I no longer had any moral certainty of what I was doing. Such a thing could give you an air of doomed vulnerability, your very weakness tempting fate to throw the works at you. If I was having trouble seeing any light in the case, not a little of it could be put down to Laura. In the effort to believe in her innocence and protect her interests, my own motives had grown tarnished. I had become unclear to myself, which is another way of saying I'd lost my luck. I didn't know that night just how badly I'd lost it. If I'd known, I would not have got out of bed the next day.

twenty-seven

I was walking across the parking lot behind my office building late the next morning, when I saw a car nose out of a space and slowly drive in my direction. When it reached the centre of the lot, it stopped, with the engine still going. It was a blue Pinto, but the sunlight striking the windscreen hid the driver from view. I walked on and started veering to the right to go around it. It reversed slowly, cutting me off. It was now sideways to me, and I could see a woman behind the wheel. Her hair was tied in a scarf covering her down to her eyes, which were hidden behind very large sunglasses. She unrolled the window about two inches and beckoned me over. I thought she wanted directions or something and then I had a sensation like a sheet of ice pressing against my chest: it was Laura.

'Get the Keplers out of town,' she said. 'Someone is trying to kill them.'

'Laura!' I pulled at her door, but it was locked.

'I can't explain now. Just please do what I say.' She was looking all around to see if we were observed. I couldn't believe she was right there, just on the other side of the window, and I couldn't get at her. It made me wild. I pawed and scratched at the glass, imploring her.

'I have to talk to you. I'm not going to do anything. For Christ's sake, don't go!'

The car began to inch forward and I walked along with it, gripping the partially opened window. 'This is dangerous for me, Thomas,' she said. 'Let go of the car.'

I felt the car surge forward. I held on and as it slowed down I scrambled up onto the hood, grabbing at the windscreen wipers for support. She reacted like a wild animal to the presence of a man on its back, swerving from side to side, sliding me back and forth over the slippery hood. It was a nightmare. I was plastered to the windscreen, my face against the glass, staring into her face a foot away from mine. She accelerated and stamped on the brakes in an effort to dislodge me. My forehead rebounded off the windscreen with a dull thud.

'Please get off!' she cried. 'Don't make me do this. Stop it! Please stop it!'

The car had stopped. She was leaning over the steering wheel with her face in her hands, weeping. I just lay there on the baking hood, my hands planted on the windscreen wipers. There were black spots dancing in front of my eyes and brutal waves of pain surging through my head. I should have done the sensible thing and rolled off the hood but some kind of terminal stubbornness held me there. She could not do this to me, appearing out of nowhere to tell me someone's life was in danger and then vanishing with no explanation. I wasn't having it. I could feel the engine humming beneath me, roaring and subsiding as she nervously jabbed the gas pedal.

'Kill me, you bitch!' I said. 'Go on. Talk to me or kill me.'

She leaned across and unlocked the passenger side door.

'Get in then,' she said.

I didn't trust her. She was sitting back with her arms folded. Concealed by the scarf and sunglasses I could only see the bottom half of her face, her mouth white and hard with fear.

'People are watching us!' she pleaded. 'Get in!'

I moved slowly across the hood, watching her hands as they rose to flex nervously on the wheel. Two rivulets of tears washed from beneath her sunglasses down the bitterly clenched corners of her mouth. My feet touched the ground but I never even made it to the door handle. She floored the accelerator and sent me sprawling in the dust, throwing up a cloud as she roared out of the parking lot. I didn't even get her licence number.·

I sat for a while in the dirt with the sun blazing down on my head. Some people had stopped on the far pavement to look at me. They pointed and shook their heads and consulted as to what to do. Maybe I was a drunk, or some kind of unfriendly maniac. They didn't know. Finally one of them took courage and shouted, 'Are you okay?'

'I am but hurt, friends,' I muttered, giving them a big wave. To prove it, I got to my feet and dusted myself off. I checked my dressing, expecting it to be wet with blood but the stitches had held. After all, it had been a relatively short ride and I'd had my clothes on. I'd been luckier than Fieldman. No bones were broken, my bruises were negligible. She must have liked me to have let me off so lightly.

Seeing me back on my feet reassured the small crowd of on-lookers. I walked upright and at an even and civilized pace towards the service entrance to my office building. I was fine, only I felt inwardly torn, violated if you like, by what she'd done. The sight of that clenched, colourless mouth, the panic that made her ruthless: it was a terrible shock to see her stripped down to those essentials. No more feeling sorry for the girl with the fancy blue eyes. If she wanted to treat me like a cop, that was her business. I didn't know what the Keplers were to her that she should risk being seen in public. All I knew was that what had just happened was her running true to form. She was on the inside and I was on the outside. She was giving me no chance, just laying some more outrageous, heavy trouble on me that might or might not be true.

Climbing the emergency stairs to my office, I cursed her. Who was it who had said that the light at the end of the tunnel is the light of an oncoming train? Whoever it was, he had described what it was to know Laura. I hadn't really even wanted to talk to her in the parking lot, I thought, I'd wanted to force her over my knee and beat terrible sense into her ass.

The door to my waiting room was wide open. A smell of good cigars and powerful, lavender cologne hung in the air. Someone had jimmied the metal plate and bolt out of the woodwork but the room was empty. The door to my office had been opened in the same manner. Some people could just not wait to see you. I eased the door open with my foot and saw two men sitting there looking at me. My desk drawers and the contents of my filing cabinet were spread around themn on the floor and they looked very much at home. The one in the client's chair was the size of a small jockey. He had not much of a chin, pale, mournful eyes, and a fat, sensual mouth with a cigar planted in its centre. He was dressed in a green rayon leisure suit and white cowboy boots. His belly plopped out of his trousers like a mould of Jell-O. His friend was in the chair by the window. He had a long leather suitcase resting on his knees. His short-sleeved shirt was open almost to his navel, showing a lot of black hair tightly clustered like peppercorns. His forearms were black with hair, too. He had a monkey face, cheerful and spiteful, with a wide mouth which was full of saliva. I knew it was full of saliva because he was blowing bubbles with it. While he was doing that, he caressed his chest with his fingertips, kneading himself, and squeezed his crotch with the other hand. He was God's gift to someone.

The little one swivelled his chair towards me, crossed his diminutive feet, and grinned around his cigar. The other one blew a bubble of saliva, watching me with an expression in his eyes that was like a view down several miles of bombed road.

'Frank Bando,' the little one said. 'This here's my colleague, Carlo. Hey, Carlo, what's your last name?'

'They didn't give me one,' Carlo said hoarsely, and giggled.

'Never mind,' Bando said. 'We just flew in from Vegas this morning especially to talk to you, Kyd. You got a little time for us?'

'He don't know how little time he got,' Carlo grunted.

'Don't pay any attention to Carlo. Underneath he's all heart. Look, you know Peaches? Sassari's mother? You talk to her on the phone once, right? She'd like us to ask you some questions. Maybe you sit down and talk a little.'

'About what?'

'Your future,' Carlo said.

'That's enough,' Bando warned him. 'Listen, we got a misunderstanding here. Peaches thinks you don't like her. You know what women are. They get an idea. They get hysterical. Me, I say to Peaches – "What, he doesn't like you? It's nothing. He likes you. I'll prove it to you." So as a favour to the lady, I come from Vegas to make the peace.'

'We're here to bury the hatchet,' Carlo said. 'Guess where?'

'Why does he keep saying these things to me?' I asked Bando.

Carlo placed his suitcase on the floor and walked around me to the door. He shut it. He stood a few feet behind me, and made a clucking sound with his lips. *'Boom-Boom!'* he said. 'Know what that is? That's the sound your head's going to make when I kick it down the stairs.'

It could have been worse; at least Carlo was talking to me. Ordinarily I imagined he knocked on your door and opened the discussion by laying a Louisville slugger across the side of your head.

'Sit down, Carlo,' Bando frowned. 'Sit down and be quiet. I don't want you to do nothing but sit and shut up.' He looked at me. 'You sit down, too. You're making everyone nervous.'

Making Frankie and Carlo nervous was the last thing in the world I wanted to do. I sat down in my chair behind my desk and by my extension tried to communicate to them that I was the most harmless yet obliging person they had ever encountered.

'Bringing Carlo wasn't my idea,' Bando said. 'But in Vegas there are certain parties with financial interests in this upcoming motion picture, *Shoot the Singer*. People are dying in Los Angeles, they tell me. Take Carlo for insurance. A boy like Carlo adds a little seriousness to a conversation.'

'Oh, boy.' I rolled my eyes.

'Don't be like that. Please, don't be funny with me.' He was disgusted. 'You're this close. Vegas wanted to send just Carlo but I talked them out of it. That's the kind of trouble you're in, mister, so please don't make with the funny faces.'

He waited for me to say something, so I nodded seriously.

'First off,' he said. 'I'm going to tell you why we don't like

165

you. We like Peaches. We've liked her a long time. Her husband was a personal friend of mine. Vinnie Sassari, Paul's father. Vinnie was in the business and he had an accident. I spent twenty large of my own money taking care of the guy who caused the accident. You understand? Peaches is family from way back. You understand the kind of people you're fucking with?'

'I'm getting it loud and clear,' I said.

'When Paul's time came, we liked him plenty, too. We financed his first two pictures. I didn't know him that good but I heard he was crazy. Temperamental. Who cares? His pictures all made money.'

'I never saw them.'

'I'm telling you a story,' he screamed. 'When I want you to talk I'll tell Carlo to squeeze your fucking throat. *Right?*'

'Right.' I nodded.

'Good. Now Peaches didn't like this Cassidy girl. Don't ask me why. She had a feeling. A girl from nowhere. A lowlife with a drug problem. Peaches didn't want Paul to marry her. She goes about it all wrong though. She don't ask our help. The rest you know. Paul married the girl anyway and one night she sticks a fucking knife in his heart.'

'Why?' I said.

'Who knows why? It's done. We don't care about "why" any more. We care about the script. That crack on the head you got wasn't from a collector. We've made inquiries. None of our people are bothering Kepler for money any more. His debts have been indefinitely postponed. So we look around to see where all the aggravation is coming from. And what d'you know? We find out you were balling Sassari's wife. That you've helped her out of the shit on previous occasions. You even had something going with Fieldman. You went over there the night he was taken care of. You asked Landau if he was willing to pay to get the script back. You talked to the cops and this morning the cops paid Peaches a visit. You gotta to be the key, mister. You're popping up all over the landscape.'

'What am I supposed to say? I didn't know she was going to kill Sassari. The only reason I went over to Fieldman's was because he called me up and told me he had Kepler's diary. Kepler was Sassari's ghost, he said. It was news to me.'

'Fieldman you can forget about,' Bando said. 'And all his ideas. There ain't no mystery about what happened to him.'

'None at all,' Carlo added piously.

'I see.'

'But I don't see.' Bando pointed his cigar at me. 'I don't know what's going on. Tell me what's going on, mister.'

'I'll tell you what I think is going on,' I said. 'I think it wasn't Sassari's wife who killed him. It was someone else. This person is the one who busted my head open at the Ocean View and probably is holding the script.'

'That's very convenient for you,' Bando grunted unhappily. 'This joker out of left field who stabs people and steals scripts and no one knows anything about. I don't believe there is such a guy.'

'What about Landau?' I said for the sake of controversy.

'Who's Landau? He don't know nothing. He don't even know where the financing comes from. Why? You suggesting he's double-crossing us?'

'No, I was just wondering how deaf and dumb he is.'

'If the price is right, Landau spreads his legs and shuts his eyes.'

'Kepler then,' I said. 'Maybe Kepler was looking to get out from under what's been sitting on his chest since college. He was doing all the work and Sassari was getting the credit. Maybe his wife didn't put the knife in Sassari. Maybe it was Kepler.'

'You're suposed to be a detective.' Bando grimaced at the ceiling. 'You're a know-nothing. The guy who hit you at the motel was after Kepler.'

'Okay, maybe I'm wrong. But someone hit me. I didn't hire anyone to damn near kill me.'

'Who knows what a guy like you would do? All I got to do is look at this office and the bandage and your way of doing things. You going to sit there and tell me you're a serious fucking individual?'

'Well, how's this,' I said, ignoring his question. 'Say Kepler suddenly grows brains and realizes he's getting taken. Say he finds out that since college Paul has been telling the bookmakers when and where to put the heat on. Because that's how it was done. Every time Kepler worked something up they dried up his credit and he had to go to Sassari and make a trade. Maybe Kepler hired someone to get rid of Sassari and that person has now turned around and started blackmailing Kepler.'

'Kepler hasn't got the balls to hire a killer. So what if he finally got wise to Sassari? What's he gonna do about it? Nothing. That's Landau and Kepler, which leaves you, and you look like a guy who has had bad ideas all his life. Ideas that just ain't gonna work. I think you and that bitch knocked Sassari off and grabbed the script.'

'Then who hit me in the head?' I said. 'You're making this up.'

Bando lowered himself from the chair and waddled to the window behind my desk. 'I don't like being confused. I don't like it. Tell me again why Carlo shouldn't kick you down the stairs.'

'Landau hired me. He represents Peaches' interests. Your interests and Peaches' interests are presumably the same. If I'm not working for you, who the hell am I working for?'

'Yeah,' he said dejectedly. 'It's what I figured. You ain't very fucking complicated. There's someone else, though, who isn't thinking straight at all. A crazy person.'

'That's what I'm trying to tell you.'

'I hate crazy people.' Bando turned and stared at me. 'I hate this fucking town. The worst scum in New York don't do the crimes they do out here. All you got here is basket cases, freaks, long-haired religious animals. In New York a guy maybe shoots you for ten dollars. In this town he takes your head off with a buzz saw for religious reasons and never even goes through your pockets. It's twisted. They find bodies all the time up in the hills. We take care of the fucking zombies in Vegas. That's a strictly on-the-level town. Everybody does business. But Los Angeles is strictly from cannibals and cuckoo clocks. How am I gonna do business with this guy if he's crazy? He don't even offer to sell the script back. Why don't he do something smart so I can kill him?'

'He wants something,' I said. 'The guy who wrote RAYMOND

K. WILL PAY on the motel room wall wants something.'

'And he *knows* something.' Bando's eyes widened. 'Because *someone is telling him things*.' He brought his face close to mine, moistened his fat red lips, and said: 'No way I can go back to Vegas with the story you've given me. Vegas don't like such stories. But it's okay if I go back to Vegas and tell them I've left Carlo in Los Angeles to take care of the problem. You understand?'

Standing up, he was not much higher than me sitting down. He had the air of a man deeply preoccupied by business worries, perplexed as to what action he should take. He looked like he really regretted everything. 'See, Kyd, someone's got to pay. I'll tell Vegas I couldn't recover the script because you wouldn't talk. So maybe we didn't get the script back but we took care of business. I'll have closed things up. Balanced the books. The way I see it, it's better than nothing. You got the picture?'

'You're going to hang it on me for lack of anyone better.'

'Maybe.' He shrugged. 'I don't know. I'm just thinking aloud. There's something about you that ain't right. You tell me you understand but I don't think you really *believe* it yet.' He turned to Carlo and said, 'Do something to his desk.'

Carlo unzipped his suitcase and removed a newly purchased axe. It still had the price tag on it. It was a full-size axe with a blade as blue as a razor. I pushed my chair back from the desk until my back was against the window, but Carlo paid no attention to me. It was my desk he was after. He swept everything off it, including the glass covering which broke into jagged sheets on the floor. Then he went to work, swinging from the heels, hewing his way down the centre of my desk. I sat there on the other side, with Bando beside me, with his hand on my shoulder. When he had sufficiently cracked up the wood Carlo stood on the desk and jumped up and down until it caved in, the two sides tilting to form a *V*.

'How much that desk cost you?' Bando took a hundred-dollar bill from his pocket, rolled it into a cylinder, and stuck it in my bandage. 'Get yourself a new one.'

He waited for me to make some comment, but what was there to say? You could not reason with the Bandos and Carlos of the world any more than you could hold a discussion with a rabid dog. He reached out and lifted up my chin, then gently patted my cheek.

'Now I think you believe,' he said in a soft voice. 'See, we ain't hard to do business with. We break something, we pay for it. We buy a screenplay, we expect to get it. That's all.'

Sure, I got it. It didn't require much imagination to understand Carlo's little allegorical performance with my desk.

'What do I do now? Take out life insurance?' I said. 'Or do you want me to price some office furniture? Or maybe I should have a crack at writing the script myself.'

'Stick to Kepler. Who knows? Maybe the crazy one will try to make contact.'

'And if he doesn't?'

Bando put his hands in his pockets and waddled to the door. 'We fit you for the part, Kyd. That's all there is to that tune.' He strolled out, leaving Carlo behind. I didn't look at him. I studied the oak desk splintered in half at my feet. I studied it for about sixty seconds and then finally lifted my eyes. Carlo got to his feet and picked up his suitcase and walked to the door.'*Boom-boom.*' He waved going out.

I sat for a long time after they'd gone, trying to get my stomach back down where it belonged. Then I went into the washroom and tried to scrub the feel of the little man's hand off my cheek. In the cracked mirror I looked like someone whose brakes have just gone out on the way down a mountain.

twenty-eight

I drove by the Keplers' house without slowing and pulled into a space at the end of the block. The sun was still shining, but the sky had darkened; here and there where the chemical concentration was highest the grey was touched with browns and smoky yellows. There was no wind and the skinny date-palms towered motionlessly above the houses and lawns.

A grey Renault with four flat tyres was parked in the Kepler driveway. The tyres had been sawed or hacked down to the steel-wire fibres. Yellow lines of epoxy glue ran along the seams of the door, trunk, and hood, effectively sealing it shut. It would take a blowtorch to get the car open again. Inside, taped to the driver's seat, I could see a square of white cardboard. It said RAYMOND K. WILL PAY.

There was the sound of a car door slamming. I turned and watched a man in overalls get out of his van and open the hood. He was across the street, parked about ten cars away. I had seen his van when I drove by, but no one had been in the driver's seat.

I strolled across the street towards him. He must have heard my footsteps approaching but he kept his head lowered, his hands busy on the engine. When I was almost up to him, he straightened and grinned at me. He was blond, in his mid-twenties, with an earnest snub-nosed face that would have looked right on an army recruiting poster.

'Marcus told me to look for a guy who looked like Kepler's car. It's Kyd, right?'

I nodded.

'Marcus said to watch the place. I'm Laker.'

'Is Kepler home?'

'He's inside,' the policeman said. 'With his wife.'

'Mind if I talk to him?' I asked.

'My orders are to watch the place. What you do is your business.'

I offered him a cigarette but he said he didn't smoke.

'Anyone see what happened to Kepler's car?' I asked.

He closed the hood and walked around to the van door and got inside. He wasn't talking. He was giving out nothing – like Kepler, like Laura, like me. Nothing but silence from all quarters. He rolled up the window and then vanished into the rear of the van.

When I reached the Kepler porch, I turned around. There was an observation window that bulged like a colourless eye out of the side panel of the van. He was watching me through it.

I rapped the sea-horse knocker against the brass plate on the front door. I waited, but nothing happened. I did it a second time and then lost patience and banged with my fist.

'Who is it?' a woman's voice said. I could sense her right on the other side of the door and suddenly had a feeling she had been there all along.

'It's Kyd, Mrs Kepler.'

'My husband isn't feeling well,' she said breathlessly. 'He can't see anyone.'

'I don't feel that hot myself, Mrs Kepler. Open the door.'

'Couldn't you come back later? I'm not dressed.'

'Are you going to open the door, or do I come through the chimney?'

She told me to wait, and I heard her footsteps recede into the house. Several moments passed. I smoked a cigarette and watched the street. There was a dead, motionless feel to the air. It wasn't the approach of rain, but there was no wind and the light was dwindling, taking the life out of all the colours.

There was a rattle of locks being unbolted and a chain being taken off the hook and then the door opened just wide enough for me to enter. I was in a dim foyer among hanging flowerpots and dark green rubber plants. Anne Kepler had already turned and moved off down the hall. She was dressed in a salmon-pink satin dressing gown, fringed in lace that had turned brown with age. It was an antique garment, with high, square shoulders in the style of the forties. At the end of the hall she turned, hands jammed in the pockets, and nodded forcefully for me to follow her. We descended some tiled steps into a small living room dominated by a bay window with drawn curtains. Plush, dark blue velvet armchairs were arranged around a circular bamboo table in front of the fireplace. Wall lamps set in arched niches provided a dim light. A vanity mirror and a number of cosmetics were laid out on the bamboo table and the air smelled of nail-polish remover.

Mrs Kepler motioned me to one of the armchairs and took the other one herself, perching on its edge, her knees pressed tightly together, her hands glued together in her lap. She had made up her eyes to look wide and startled, but it hadn't altered their flat, beseeching stare. Her mouth was compressed. Nothing in her face moved except her nostrils, which flared errati-

172

cally. She was breathing with difficulty, using only the upper part of her lungs like an asthmatic.

'Is your husband here?' I kept my voice low, gentle.

'In his study.' She stared at me with a fixed vacancy. 'After the police left this morning, he went in there with a bottle. He won't talk to me. I've had to send the children away in case the man who did that to the car comes back again . . .' Her upper lip quivered and began to retract in a trembling circular motion over her front teeth. She put her hand over her mouth and bent her head. Silently her eyes gushed tears, washing rivulets of mascara through her face powder.

'I was making up.' She took a breath. 'I couldn't think of anything else. I don't know what to do any more.'

'Why won't your husband talk to you?' I asked.

'He just stares at me like he doesn't know who I am and he says . . . such horrible things. When I ask him what he means, he just laughs.'

'He must have a cast-iron sense of humour. I've found out quite a lot about your husband in the last few days. His relationship with Sassari, for instance. Weren't you aware your husband ghosted Sassari's work?'

'Aware of it? Don't you think I begged him to stop gambling? Don't you think I know what it's like to have men threatening him in the middle of the night? Sassari took advantage of his weakness.'

'It would have been nice if you and Landau had told me that in the first place.'

'What does it matter?' she said bitterly. 'What could you have done? They're trying to kill my husband.'

'Who is?'

'The people who did that to the car.' She blew her nose with some tissues from the table. 'He won't tell the police their names. He won't tell me.'

'Your husband isn't being harassed by gamblers. That's past history.'

'Well, who are they then? He doesn't have the script. What do they want? We don't have anything. We've never had anything.' She sank back in her chair and groaned. 'Don't you understand? My husband won't speak to me. He just stares at me like I'm some kind of monster.'

'Maybe he's jealous of Landau,' I said curtly.

She just glared at me in cold indignation and then folded her arms and stared grim-faced at the wall.

'Well?'

'Dix Landau has wanted to marry me for two years. I've been faithful to my husband all that time. I've stuck with Raymond through his gambling, his drinking, and the destruction of his talent. I've believed in him when any sane woman would have realized that he wasn't going to change. Dix would give me . . . anything. Don't ever tell me I've given Raymond grounds to be jealous. Don't ever tell me that. If you're going to talk to me like that, you can get out of my house.'

I pulled myself up out of the chair and moved to the bay window. I cracked the drapes. There was a golden Labrador standing on the Kepler front lawn, its forepaw raised, alertly staring at the front of the house. It held itself absolutely still except for its tail, which twitched in a small arc. We stared at each other for several moments, having our different thoughts. I let the drapes close, turned, and looked at Mrs Kepler watching me from her chair. She had the zombie expression on her face again, the features slack, the eyes hollowed out by the wasting energy of shock. I thought of the way Carlo had looked at me in my office. I'd seen his sort of eyes before: killer's eyes, as remote and mysterious as the floor of an ocean. I was in a maze. I could sense the exits closing one after another, my avenues of escape being sealed shut. How had I ever fallen into it? What did saving Laura Cassidy from a beating have to do with what had followed? It was too late to think along those lines. Maybe from high above there was a perspective on it all. Maybe some thread of fatal purpose ran through it all, but I didn't believe it. When the cops found me in the trunk of a stolen car with one of Carlo's bullets through my head, it would be nothing but one more unsolved murder. The prospect didn't exactly endear me to Mrs Kepler.

'You're in a state of shock.' I leaned down close over her. When she drew back I leaned even closer. 'It's funny. Since you

174

hired me everyone seems to be dead, walking wounded, or in shock. You cry beautifully. It doesn't do anything for me any more.'

Her neck was smooth and pale and eminently touchable. A pulse pounded in her taut throat as if there was a hammer under the skin.

'I think you should go.' She turned her face away and drew her dressing gown tightly closed.

'I'm not a nice man. I was lied to and that's made me even less nice than I normally am. If you wanted a fall guy, you should have hired someone else.'

'Dix hired you,' she said. 'I'm sorry you were hurt but that's not my fault. What do you want from me?'

'Oh, I forgot.' I smiled at her and she pressed herself further backwards in the chair. 'Of course. Landau was the one who hired me. But then Landau works for Peaches and Peaches answers to her syndicate friends in Vegas, so I guess I was working for the mob the whole time.'

She looked totally puzzled.

'But you don't get it,' I said.

'I don't know what you're talking about.'

'Let me give you a crash course. I just had a visit from two corporation hoods. They're very upset about this missing script. They seem to think I have something to do with it. One of them is an old friend of Peaches'. The other one kills strangers for fun and profit. If I don't come up with the script or some explanation, they're going to kill me. Do you feel like dying, Mrs Kepler? I don't.'

'Are you abusing my wife?' Raymond Kepler paused in the arched entrance and then sauntered a few steps forward. He was dressed in striped pyjamas and a tartan bathrobe slung loosely over his shoulders. There was a glass of liquor in his hand. 'First the police and now you.' He shook his head in mock annoyance. 'What a lot of abuse we're getting. You'd think we'd done something wrong. Have a drink, Kyd.'

'Drop dead,' I snarled.

'All in good time, old man.' He placed his glass on the mantel. 'How's the head? What a lot of trouble you'd have been saved if I hadn't gone out to that liquor store. I'd have been dead and you'd have had the relatively simple task of finding the body. Sorry about that, Kyd.'

'Who did that to your car, Kepler?'

'God knows. A talented maniac I'd say.' He laughed. ' "Raymond K. will pay." It rhymes. The poor fellow's a poet.'

'Maybe you did it yourself,' I said. 'That would be sort of in character.'

'You're not even warm, old man. Sorry. Top marks for trying but 'twas not I who perpetrated the foul deed. Was it, darling?' He smiled horribly at his wife. 'Tell him it wasn't little Waymond who did it.'

She didn't respond to his baiting. The leer tightened on his face and his eyes narrowed. There was no doubt he hated her, hated her with that sour fury that only grows between men and women who once passionately loved each other.

'Too shy to speak,' he said. 'She's just a little mouse. A poor little mouse having a nightmare. Never mind her.' He patted the pockets of his robe in a forgetful abstracted manner and fished out a small-calibre automatic. He held it out to me in the palm of his hand as if it were some fascinating gadget he wished me to admire. 'Marvellous things, aren't they?' He sighed. 'So small, so heavy, so serious. I should say this is the most serious object I've ever held in my life.'

I asked him if it was loaded. He smiled at me, lifted it to his temple, and pulled the trigger.

'No.' He laughed.

'That's a lousy joke,' I said.

He took a clip out of his pocket and snapped it into the handle. He held the loaded gun at his side, with the barrel pointing at the floor. The loose, crazy smile didn't leave his face.

'You ought to leave, old man. Nothing here for you. We've got the forces of the law and order protecting the house and Anne and I have each other. No offence, but you're out of your depth.'

'Do you need a gun to tell me that?'

'Not at all. I can see you don't understand me in the slightest. No, I don't go in for the manly aggression bit. No, I tend to–

wards the opposite. Martyrdom, old man, suicide in its slower forms, that's my game.'

'I once read that when someone kills himself, he's simultaneously murdering another person. Who are you trying to kill, Kepler?'

'We are waxing theoretical today, aren't we?' He laid the loaded gun on the mantel. 'Let's just say that after certain things one has a moral obligation to just go to hell. After certain things a preoccupation with survival seems in rather bad taste.'

He was drunk but the drunkenness gave him a canny neurotic's advantage. He wasn't just rambling. He was alluding to something specific but in riddles. It obviously provided him with some low-order amusement to feed me scraps of the truth with the knowledge that I wouldn't be able to guess what they meant. Another intention was there, too, I thought, below the game-playing and contempt. Kepler was suffering. You didn't have to be a doctor to see that his whole performance was a plea to have his secret discovered.

'What about indifference to other people's survival, Kepler? Or is that not important?'

'I warned you to stay clear of this mess. No one asked you to come here.'

'The hell they didn't,' I said in an icily controlled voice. 'Something's got you by the balls so hard you're ready to die just for a little relief. I don't know what poisoned you, Kepler. I don't know what you did, but you're sure as hell not taking me with you.' I hadn't realized quite how mad I was at him. I could feel the blood thumping in my face, my eyes staring, an oppression in my throat. I had a terrible desire to get my hands around his neck and shake him.

'For what it's worth,' he said, 'you have my apology. You at least are a victim with all the victim's advantages – good conscience, the right to be indignant, etcetera. You have no idea what a luxury innocence is.' He gave his wife one of those jeering smiles which she met with a look of uncomprehending misery on her face. 'Well, then.' He made an elaborate performance of tasting his drink. 'I'd better go see about moving that car.'

He left the room and came back a moment later with a fresh

drink and tyre iron. He walked past his wife and me, whistling briskly, paused in the foyer, bowed superciliously, and was gone.

Anne Kepler was crying into her hands. I put the automatic into my pocket and left the room.

Raymond's study looked out onto the back garden. The walls were lined with floor-to-ceiling bookcases. There was a rumpled sleeping bag on the couch and a nearly empty bottle of Wild Turkey on the desk. The fireplace was still warm, but there was no sign of any wood, nor any implements for tending a fire. I sifted through the ashes with my hands; it was all soft powder and bits of burnt paper. At the bottom I found the charred remains of what looked like several hardbound accountant's ledgers. He'd burned papers after the police had questioned him. Was it the script? His diaries?

I checked under the couch, patted down the curtains, and removed the screen from the heating duct. I felt up inside the fireplace. I rifled through his desk drawers but they were empty or filled with bills and writer's paraphernalia. In the bottom drawer I found another clip for the gun which I kept. It probably didn't matter. Not having a gun never stopped anyone from taking himself or anyone else over the edge.

I heard a sound of metal shrieking followed by a dull pounding. When I returned to the living room I found Mrs Kepler standing in the middle of the floor, staring at the curtained window with her hands over her ears. Whatever Raymond was doing to the car, it sounded awful.

She dropped her hands when she saw me, closed her eyes tight, and let out a strangled cry of misery. I thought she was going to scream. I touched her shoulders. She shuddered horribly and pressed herself against me, all of her. There was nothing soft or sexual about it. It was like embracing someone whose muscles are rigidly supporting a terrible weight. Her breath rattled in her throat. Suddenly she pushed me away, crying, 'What am I going to do? Is my husband crazy? Do I have to have him put away?' She sank to the floor in a heap by the armchair. 'Why is he doing this?' she whispered.

'I don't know what's bothering him. Maybe he's holding up really well.'

Her face lifted up out of her arms, crumpled, nakedly weeping.

'You don't care. You don't give a damn what happens to him.'

'Does he have any other guns in the house?'

'How can you despise him like that? What did he ever do to you?'

'Your husband despises himself, and I'm starting to see why. Don't tell me he was exploited. He hung around Sassari just like Fieldman, eating dirt because he thought he could get something out of it. But Sassari was better at that game than either of them. There are people who like being exploited, who like being losers. There are women who like being married to them.' I lashed out at her and didn't care how much it hurt. I wasn't asking her to face up to anything that I hadn't myself suffered – there were people like me who had a perverse weakness for girls like Laura Cassidy.

She was prostrate on the floor, sobbing, talking brokenly to herself. I felt dull and soiled, made degenerate by my work. My mouth was so dry, my lips were stuck to my teeth. I picked up the glass Kepler had left behind on the mantel, but it was empty.

'When I got out of the army,' I heard myself saying, 'I lived with a girl called Natasha. That wasn't her real name. Her real name was Rebecca. She was crazy about Russian novels and one day she just started calling herself Natasha. I lived with her for about six months. I don't know why I did it, because at the time I wasn't fit to live with anyone. I wasn't very good to her. I was there but I wasn't really there, if you know what I mean. She drank a lot, this girl, and did a lot of drugs. I tried to get her to slow down, but it never did any good. That's how she was. She had to get high. I used to like making love to her. I was just out of the army. I did it all the time. I figured, whatever else, I was taking good care of her in the sack. I was really handling my end of things there. One night I came home and found her on the floor in the bathroom. She'd taken an overdose and hacked up her wrists with a razor. I got her to a hospital and they pumped her stomach and bandaged her up. I stayed there all night waiting for her to come around. I just sat there smoking and drinking coffee and thinking what a mess she'd made of it and how screwed up she must have been to try something like that. I was mad at her, you know, for boxing me in like that. I thought she'd tried to stick me with a lot of guilt. In the morning a shrink came around and asked me if I was the guy she was living with and would I come into his office, because he wanted me to be there while he talked to her. It didn't seem like it was necessary for me to be there because, after all, she was the patient. But I went in and we both sat down, Natasha and I, and the doctor looked at me and said, "I just want you to know that I consider you directly responsible for at least fifty per cent of what happened last night. You cut one of her wrists. You put half those pills down her throat." '

'Many thanks,' Anne Kepler said in a soft, bitter voice. 'Many, many thanks.'

'It's just a story, Mrs Kepler. When someone told me that, I didn't care for it either. Maybe there are people who just spontaneously fall to pieces by themselves like exploding stars. Everyone usually needs help though, even to go down the drain.'

There was a sharp crack and the sound of glass shattering from outside. I pulled open the drapes and saw Kepler raising his tyre iron to knock out the remaining shards of glass in the side window on the driver's side. He had put his drink on the top of the car. Alone in the middle of the afternoon in his pyjamas on a quiet, residential street, Kepler was breaking into his own car like a drunk vandal. He was obviously determined, in the way that drunks get. He reached into the car and released the emergency brake and put the car in neutral. Then he tried to push it out into the street but the flat tyres wouldn't roll. He strained with all his might and abruptly stopped. Then he stared sort of vacantly and sadly at the car, at a loss what to do. Then suddenly he started all over again with redoubled energy. His hand was cut where he'd raked it against a splinter of glass, and he kept using it to wipe the sweat from his face. His skin was deathly white, with dark smudges under the eyes, the face itself all anguish and stupefaction. He knew it was useless. He knew he was just wearing himself out. But he couldn't stop. He couldn't even get angry. He was a weeping lunatic steadily and helplessly banging his head against a padded wall.

Drawn by the noise, a few neighbours had come out on their front lawns to stare at him and exchange meaningful glances with each other. His wife was on the floor crying. He was outside, his face streaked with blood and sweat, trying to summon the coordination and strength to beat up his car. It was like a soap opera by the Marquis de Sade.

A man came jogging down the street, one of those over-equipped joggers you see in Los Angeles in a yellow and magenta track suit, with a matching wrist- and headband and forty-dollar running shoes. Kepler was making a terrible noise trying to pry the side door open with the tyre iron. The jogger slowed down, staring at him, and then kept going when he saw Kepler lose his grip on the tyre iron and sit down backwards in the driveway. It was cruel slapstick.

'I'm going to bring him inside,' I said, 'before he hurts himself.'

As I stepped out the front door, I saw Laker, the blond, snub-nosed policeman, rushing across the street with his weapon drawn. He screamed 'Kepler!' and started sprinting down the pavement after the jogger.

Kepler was lying flat on his back with his head angled against the front flat tyre. I let his head down carefully and as soon as it touched the tarred road, a pool of blood spread out. The red and blue hole between his eye and his slack mouth was hardly bleeding. His heart beat in weak, erratic flurries. His lungs weren't even trying. His eyes were soft and immobile and unfocused. The side of his mouth hung open like a sleeping person's. And then he went for good, without a fight, or a shudder, or a last sound for anyone, like someone passing quietly from exhaustion into the deepest sleep. One second his soft, shining eyes were alive and then they were just fixed objects in his face. In that moment, like a camera, death froze his image for all time.

Down the long, deserted street gunfire cracked. I left him lying there and kept low, moving down to the cover of the cars. About fifty yards up ahead I could see Laker braced over the hood of a panel truck pouring fire into a walled-up porch and staircase across the street.

A car driven by an elderly woman turned into the street and went by at an agonizingly slow speed, passing miraculously through a burst of return fire from the walled-in porch. She went another thirty yards and then obviously had a delayed reaction and stepped on the gas.

I ran, bent over, along the line of parked cars until I was about ten yards from Laker. A bullet took the glass out of the window of the panel truck he was hiding behind. Another ricocheted off the pavement separating us.

'Safety's on,' I shouted, throwing him Kepler's automatic.

He jammed it in his waistband and told me to go call for assistance. When he started firing his gun again, I backed away on my knees behind the cover of cars. I had to fight to get my body to move. It didn't matter: the jogger wasn't waiting for backup units to arrive on the scene. After Laker's last round, he must have thought the policeman was out of ammunition, because he suddenly broke cover and streaked across the lawn towards the cars on his side of the street. Only he didn't stop; he went between them, squeezing off shots, coming at Laker full tilt. The policeman waited until he was almost to the panel truck and then lifted up and emptied Kepler's automatic point blank into the charging man. It was a lady's purse gun: it made five flat plops. The first ones slowed him down and the final ones brought him to a halt. He went down as if he was trying to regain his balance in some heavy liquid that kept getting thicker and thicker.

Laker's head was twisting around on his shoulders and his feet were pawing the ground. His face wasn't any good for any army recruiting poster any more. His eyeballs were trying to roll back and his lips were flattened in thin snarling lines over his gums. All the human colour had been sucked out of his skin. He came forward in a crazy series of crouching jumps until he was right over the body, pointing his gun at it.

'Come on, you son of a bitch!' he cried. 'You want me? You want me?'

I got in front of him and tried to move him back from the man lying face down in the street. His arms were shaking but when I gripped his biceps they went as hard as stone. It took all my strength just to hold on to him.

'I'll kill him,' he sobbed, 'running at me like that.'

I shook him and then grabbed his jaw and shook that and forced him backwards. I crooned to him and shouted in his face. I don't know what I said. I don't think he knew either. It was just some human noise to get him away from the abyss he was staring into. Suddenly he went from snarling violence into utter limpness. He said, 'I'm tired.' He sat down in the street with his back against the panel truck and cradled his face in his hands.

I flopped the jogger on his back and ripped open his track-suit top and tried to get his heart going. I pressed the heels of my hands down hard on his chest and shoved rhythmically. His mouth jerked open in response. He had five holes clustered to the heart like a perfect score on a police-range dummy. I checked his other vital signs but I might as well have searched for a pulse in the tarred road he was lying on.

The golden Labrador I'd seen earlier had caught the scent of the dead man. It stood at a distance, its tail curled between its legs, whining hoarsely. I got to my feet. The front lawns all along the block had filled with silent groups of onlookers. Where had they all been five minutes ago? They seemed to have come from nowhere. Laker had already started walking back towards Kepler's house. I followed him, with the whining dog at my heels. There was a crowd of neighbours gathered in a circle around the dead writer. Through their legs I could see Mrs Kepler clutching her husband's head. When the dog caught the scent of the second dead man it let out a howl and took off down the street. By the time the first sirens could be heard, it was three blocks away and still going strong. I came up close and stared down at the dead man and then I took his drink off the top of his car and swallowed it. No one saw me do it, but I knew I'd remember it for the rest of my life.

twenty-nine

It was an airless overheated room with wire-mesh screens over the barred windows and a large conference table with its legs bolted into the floor. There was a cork notice board with nothing on it and a ball-point pen attached by a chain to a fixture in the wall. The window had been permanently sealed shut; it looked out on an airshaft of grimy yellow brick. The single bulb in the ceiling was fixed inside a screened-off niche full of dead flies and moths. Half a dozen straightbacked chairs were set around the table and after counting them and reading the initials carved in the tabletop there was not a lot else to do in the room. I suppose that's why it was called a waiting room.

Every couple of hours a different policeman brought me a cup of coffee and a ham and cheese sandwich in a clear plastic container. Politely but firmly they all refused to answer any of my questions. For the second that the door was open, I heard the night-time sounds of the station house, the wash of men's voices and the clackety-clack of typewriters being used to write up the day's reports. I don't know if the door was locked. I never once tried it.

I sat with my elbows on the tabletop, my chin in my hands, and studied the row of Styrofoam coffee cups. I hummed. I brooded. I went through my wallet for the tenth time and tried to convince myself that my driver's licence and Social Security card were interesting reading material. I studied a dollar bill and tried to recall what ANNUIT COEPTIS meant. NOVUS ORDO SECLORUM I could roughly translate as 'the new order for all time'. IN GOD WE TRUST spoke for itself. E PLURIBUS UNUM meant 'from many came one'. I'd never bothered to count the lies printed on a dollar bill before, and even now my Latin wasn't good enough. I looked at Washington on the reverse side and tried to analyse what it was about his face that had always faintly depressed me. Perhaps it was appropriate that they'd put him on the dollar bill. There was something about those fishy, pitiless eyes and that parsimoniously pursed mouth of his that would have looked right at home behind a bank manager's desk. I wondered if Egyptian paper money had pyramids on it, too. Then I slept.

When I awoke, the door was wide open and something distantly related to fresh air was circulating through the room. A moment later Marcus entered, set down a cup of coffee, a yellow legal pad and some freshly sharpened pencils. Marcus liked to stare at you before speaking. It was one of his gambits, just a dead, expressionless stare of inflexible moroseness. It seemed to suggest that everything was finally over and understood and irretrievably lousy for you. Even if he wanted to, there wasn't anything he could do to help you. That's how he looked down at me. That's probably how he'd looked at the doctor who delivered him.

'Sorry we kept you waiting.' He settled himself in a chair and bent over his legal pad, writing something down. 'Laker says you saved his ass. He appreciates it. He'll probably call you.'

'He handled himself great.'

'Sure, he's the best. If we had more cops like him and courts that cared as much about the victims of crimes as the criminals, it might be safe to walk on the streets.' He lifted his face from the legal pad and said, 'You're free to go now any time you want.'

'I am?'

He pushed his chair back from the table and stretched his shoulders.

'Sure,' he said. 'We just had to detain you while we checked some shit out. What's the matter? You like it here?' The crummy grin was back on his face and the contempt had hardened in his eyes. 'I'll bet you like it here a whole lot better than on the street though.' He rose, took two giant strides to the door, and slammed it shut. 'I got a statement from Mrs Kepler, alleging you told her that your life had been threatened by two Las Vegas hoods about the script of *Shoot the Singer*. It's funny you never mentioned that script to me. Your ex-client told me right away.'

'Four days after it disappeared isn't right away.'

'We'd be interested, of course, in knowing a little something about these people from Vegas,' he persisted.

'They never told me their names.'

'If they're what they sound like, chances are we got pictures of them.'

'Thanks, but no thanks. These guys are off the assembly line. If they don't work out, the factory sends replacement parts. You picking them up wouldn't do me any good and you know it. Their lawyers would have them out within twenty-four hours and the only difference would be they'd be a little madder.'

'You don't know their names and you refuse to look at any pictures.'

'You work for the second biggest organization, Marcus. They just carry a little more clout these days. When they tell me they're going to knock me down, I believe it. When you tell me the police can guarantee my safety, I don't believe it.'

He didn't question that.

'Are these characters armed?' he asked.

'They drive a tank. They sleep with bazookas under their pillows.'

'Something finally scared you, Kyd.' He nodded to himself. 'It's too bad you don't want to cooperate.'

'How you doing on the Fieldman case?' I demanded. 'You got a murder weapon? Any prints? Any witnesses? I doubt it. You got an unsolved murder. What happened to Fieldman could happen to me. Nothing you could do about it.'

'They killed Fieldman?'

'These guys acted like, you know, who put Fieldman to sleep was of no interest to them. Which is to say, there was no mystery there. 'Cause they did it themselves.'

He yawned extravagantly and rubbed his eyes. 'Well, I guess you know what you're doing, Kyd.'

'Me and the guy who designed the Edsel.'

He smiled at me with apparent fondness and squelched another yawn. 'You wouldn't happen to know anything about the identity of that prick in the track suit?'

'No.' I tried to sound as casual as him, but of course it was the one thing that interested me. For all I knew they could have already recovered the script and Marcus was just putting me in the hot seat out of principle.

186

He rubbed his eyes. 'We've sent his prints to the FBI and the armed forces but it'll take time. The gun's a dead end. Serial number filed off. Some traffic cops saw him running along Wilshire in Westwood earlier in the day.'

'That's a long way to run to Kepler's house.'

Marcus studied his legal pad, frowning. 'From the preliminary autopsy report it looks like the guy was a sex freak of some kind. He had welts all over the upper part of his body. Old ones and fresh ones. The coroner says they look like they were made with a steel-tipped whip. That mean anything to you?'

'Not a lot.'

'It's funny how no one seems to know anything about this guy. We're hoping he may have the script and Kepler's diary.' He looked at me derisively. 'Yeah, Landau told us about Kepler's diary, too.'

'I'd like to know why he's so talkative all of a sudden.'

'I'd like to know why people in Las Vegas got you on their shit list.'

'Sassari's father was some kind of hood, that's what I heard. He got bumped off. The family's got some kind of syndicate connection going way back. There's underworld money invested in *Shoot the Singer* like there was in Sassari's other pictures. I wouldn't know where to start investigating that, but Landau might be a start. It's probably perfectly legitimate business, though the money's from a dirty source. The guy who threatened me just said he had to kill someone if he didn't recover the script. He had to frame someone and knock him off so it would look like he'd done his job. They don't like unsolved crimes any more than you do.'

'If the people from Vegas feel anything like the D.A. does about what's been happening,' he smiled cheerfully, 'I'd say we'll be finding the body of a private detective within the next few days. And frankly it won't worry me a hell of a lot because you've been bullshitting me from the day I met you. Sure you don't want to give me their names?'

'I don't know their lousy names.'

Marcus went to the door and shouted for a policeman to take me to my car.

'Nothing else in the autopsy report?' I asked.

'Yeah, a riddle. What would a man do to make his right leg three inches thicker than his left?'

'Maybe he pedals something.'

'Could be. But his whole body's out of alignment right the way down. We think it's from some industrial job, maybe some machine he worked that's produced the distortion.'

'I'd like my gun back,' I said.

'The property room's closed.' He leaned against the doorframe and scratched the back of his neck. 'You're going to have a lot more questions to answer before we're through. Don't leave Los Angeles.

'I'll be around – somewhere.'

'Give my regards to your girlfriend, Kyd.' He stepped back into the room, watching me, and then eased the door shut with his foot.

A young police officer escorted me to the station house steps and pointed across the street to where my Mustang was parked.

'The keys are under the front seat.' He frowned and wiped his hands on his thighs. 'Hope it works out, Mr Kyd.'

'I must be getting old,' I said. 'Policemen look younger and younger to me.'

'Laker's a popular guy in the division. We're all grateful for what you did.'

I thanked him and then we shook hands. It was almost like we were normal human beings doing a natural thing that men all over the world do. I couldn't remember if I'd ever shaken a policeman's hand before. He watched me walk to my car and get inside and then waved and vanished back into the station.

I drove slowly in case there was a police tail on me. It might be like Marcus to do it without telling me. I hoped he'd done it. I moved along well-lighted, nearly empty streets. The shop fronts lay behind iron bars and steel-mesh screens. There were liquor stores on every corner, each a fireworks display of flashing neon lights. I rolled down the window and the night air blew in chilled and damp and still tainted by the day's traffic. It seemed to carry a message from afar of something weak and rotten yet to come in the night. Some headlights stayed in my rearview mirror for about six blocks and I convinced myself it was a cop. A beautiful, alert, deadly cop with orders to protect me. A crackshot with X-ray vision. A genius bodyguard. A cop of the mind who would let nothing harm me. Hope plays cheap tricks on the imagination. Whoever it was pulled off at a drive-in movie where they were showing *The House of a Thousand Dolls*. There wasn't anyone following me. There wasn't a single person in the city who knew where I was. It was just me and the night and my paranoia.

thirty

I took off my clothes and dropped them on the pink shag rug. I unpacked the toothpaste, safety razor, and shaving cream and laid them out on the glass shelf over the sink. I tore the water glass out of its hygenic wrapper and filled it with three fingers of Scotch. Drinking alone in motel bathrooms isn't my idea of civilization, but it beats getting shot in the head at home. The Scotch tasted like medicine and the room reminded me of a hospital: the white vinyl wallpaper, the sheath of hygenic paper around the toilet seat, the odour of disinfectant. The mirror was clean, the sink and faucets sparkled. The electric light bounced hard off the shiny white surfaces, far too much light, as if the management had to prove there wasn't a single speck of dirt on anything. Who was I to be critical? It was perfect: the hot and cold taps both worked, the toilet flushed obediently, the towels were freshly laundered. Even the mirror worked. When I looked into it, I saw a battered, naked man in his mid-thirties, with a tired, apprehensive face, and I had to concede it was me. I showered with a towel wrapped around my head to keep the dressing dry. Then I drank some more of the Scotch while I was shaving and thought of the other man lying naked in the morgue refrigerator downtown. I pictured him lying naked on a bed and being repeatedly struck by a woman with a steel-tipped whip. I imagined him tossing and turning, taking some of the blows on his back, others on his arms and chest. It was odd that he should only be hit above the waist. It was usually the legs and buttocks that were receptive in bondage and discipline types. What did I know? Maybe it was just what he needed after a hard day's jogging. I looked down at my legs and tried to conceive of some action that would strengthen only the right thigh. I lowered myself slowly, taking all my weight on my right leg, my left leg extending backward like a Russian dancer. I held the pose until my right thigh began to ache then I stood up. It didn't suggest a thing to me.

It was after I'd hung my clothes up in the closet that I tried it again. There was a full-length mirror on the back of the closet door and I experimented naked in front of that. This time I took most of my weight on my right leg, bending at the knee and let my left leg drag behind. I lowered myself slowly, my arms came out to balance me. I was semi-crouched, my right leg forward, bent almost at a ninety-degree angle at the knee. When I glanced in the mirror what I saw was a man executing a lunge. The pose exerted a tremendous strain on the right thigh.

What kind of protective clothing did fencers wear? Was it thin enough that a blade might mark the skin through the material? Would that account for the old and fresh welts above the killer's waist?

I phoned an old friend who kept odd hours. I hadn't spoken to him in several years, but he was the kind of character who considered it normal to be called up at two in the morning and asked to look up fencing in his encyclopedia. It took about ten minutes to get the salient information and by then I was perspiring a little from excitement.

Marcus's wife answered on the ninth ring and didn't think she could conceive of anything so important it couldn't wait until morning and then Marcus came on the line himself and said, 'This better be good, you son of a bitch. I haven't slept for a week.'

'He's a fencer,' I said.

'I don't care if he sucks sewer water. *What?*'

'Fencing would increase the size of his right thigh.'

'My wife hates you, too, Kyd. Tell me who says he's a fencer?'

'Those welts on his body are from fencing.'

'They wear stuff. Fencers. Don't they wear protective padding?' He went off the line for a moment. 'She says they wear padded jackets.'

'The jackets can be very thin. You said all the welts were above his waist. There are three fencing weapons: épée, foil, and saber. The épée and foil would make round marks because you only hit with the point. If it was épée, he'd have marks on his legs because the whole body is the target.'

'The marks are like little whip marks. They're not round. Mainly on his arms and shoulders.'

'Then it's got to be sabre. The sabre's a cutting weapon. If he's got fresh welts, it means he's a practising fencer. If his right thigh is that overdeveloped it means he's an experienced fencer. How many experienced, practising fencers can there be in this town?'

'*If* he's a fencer. *If* those jackets they wear don't fully protect them.'

'He's a jock. He runs. Why wouldn't he be a fencer?'

'Because you think he is,' Marcus growled. 'That good enough for you?'

'I think the earth's round. That doesn't make it flat.'

He spoke to his wife: 'Honey, the earth's flat.'

'Okay, Einstein, have it your way. I say the guy was a fencer. I say tomorrow morning I start finding out who he was. You can sit in your office trying to think of some industrial machine the guy worked, something he pedalled so hard it made his right thigh three inches thicker than his left and whacked him across the arms and shoulders every sixty seconds with a steel whip . . .'

'Just be in your goddamn office at nine o'clock. If there's nothing on his prints, we'll take his photos around in the morning.'

'Admit it,' I said.

'Admit? What admit? That you got more luck than brains. A guy has to be retarded to get himself into a position where he needs your kind of luck. Think about that, crackerjack.' He slammed the phone down. I don't know what he did after that. He probably hit his wife with an uppercut and went to sleep in the den.

thirty-one

I had done nothing about my desk, the scattered papers, and broken office doors after the visit from Bando. I had just walked out. Maybe I'd even hoped that vandals would clean me out, steal the files, the telephone, the framed investigator's licence on the wall, and give me an excuse to go out of business. In the morning it was all just as I'd left it, of course, because there was not a damn thing in the office to interest even a prowling wino.

I ignored the mess and noted down what I could find in the Yellow Pages under fencing. There were a number of sporting goods stores that dealt in fencing equipment and two fencing schools listed, in Hollywood and Gardena. To spare myself listening to Marcus's reaction to the state of my office, I went downstairs and waited for him in front of the building.

He showed up a quarter of an hour late, looking badly slept, and angry with the human race.

'The only reason you're coming with me,' he told me at once in the car, 'is I don't want you screwing up behind my back.'

'The only reason I'm coming with you is I don't think Las Vegas would try and hit me with a Captain of Detectives.'

'This is a police investigation,' he said. 'I'll do all the talking. You better get that through your head.'

I lit a cigarette and looked out the window as we broke the speed limit down Western.

'Did you hear what I said?' he insisted.

'I'm unemployed. I don't get a gold star after my name for solving this.'

'Just so we understand each other,' he said grimly. 'I don't want you getting any ideas . . .'

I didn't answer. He lit a small, stumpy cigar and started humming. He was feeling better, you could tell. After a moment, he looked over at me and leered.

'You know what you remind me of?' He chuckled. 'You remind me of a bug that flew into a space capsule and got sent to the moon. You don't belong. You're out of your depth. That nickel-and-dime operation you run is for finding lost cats. Yeah, a fly in a space capsule and everyone looking to swat you. *Buzzzz . . . buzzzz . . .*'

He pulled up in front of a sporting goods store on Santa Monica Boulevard near the Hollywood Freeway. There was a sign on the door saying the place was only open on Thursdays and Fridays from four-thirty to seven-thirty. Through the window I could see walls hung with fencing masks and modern and antique weapons. Marcus rattled the doorknob and banged on the plate glass.

'What kind of working hours are those?' he said. 'Six lousy hours a week. I'm telling you, this country's going to the dogs.' He peered through the window. 'How you supposed to investigate a crime, huh? The whole fucking country's on welfare or vacation.'

Our next stop was an exclusive sporting goods store on Little Santa Monica in Beverly Hills. There was a young woman behind the counter in the fencing section. Marcus plunked his badge down and hoisted up his trousers and said, 'Captain Marcus, L.A.P.D.'

'Is something wrong?' She blanched.

'See this man.' He slid some photos of the dead jogger over the counter. 'He's a murderer. Have you ever seen him before?'

'No . . . I don't think so.'

'That's funny. He used to buy fencing equipment here.'

'What's his name?' She tried not to look at the gruesome photos.

'That's what we want to know.' Marcus leaned over the counter and drilled her with his eyes.

'How long have you worked here, Miss?' I asked.

'This is my third day.'

'Get me the manager,' Marcus said.

'I am the manager,' she said weakly.

'You the only person who works here?' he demanded.

'There's a boy but he's on vacation.'

'See what I mean?' Marcus looked at me. 'No one works any more.'

I inspected some of the fencing jackets hanging on the walls.

The material was thin around the arms and shoulders.

Marcus took down the name and address of the boy who worked in the store and we left. The streets of Beverly Hills were clogged with Rolls-Royces and Mercedes-Benzes, the pavements thick with exotically dressed pedestrians shopping in the world's most expensive stores.

'If they don't work,' Marcus said, 'where do they get the money? I'll tell you something about this town. Per square foot there are more phonies walking the streets of Hollywood and Beverly Hills than any place in the world. You think these people have money? You think they own those cars? You think they've paid for those clothes? They don't own their fucking sunglasses! I worked Hollywood Division five years. Nothing but deadbeats trying to pretend they're out-of-work actors. I'd like to round them all up and stick them in Death Valley. Give them some water, some seeds, and tell 'em to make it green like they done in Israel. You think I'm some kind of fascist talking like that? You're wrong. I'm a fucking visionary. People with nothing to do get into trouble. This town is full of people who think they're special. People waiting to get discovered. You got a whole town here waiting for a lucky break. That's their profession. They ain't really pumping gas and waiting on tables. Hell no, they're just filling in time until they can do what they really want to do. Be in some dumb TV shows. Big fucking deal! Who can watch that garbage anyway? Me, I'm just waiting for the earthquake. That's what keep me going. I'm just waiting for the day when the whole thing gets the shit shaken out of it.'

'You're a philosopher,' I said.

'Naw, I'm just a crazy optimist. There ain't never going to be an earthquake. This town's just going to get worse forever.'

Marcus parked in a loading only zone on Hollywood Boulevard just past Wilton and we walked about thirty yards to the Faulkner School of Fencing. It was flanked by a theatrical costume rental store and an amusement arcade. We were close to my end of Hollywood, where the climate is hotter and the ragpickers and pimps flourish. Faulkner's took up three storefronts. The windows were filled with tarnished, dusty fencing trophies and a jumbled collage of yellowed photographs of movie stars and former fencing greats. The main reception room was empty but you could hear various dancing classes in progress behind the closed studio doors. Marcus opened the one on the left and glared into a room of startled young women in leotards being instructed by a flamboyantly gesturing teacher.

'Can I help you?' The teacher fixed him with an arch glance.

'Where's the fencing go on?'

'In the rear.'

Marcus shut the door and shook his head. 'See what I mean? It's Fruit City. All these broads learning how to tap-dance. We got a depression on and they're paying some fruit to teach 'em tap-dancing.'

We walked down a narrow corridor lined with glass cases filled with photographs of early movie stars in fencing poses.

'Fencing,' Marcus snorted, 'that gets the Useless Prize of the year. Didn't they ever hear of the atom bomb? Some guy fucks with me, I'd rather know karate. I'd rather put a bullet in him.'

'It's a sport,' I said.

'So's tiddledywinks. That don't mean nothing to me either.'

The corridor opened into a small, enclosed patio with a lawn and a trellised arbour. Beyond that was a large corrugated-tin building that resembled an airplane hangar that had been converted into a gymnasium. The wall facing the patio was a huge sliding door that had been rolled open. Inside you could see a dull hardwood floor and long tarnished mirrors along the walls, interspersed with a variety of fencing dummies. I had expected something more exotic; the fencing salle had the seedy, Spartan atmosphere of an abandoned boxing gym. At the far end two men in masks, padded jackets, and shorts were duelling on a strip marked off with white tape. They moved backwards and forward, taking short, crouching steps, and suddenly came together in a blur of clashing blades. It was impossible to distinguish whether either or both of them had been hit. My main impression was of phenomenal speed and lightning reflexes.

Marcus watched silently, the cigar dead in his mouth, his brows deeply furrowed. After a moment it became clear that the larger of the two men was giving the other a lesson. At certain moments he would abruptly drop his sword and offer his head as a target and the pupil would strike it in response. The steel blade hitting the leather reinforced mask made a clanging pop. Each attack was punctuated by a shout, high-pitched and triumphant on the part of the attacker.

'You are hitting too hard,' the teacher said. He had a deep gruff voice, with a well-bred but distinctly foreign accent. Over his padded jacket he wore a scarred leather breastplate. For such a large man he had almost menacingly swift reflexes. He would wait until his pupil's blade had almost touched him and then parry and riposte with a blinding movement.

'This is medium speed,' he said. 'Now I'm going to increase the pressure.'

'Hey, fella.' Marcus sauntered across the deserted floor, hands in his pockets, shoulders hunched. 'Leave the swordplay for a minute. I want to ask you some questions.'

The teacher slowly removed his mask. He had black hair, a black cossack moustache, flushed cheeks, and brown, dangerously vivid eyes. He had what you rarely find in the best American athletes: perfect carriage.

'What can I do for you?' His dark eyes swept us both, took in the clothes, our posture.

'Captain Marcus, L.A.P.D.' Marcus flipped his wallet open and held out his badge.

The fencing teacher didn't bother to look. His eyes stayed right on the policeman.

'Yes?'

'You're pretty quick with that sword, fella. This how you make your living?'

The teacher bent at the waist and laid his sword and mask on the floor. When he stood up he seemed considerably larger than before. His handsome face looked pained.

'Please get to the point,' he said forcefully. His eyes darted from Marcus to me.

'The man's busy,' I said. 'Why don't you show him the pictures?'

Marcus turned and looked at me and then drew out the photographs and handed them to the fencing teacher. He studied them, frowning rigidly.

'What has happened?' he said.

'You know this guy?' Marcus said.

'Sure.'

'What's his name?'

'Bomberg. Carl Bomberg.'

'Yeah, where does Bomberg live?'

'I'm not sure any more. He used to live at the Veterans Hospital in Westwood. What has happened to him?'

'You a friend of his?'

'He studied with me, sure.'

'Why did he live at the Veterans Hospital? Something wrong with the guy?'

'He never talked much about his private life. I think he suffered badly in the war. He was a lonely fellow, wrapped up in himself, and mentally strange, you know . . .'

'Sure he was strange.' Marcus glared at the fencing instructor as if he was personally responsible. 'He killed two people. That's right.' The policeman turned to me. 'I showed his pictures to some of the people at Sassari's party. Bomberg was there that night. No one knew who he was. He left before the police arrived. It looks like your girlfriend didn't do it, Kyd.' He studied me with shrewd cold eyes, waiting for some reaction. I mumbled something about Bomberg, wondering who he was. The policeman said he was going to phone the Veterans Hospital and left.

'Are you also a policeman?' the fencing instructor asked.

'I'm just helping with inquiries.'

'This is a terrible thing. There is no doubt – Bomberg has killed two people?'

I nodded, thinking what a blunt, unlovely name Bomberg was, not at all the kind of name for a girl like Laura. Cassidy was better – it had a ring to it redolent of Irish romance. Even Sassari was not a bad name.

'Did Bomberg have any family?' I asked casually. 'Brothers or sisters?'

'He was an orphan.'

'Married?'

'I don't know.'

Marcus returned, pleased with himself now, with that vindictive glint in his eyes that was the closest he ever got to happiness.

'Bomberg's an in-patient at the Mental Hygiene Clinic. They didn't even know he was missing. No point talking to his doctor without a subpoena and a warrant to seize his property.'

It took Marcus about three hours at the D.A.'s office to get what he needed. While he waited, he ran a make on Carl Bomberg: it turned out he had a drunk-driving conviction and his licence had been lifted a year ago. He had also been arrested for assault on a hypnotist in Hollywood at about the same time. The charge was dropped on the condition Bomberg return to the hospital.

thirty-two

It was clear and sunny in Westwood and from the elevated grounds of the Veteran's Administration you could see an oil tanker lying off the docks of distant El Segundo. It was a lovely enough spot: the pale Spanish-style buildings with orange-tiled roofs, the landscaped lawns, the whispering eucalyptus and palm trees. Here and there men in pale green pyjamas and striped robes sunned themselves on the grass and looked out over the city to the sea. I'd done a stint there there years ago when it was more crowded. On the surface it looked all right but after a while you noticed that there was something wrong with a lot of men's eyes. They were permanently blocked on tranquillizers and downers. It was a pill factory. You came back wounded or crazy from Vietnam and they gave you a big Valium prescription and some mood elevators to keep you awake. The place was like a museum; there were First World War veterans there who'd never recovered from poison-gas attacks and buildings originally built to house the wounded from the Spanish-American War.

I directed Marcus to the Mental Hygiene Clinic opposite the

canteen. From there we went to another building which housed the in-patient clinic and an enclosed ward for the more serious cases. The D.A.'s office had already contacted the hospital and we were met by a small dark-haired psychiatrist called Dr Abrahamson who led us into a waiting room where Bomberg's effects had been collected.

'I suppose there's no doubt at all that Carl killed these two men,' he said.

'That's how come we're here.' Marcus turned his back on the doctor and began rummaging through the cardboard boxes stacked on the table. They were filled with a jumbled assortment of clothes, tape cassettes, fencing equipment, books, and war souvenirs. Everything was dated, a product of the last period of the war. Looking at Bomberg's things, you would have guessed they belonged to a man who had died the year the Americans pulled out. At least that part of him that took an interest in the outside world, in music, books, and clothes had ceased functioning when the fighting stopped. There were boxes filled with the mementos so many grunts picked up in the Saigon tourist shops: brass opium pipes, saffron-coloured silk robes worn by the Buddhist monks, fake-ivory carvings. At the bottom of one I found a picture of him in the jungle, a Polaroid snap taken with a flash. It was night and he was loaded up to go out on patrol. His face was daubed with nightfighter cosmetic, his matted blond hair hung to his shoulders; there were leaves and twigs woven into the mosquito netting on his helmet. The front of his tigersuit bristled with grenades, knife, handgun, ammunition clips. With the freaked-out blond hair, the makeup, and his eyes turned a bright orange by the flash bulb, he looked like a hallucination, a monstrously camouflaged figure that had materialized out of the jungle and would melt back into it.

'Did Bomberg have permission to come and go as he pleased?' Marcus asked.

'It depended. He's had periods in the enclosed ward and times when he lived in an apartment and just came in for therapy. His condition fluctuated.'

'You got any record of his exits and entrances?'

'Yes,' the doctor said with distaste.

'Get it.' Marcus jerked his head. 'It ain't no tragedy about Bomberg, Doc. He fluctuated right off the bottom of the chart and he took two people with him.'

'He took a lot more than two,' the doctor said. 'That *was* his tragedy.' He left the room and Marcus pointed to one of the boxes and told me to go through it. Beneath some underground comic books I found a flak jacket with, IT'S ALL RIGHT, MA, I'M ONLY BLEEDING stencilled across the back in Day-Glo paint. Older graffiti which he had failed to rub out, or which had just faded with time, covered the garment; PRAY FOR WAR, WIDOW-MAKER, TIME IS ON MY SIDE; sayings that turned up on GI helmets and jackets in every combat zone like brand names or magic charms against death. Wrapped inside the flak jacket was the bound screenplay of *Shoot the Singer*, with Paul Sassari's name on the title page. Bando and Carlo would be pleased to get it back, likewise Landau and Peaches. It was a reprieve of sorts for me, but only a marginal one: there was still the matter of who Bomberg was to Laura, and why he had the script. Hidden in the answers to those questions were bound to be revelations that would hurt me, show my hand in a tarnished light. I was with the policeman but I felt at any moment he was going to find something to implicate me.

The doctor returned with a large ledger which Marcus took from him and studied. He checked it against his notebook

'Bomberg was out the night you took a beating.' He turned to the doctor. 'You got a file on this character? You write down his dreams and all that stuff?'

'I'm familiar with his case. You're entitled to see *his* things. My notes are another matter.'

Marcus nodded. 'I've got lousy manners, Doc. All day long I do nothing but step on toes and ride people. I had a police guard on a man, a writer, and a wife and two kids, and Bomberg killed him yesterday. He also tried to kill one of my men. I've got no reason to love the guy, you understand, but I'm willing to try and understand him. Help me.'

'No one is ever going to understand Bomberg now.'

'Why's that?'

'Because even Bomberg didn't know the whole truth about

himself, and he's the only one who could tell you.' Dr Abrahamson picked up the photograph I'd been looking at. 'Bomberg came to us from a V.A. hospital in Virginia. According to his medical record, he was suffering partial amnesia and chronic depression, and had twice tried to kill himself. According to his service record, though, he had a very uneventful war as a filing clerk and never saw any action. He himself was very vague about it, couldn't seem to remember more than three or four incidents out of his whole time overseas. We call guys like Bomberg *sleepers*. They've been officially put to sleep.'

'I don't know if I get this,' Marcus said uneasily.

'Hypnosis combined with drugs, Captain. You have no idea what we can do these days. Take murder, for instance. Say the army wants Bomberg to eliminate a Vietnam black market racketeer. They hypnotize him to do it and at the same time they programme him to forget the whole thing afterwards. They go better than that – they hypnotize him in such a way that any attempt on his part to remember throws him into a violent depression, makes him suicidal. He's a perfect agent. He self-destructs after doing the job like one of those letters that re-composes ten seconds after it touches the air. You think this is science fiction I'm talking about – it isn't. This place is crawling with sleepers. And God knows how many there are outside, walking the streets – guys who've had their minds fucked with, guys who cannot remember who they were and what they did over there. The problem is, in their sleep, they do remember; they suffer fragmented versions of all this repressed experience, horror shows, nightmares. That was Bomberg all over. He was one of the unlucky ones – they botched the job, didn't fully erase him. Most sleepers are afraid to do anything about it – they don't want to know. Bomberg tried to remember. I've hypnotized him over seventy times. Probing his memory was like going to hell, like following a sewer back to the septic tank. He had a war all right. Every time I put him to sleep, the dead bodies just floated to the surface. But not painlessly. His mind was rigged like a mine field and he had to fight for every square inch that he recovered. He was different people with different names and they had all done different things. Some of them were real, some of them were just to make sure no one ever got to the bottom of him.'

Everything in Marcus wanted to dismiss the doctor's explanation as a crackpot, left-wing fantasy. How could the American Army do such things to its own soldiers?

'If this is true,' Marcus asked, 'what are *you* doing here?'

'Sleepers are my speciality. I'm not very successful at the work – it's an almost incurable condition so they tolerate me. I got transferred out about a year ago. Bomberg took his problems to some hypnotist, a woman who claimed to cure people of smoking and impotence. She couldn't handle the kind of problems he had, so I came back. If you're suggesting I'm a subversive, Captain, I'm flattered.'

'You ever hear about anything like this, Kyd?' Marcus frowned.

I said it was not uncommon, but I didn't mention the boy Laura had told me about, the one she hadn't seen for years who had grown up in the orphanage with her in New York.

Dr Abrahamson picked through one of the boxes and came up with a clear plastic bag containing a tortoiseshell comb, a sheaf of black hair, and a pair of jade earrings. 'This one was Bomberg's worst nightmare – his number one exhibit against himself. During the war he fell in love with a Vietnamese girl, a nightclub singer. One day he went to her club and found it had been blown up, with her inside. He spent his entire leave in Saigon, trying to find out what had happened to her. To cut a long story short, his investigations led him back to people in his own organization. In fact, he found out that he had blown up the club himself on a sleeper mission. Bomberg wasn't any use to anyone after that. They debriefed him and sent him home. The worst part of this story is that Army Intelligence or the CIA or whoever was using Bomberg wasn't even after the girl. They wanted to get the owner of the club. The girl was only in the club that night because she had come to beg with the owner for Bomberg's life. His cover was blown. They already knew he was an assassin.'

'Jesus Christ.' Marcus grimaced. 'What kind of sick story is that?'

'That's the plot of *Shoot the Singer*,' I said. 'This screenplay is based on Bomberg's experience. It says Sassari wrote it, but if it's like the rest of his work, it was ghosted by Kepler. Somehow Bomberg's tragedy, which pushed him over the edge, ended up in this film script.'

'Wait a minute.' The doctor started thumbing through Bomberg's file. 'A year ago, he showed me something he'd written about the experience. Bomberg hadn't had much formal education. His mind had been so tampered with, it was hard for him to write, but he did it something like a scenario. I remember it because he had a quote at the beginning. "Every man kills the thing he loves." It was sort of gruesomely appropriate. He asked me my opinion. It was very realistic – the characters sounded like real GI's. I thought it was a little too real for Hollywood, but I encouraged him to try and do something with it. It was just twenty pages or so but every line had been fought and paid for. He was a guy struggling to remember things that were only going to torture him – I admired that.'

'What did he do with it?' I asked.

'I don't know if he ever did anything.'

'What was it called?'

'*The Sleepwalker of Saigon*. After that he freaked out with the Hollywood hypnotist and got put back in the enclosed ward. He never mentioned it to me again and I didn't either because he probably thought it was another failure.'

'What about friends?' Marcus asked. 'Girls?'

'A washout. He was severely withdrawn. He talked about his fencing teacher once in a while. He said fencing was the only time he forgot himself. He'd been married before he was drafted, but his wife divorced him. He didn't hold it against her – he used to tell me he was unfit for human consumption.'

Marcus excused himself to go use the telephone while I continued to search through Bomberg's effects.

'He must have got married very young,' I said.

'He was eighteen. The girl was even younger. I don't have any idea how to get in touch with her. Maybe she'll read about it in the papers.'

I took the thick lock of glossy Asian hair from the cellophane bag, wondering how many times Bomberg had done the same thing himself, held it to his face, smelled it, tortured himself for what had happened. It had no smell whatsoever now.

'The damn Screenwriters Guild won't give out any information.' Marcus returned. 'Someone from the D.A.'s office is going to meet us over there with a court order.'

In the car Marcus asked me what I thought of it all.

'Looks to me like someone stole Bomberg's idea. He was a time bomb. Getting that story stolen triggered his fuse.'

'Yeah.' Marcus had become remote and quiet under the weight of what we'd learned in the hospital. The ugliness of it flattened me, too; it lay on my mind like an oil slick on the sea, making a dead unnatural calm.

'They looted him like a corpse.' Marcus threw the car violently into gear. 'It was stealing from a dead man.'

thirty-three

A trim, grey-haired lady rose from behind her desk as we entered the Screenwriters Guild and motioned us towards a door. We were shown into a small, deserted office with no windows. Two film scripts in different coloured bindings rested on the table each with dated and signed receipts attached.

'That is not all the material requested in the court order,' the grey-haired lady explained. 'You asked for all properties which had been registered with us by Dix Landau, Raymond Kepler, and Paul Sassari. Certain of these properties have been withdrawn. However, we keep microfilm copies of all material submitted to us.'

She showed us how to work the microfilm viewer and explained what we were looking at as the pages appeared on the screen. 'This is the earliest version we have. It's untitled, or at least the title page is missing. It was submitted a little over a year ago, and authorship is credited to Dix Landau.'

Scanning the pages, there was no doubt we were looking at Bomberg's crudely written original. The typing was erratic, the grammar that of a man without much formal education. The dialogue, however, had the genuine obscene ring; it was the language of American soldiers in Vietnam. Only someone familiar with the street life and layout of Saigon could have written it. This early untitled version had been withdrawn at the request of Dix Landau some three weeks after it was registered. There was a signed letter on his office stationery to prove it.

The next version was on the table, bound in a red cover, titled *The Sleepwalker of Saigon,* with Raymond Kepler registered as author. It was seventy pages long, in first-draft screenplay form, obviously the work of a professional. Kepler had changed the names of the characters, expanded the incidents, and purged Bomberg's dialogue of some of the gamier turns of phrase. But it was the same story and some of Bomberg's atmosphere of death and hallucination still shone through it.

The third version was in a white cover, over one hundred pages long. Sassari was credited with authorship. It was titled *Shoot the Singer.* In form it was close to the copy which Bomberg had stolen from Sassari's home and hidden among his effects at the hospital.

'It looks to me like Bomberg submitted that first rough version to Landau who tore off the title page and registered it under his own name. Then Kepler wrote this expanded version called *Shoot the Singer* and registered it under his own name.'

'There's a letter attached to that version,' the lady pointed out. 'Mr Kepler relinquished his rights to the property some time ago. The only valid credit on file is Mr Sassari's.'

'It was the old routine,' I said 'Kepler got in the hole, the bookmakers started to squeeze him, Sassari bailed him out in exchange for the credit. Only this time Kepler wasn't his usual martyred self. All those years of having his original work stolen by Sassari must have finally rubbed off on him. Kepler was going to be smart this time. *He* was going to steal someone else's work.'

Marcus tossed the scripts down and scratched furiously at the back of his neck. 'I can see how it got from Bomberg to Sassari.

The only thing I can't figure is what the hell Landau was up to at the beginning.'

'He's got eyes for Kepler's wife,' I said. 'I think he must have given Kepler the original and then told Bomberg that Kepler had stolen it. He wanted Kepler out of the way. He counted on Bomberg doing it for him. But by then Sassari had stolen it from Kepler like he managed to steal everything Kepler ever wrote. And Bomberg wasn't controllable. He went after both Sassari *and* Kepler. He went after everyone who was trying to exploit what happened to him that night in Saigon.'

'It sounds like a helluva lot of crazy shit for one literary agent to pull,' Marcus grumbled.

'It must have snowballed on him. Maybe Bomberg confronted him and to save himself he blamed it on Kepler and Sassari.'

'Then tell me why Landau would hire you to find a missing script when he knew where it was all along?'

'Maybe it was just a blind. Maybe he wanted me to find Kepler . . . *for* Bomberg.' I glanced at the lady with the grey hair. She had rather wide-open blue eyes with a slightly lunatic gleam. She was following our conversation with a look of slack-jawed wonder, turning her head back and forth.

'If your girlfriend was innocent,' Marcus persisted, 'what the hell did she run away for?'

'She's not my girlfriend. She wasn't innocent. She's wanted in New York on an accessory to murder charge.'

'Once Landau found out Kepler was holed up at the Ocean View Motel, presumably he told Bomberg where he was. What was the point of sending you there?' He sneered.

'You're the brilliant one. You figure it out.'

'No, I'm interested in your opinion, *really*.' The corners of his lips turned up and he batted his eyelashes. 'You see, Kyd, I have this sneaking and completely insane idea that everyone is guilty.' He was smirking so foolishly at me I didn't know how to take it. He looked grotesque, nodding at me with his eyes closed and a knowing simper on his lips. 'That's what I'm after. *Everyone*.' His eyes snapped open and played over me with their shrewd, sullen gaze. When he said everyone he was including me.

It was not a bad moment to tell him that Laura's passport was made out to an Eva Bomberg who was the ex-wife of the man whose original story had been stolen. After all, what difference would it make? By now she would expect me to have given her away. She would certainly not be using that name any longer. If they couldn't catch her as Mary Dana Thompson, they weren't likely to get her as Eva Bomberg. It did matter, of course. Telling the policeman would just be a good way of losing my investigator's licence and going to jail. I was just not made out of the noble stuff that turns itself in to the Marcuses of the world, not in this reincarnation at least.

'For someone with three murders who hasn't even made a single arrest, you're pretty damn ambitious,' I smiled.

Marcus swept up the scripts and registration slips and letters of withdrawal in his arms, thanked the lady, and headed out the door. I followed him. Where else was I going to go?

thirty-four

Kepler's street was crisscrossed with white chalk marks diagramming the trajectory of the bullets fired in the shootout. Other red and yellow chalk lines followed the movements of the participants; the place where they had stopped breathing and their final position had been carefully preserved by a chalk outline of their bodies. If you didn't know what had happened, you might have thought the street had been the scene of a hopscotch festival.

Marcus killed the engine and glided to a silent stop outside the Kepler house. A yellow Porsche was drawn up in the driveway behind the vandalized Renault. We got out and walked over the coloured chalk lines. High above our heads the crowns of the elongated palm trees rustled in a breeze that was barely perceptible at street level.

Marcus ignored the brass knocker and instead slowly banged his fist against the door.

'Who is it?' Landau's voice asked.

'Police,' Marcus said. 'Open up.'

The agent opened the door and looked at Marcus in angry bewilderment. He ignored me.

'Mrs Kepler doesn't want to be disturbed. I would have thought this could wait.'

'We're not planning on disturbing the lady.' Marcus unceremoniously pushed past him. 'We just have something which you're going to find awfully hard to explain.'

'You can't barge in here like that.' Landau followed the policeman into the living room.

'You can talk to me here.' Marcus wheeled around. 'Or I can handcuff you and throw you in the back of the car.'

'What *is* this?' He was still full of indignation.

'Just shut up and listen.' Marcus shook the script of *Shoot the Singer* in the agent's face. 'We got you your script back, Landau. The guy who killed Raymond had it. He was a Vietnam veteran called Carl Bomberg. He was also the one who killed Sassari and swiped it from his study. This is another script, mister. Written by your lady friend's late husband. Actually they're both written by Kepler. Sassari probably never changed a word. He just gave Raymond something under the table for the privilege of having everyone think he'd written it himself. It happens all the time. A deal was made.'

'You're right.' I spoke for the first time. 'It's crummy, it's low, it's how suckers like Kepler get screwed every day but it's perfectly legal. Some mob bookmaker suddenly puts the pressure on Kepler and he goes to Sassari for the money. Sassari's very helpful. He gets his mother to give Raymond a valuable drawing and in exchange demands the credit to *Shoot the Singer*. After all, a screenplay by Paul Sassari is worth something – he's got a name, a track record. It doesn't matter that Sassari can't write worth a damn. All he cares about is that people think he can. As his agent, that's all you cared about, Landau. You were happy to keep Kepler out of it for other reasons, too. It made him look like a loser to his wife, and you were all for that. It wasn't legitimate but it was legal. Only that,' I pointed to the letter of withdrawal, 'that, Landau, is illegal. That is your ticket to the slammer.'

He took the letter from Marcus, scanned it quickly, and handed it back.

'What is that?' he snorted. '*The Sleepwalker of Saigon*. I never wrote that.'

'I know you didn't. Bomberg wrote it. He submitted it to you and you registered it at the Screenwriters Guild under your own name. You withdrew it a couple of weeks later right about the time Kepler registered his version. Too bad the Guild keeps microfilm copies of everything they get, or you would have got away with it.'

He took the letter back and licked his lips. It rattled in his hands. In the silence I heard the sound of bathwater being turned off and the click of a door closing.

'I've never seen this letter before,' he whispered. 'I've never heard of Bomberg or *The Sleepwalker of Saigon*.'

'Was she worth it, Landau?' Marcus scoffed.

His homely, pensive face had lost all its prim authority. He had the slack, shocked look of someone who has just been slapped across the mouth and doesn't understand why.

'I wasn't even in the country when this was registered,' he said.

'Can you prove that?'

'I was at the Munich Book Fair, meeting with foreign publishers.' He opened his mouth and panted a little, his eyes wandering. He was only forty-five or so but he already had the appearance of an old man. He put his hand to his chest and swallowed and then fumbled out his wallet. 'Look in there if you want examples of my signature,' he said meekly.

Marcus compared the letter of withdrawal with one of his credit cards, shrugged, handed the wallet back. 'We got experts to decide these things. It looks close enough to me.'

Landau hardly seemed to notice what the policeman had said. 'I have to . . .' He gestured vaguely with his hand. '. . . See about her.'

We followed him out of the living room down a corridor where he stopped outside the shut bathroom door.

'Anne?' he said. 'Anne?'

There was no answer. Landau tried the door, but it was locked.

'Open the door,' the agent pleaded.

Marcus moved him aside, stepped back, and kicked the lock until the door splintered open.

There was so much steam that at first I could barely make her out. She was lying in the tub with her head propped up on a contoured plastic cushion but she wasn't naked. The salmon pink robe she wore had loosened itself around her breasts and thighs and in the steamy air it was hard to distinguish between the material and her pink flushed skin. It was a long bathroom done in terra-cotta tiles and rust-coloured wallpaper and we stood there gazing down its length at her.

'What are you doing, Anne?' Landau whispered.

As the air cleared I saw she was holding something in her hand pointed at us. It looked for a moment like a strangely shaped pistol but it was a long-barrelled hair dryer. A white cord ran from the handle over the rim of the tub to an outlet in the wall next to her.

She pulled the trigger and the hair dryer began blowing.

'If you come any closer,' she said in a far away voice, 'I'll drop this in the water.' She pulled the trigger again and put it on high. 'I want to be alone.'

Her head lurched a little as she spoke and there was a petulant, sleepy whine to her voice, as if she'd been woken in the middle of a nap.

'Please, Anne.' Landau took a step forward and she lowered the muzzle of the hair dryer towards the steaming water.

'Go *away*,' she hissed and to emphasize her threat smacked her hand down on the water, spraying it over the walls, wetting the plastic hair dryer.

'Let her be,' I said. 'It's too late now anyway.'

'Shut up,' Landau raged. 'There's a reason. There's an explanation.'

'Forget it,' I said. 'You never meant anything to her. You never meant anything more to her than Bomberg did. That's a very ambitious lady there.'

'For Raymond.' She stuck her head in our direction, and

210

squinted. 'I was ambitious for Raymond, you stupid man.' She was trying to snarl the words but her mouth contorted with a slow clumsiness as if deadened by Novocain.

'You and Lady Macbeth.' I sneered.

'Stupid man. Go away, stupid.' She sounded like a four-year-old, a drunk four-year-old. I could see an empty bottle of pills lying in the sink and I wondered how many she'd taken. She seemed to be very close to sinking into a coma. Electrocution wasn't a woman's way of committing suicide. Men blow their brains out or hang themselves but women are more sensitive to how they will look as corpses.

'She did love Raymond,' I said. 'She loved him so much, she even stole another man's script and gave it to him. And her sad sick husband never appreciated it. He went and lost it to Sassari like all the others. And when Bomberg confronted her, where an ordinary person might have given up, she had a stroke of genius. She told Bomberg it was Sassari who stole it.'

'What are you saying?' Landau said. 'Anne wouldn't . . .'

'You bet your ass, she would. Her only problem was Raymond. Raymond was a little alarmed at all this stuff she was doing for him. He already felt like a heel for stealing another writer's work. That was the kind of crummy thing that Sassari did. Raymond wasn't made for the role of exploiter. So long as he was the victim, he had some perverse sense of integrity. In his heart he knew he was superior to Sassari. And sudenly she took all that away from him.'

'I wanted him to be a man,' she cried.

'If he'd been a man he would have turned you in, but he couldn't do it, not his own wife. That was his big mistake. Because you had Bomberg kill him just like you had Bomberg stab Sassari. And I think Raymond knew it all along. He just sat in this house waiting for it to happen. It was going to be his final revenge on you. It was going to show that you were a murderous cunt and he was too good to live.'

'I always loved Raymond,' she said doggedly. 'I never told Bomberg he was at that motel. Raymond told him himself because he wanted to *apologize*. He was such a fool. He wanted to apologize.' She sobbed and beat her fist against the water. 'Apologize.'

Landau tried to go to her but I restrained him.

'Let her fry,' I said. 'She never even cared about Raymond.'

'I loved him!' she shouted.

'Bullshit. I can't even stand to listen to it. She loved her husband so much she had him shot in the head.' I shouldered my way out of the bathroom, with the sound of her angry yelling in my ears. I hoped Marcus had the brains to keep hammering at her sore point. She didn't want to die misunderstood; some final egoism would make her want to talk her suicide note.

I ran into the kitchen and searched for a fusebox. Maybe it was outside. I tried the kitchen door but it was locked. I opened a window and climbed out onto a shed covering some garbage cans and jumped to the ground. I ran around to the back of the house, past Raymond's study to the bathroom window.

I could hear her whispering fiercely and Marcus guffawing in derision. Through the drawn drapes I could see the policeman and Landau backed up nearly to the bathroom door. Mrs Kepler was sitting upright in the tub. The back of her head was just below me on the other side of the glass. I smashed my hand through the pane and grabbed the hair dryer and hung on. She went wild, pulling it downward with both hands, biting at my hand. I couldn't see anything but I could feel her teeth biting my fingers, water splashing dangerously, and the insane strength of her hands trying to plunge the hair dryer into the bath.

'Let go, Kyd,' Marcus yelled. 'It's disconnected.'

I got my hand out and leaned against the side of the house. There was a fight going on in the bathroom: screams, groans, dirty language, splashing water. My hand was a mess. I put it to my mouth and tasted warm salty blood. I stumbled around to the front of the house and leaned on the doorbell. It seemed like I stood there a long time before Landau finally let me in. He was drenched with bathwater.

Marcus stood next to Mrs Kepler in front of the fireplace in a pool of water. They were both completely soaked and panting. Marcus's face looked like he'd been savaged by a cat. Mrs Kepler's eye was black. Their shoulders were touching and their wrists were connected by chromed handcuffs.

'You can't make me live,' she said in a dull voice, and sank to her knees. The violent exertion had speeded up the effect of the pills she'd swallowed.

'If living is harder for you than dying, lady, I'm going to make sure you live.' He pulled her up and glared at me. 'Well? Call for assistance, goddamn it.'

I telephoned and went into the bathroom and wrapped a towel around my hand. The floor was awash with water. Just enough blood from my cut hand had dropped in the bath to shade it pink. Broken shards of glass gleamed obscurely at the bottom of the tub where the hair dryer lay. The curtain flapped against the window, flapped and bunched, as if the night was trying to swallow it through the mouth of the jagged pane.

When I heard the sirens wailing in the distance I went back into the living room and looked at the three people there, the woman and the policeman hunched together in a spreading pool of water and the man collapsed in the armchair with his face in his hands.

I wondered what the hell assistance was, and who you called when you needed it. Whatever it was, it was too late and there was too little of it.

I left the front door open and went to wait on the pavement for the ambulance. Clouds were on fire over the ocean in the west but dusk had already settled over the Hollywood Hills. Where the sun was setting it looked like a giant vein had been opened in the sky.

After the ambulance arrived and the medics went in with the stretcher, it was silent for a while. The shadows of the trees lengthened over the lawns. The air lost its last twilight warmth. As I stood there all the lamps along the street silently came on at the same time and glowed weakly in the remaining daylight, a desolate, unreal light that did nothing for the pale stucco houses and skinny palm trees.

thirty-five

Anne Kepler survived the overdose. Her stomach was pumped out and when she came around, she waived her right to an attorney and made a full confession of the role she had played in the theft of the original screenplay and the murders of Paul Sassari and her husband. She admitted to forging Landau's signature and absolved him of any involvement in her crimes. The only place Laura's name surfaced in the confession was in Anne Kepler's description of her own first meeting with Carl Bomberg. The Vietnam veteran had come to Landau's office one day and asked her to submit his script to Landau. When she asked who had recommended him to the agent, Bomberg had replied evasively that it was someone who knew the wife of Paul Sassari. Anne Kepler later questioned Laura, who seemed to know nothing about him. As far as the police were concerned, that was Laura's sole part in the story. The only time Anne Kepler showed any emotion in her confession, according to Marcus, was at the mention of my name. Apparently what I'd said about her not really loving Raymond still enraged her.

They had removed all potentially dangerous objects from her room and stationed a guard to check her every half hour. But they had not counted on the fierceness of her will to die. She managed to pry loose a strand from a steel bedspring and used it to open a vein in her wrist. She spent the last minutes of her life huddled on her side with her face to the wall. Even with her strength ebbing, she managed to write Raymond's name sixteen times on the wall in blood. Maybe it was partly her way of answering me, of proving she had loved Raymond. I don't know. I don't know if the word *love* covers that kind of behaviour.

I never heard anything more from Frankie Bando and Carlo. They had their script back but it wasn't such a hot property any more. The three men who had worked on it were dead. Establishing which of their heirs actually owned the thing could only be resolved through lengthy paper wars which might do nothing but make some lawyers rich. Other studios had Vietnam war stories in the works and, before long, the moment was past. Vietnam proved not to be such good box office as the trend-spotters had forecast. *Shoot the Singer* ended up as a tax write-off for someone in Las Vegas who had probably made so much money that year he was grateful to lose some.

I had the bad taste to send Landau a bill for my services. After he'd failed to acknowledge my third reminder I had the bad taste to have my broken desk professionally packed and delivered to his office. I stuck the blood-stained bandage from my head in the right-hand drawer along with a letter from my attorney advising him of my intention to sue. I got a cheque from him the next day.

When no one asked me to give back the Picasso drawing I returned to Sotheby's. The English girl had been transferred to their New York branch, but she had left instructions with her replacement. The drawing wasn't on their list of stolen works, and I was free to sell it. Something in me wanted to keep it, but I'd lost confidence in that part of myself. It went for five thousand dollars and after paying my back taxes there was about eight hundred dollars remaining, enough to buy a second-hand desk and get my office painted.

In May that year I was approached for what seemed like an interesting assignment: A consortium of jewellers wanted me to fly to Israel and escort a consignment of diamonds back to Los Angeles. We had two conversations on the phone and then made an appointment to meet the following evening at the home of the consortium's treasurer.

His house was in the Hollywood Hills on a steep, winding street that offered a view of the whole city. Perhaps because I was going to get out of town, the sight of all those blazing lights made me like Los Angeles. It looked like a pinball machine below me spreading to the edge of the ocean, curving southward down the coast, all brilliantly lit but so distant, you heard nothing but a kind of faraway whisper from the millions of cars.

I climbed some steps through a garden up to the house. It was pink and Spanish and rather modestly sized for the acre of property surrounding it. The porch light was on and so were the garden spots, but the windows were shuttered. I rang the bell several times and walked around to the back and tried the

215

kitchen door. I checked my address book. It was the right day, the right house, the right hour.

I hung around for about five minutes, disappointed because I'd been excited at the prospect of a trip to Israel even if it was only for forty-eight hours. Then I left a note on the door and returned to my car.

'Hello, Thomas.' She was sitting in the passenger seat; the glow of her cigarette momentarily lit her face, and then she was in darkness again. Her perfume filled the car. There was a silky, rustling sound as she shifted in her seat. 'Can we talk?' she said anxiously. I heard a car up the hill. It was turning around and a moment later it went by us, illuminating us with its headlights.

'Are you alone?' I asked.

'I am now,' she said.

I got in next to her and snapped on the dashboard light. She was dressed in a pale grey silk suit, a very classical thing, with a waistcoat and crisp, pointed lapels. Her hair was short, black again, pulled back from her face and neck into a topknot. It gave her eyes and bones a look of soft, naked simplicity.

'You look very beautiful, Laura, also prosperous.'

'I'm sorry about the Israeli business,' she said. 'I wanted to see you alone, somewhere quiet. I didn't even know if you would see me. You look marvellous.' She reached out and laid her hand on mine. Her eyes were huge, sexual, and shining with fear. 'Carl was my husband,' she said.

'I know.'

'I couldn't abandon him. I never even knew he had written that thing. I was telling him about Paul's latest project one day, and he went funny, but I didn't think anything of it. It was Anne Kepler . . .'

'I know that.'

'I couldn't turn Carl in, not after what they'd done to him. I didn't have to warn you Carl would try and get the Keplers. I tried to keep faith with Carl. I tried to keep faith with you. I didn't want any of this to happen and once it started, I just couldn't catch up. Don't you see that?'

'It was Bomberg who picked up the passport, right? He made the weird phone calls to me.'

'I thought I could control him.' She nodded. 'They made him a killer over there. He was just a sweet kid when I married him. I gave him money. I got him a car, an apartment. I paid for shrinks. I took care of him but it wasn't enough. That's why I married Paul – so I'd have the means to take care of Carl. Don't you understand that?'

'Yeah. I see it. Poor son of a bitch was probably ashamed at being such a burnt-out case. That's why he wrote that screenplay in the first place – to show you he could do something, the kind of thing your husband did. He was trying to compete in his institutionalized, humble fashion.'

'It's true,' she said quietly. 'He was.'

'Well, I feel sorry for him. Seems to me he got just about the rawest deal a kid can get from the day he joined the army to the day I helped that cop whack him out.'

'Everyone got a raw deal,' she said tonelessly. 'Everyone.'

'Sure. Look at Fieldman. Not one of the brightest or most honest specimens, but I kind of liked him. He thought he knew what was going on. First time in his life he thought he had the world by the balls. All full of himself. He's going to get his, and he gets shit.'

'That was terrible what they did to Morris,' she said with a desperate plea in her voice. 'But it wasn't me. They did that. I had to . . .'

'Hey.' I laughed. 'What is this? You survived. You did what you had to do. I nearly got killed and five people died, but that's cool.' I started the car and steered it down the hill.

'I lost everything, Thomas.' She watched me for a reaction. 'I lost you.'

'I lost my self-respect. It's like an appendix – it hurts when it goes bad, but then you find you can live without it.'

'You're really bitter, huh?'

'What do you want from me? Right now? Why are you here?' I looked over at her. 'Don't think up something, just give it to me simply.'

'You were the only one I ever trusted and I hurt you. To make it better, I suppose.'

'You really trust me, huh?' I came out onto Laurel Canyon

and turned right into the light traffic. I wasn't going anywhere. We just cruised in silence.

'Yes, I trust you,' she said. 'You could drive me to the cops right now. I'm giving you the chance.'

'It's a bit late to straighten things out. You got any alternatives?'

'We could drive to the airport. We could take that trip to Israel.' She gave me her best and most poignant smile.

I pulled the car over to the kerb and got out and walked around and opened her door. 'Get out.'

'What's happening?'

I grabbed her arm and roughly pulled her out. She tried to hang onto the door but I dragged her off it.

'What are you doing?'

'I want to see how much you really trust me.' I started dragging her along the pavement.

There was a squeal of brakes and a car pulled up in front of mine. The door flew open and a man jumped out. His blue-black hair was brushed straight back from his forehead. He had lively, dangerous eyes but the rest of his face was suavely good-looking. He was dressed in a white three-piece suit, with a midnight-blue shirt open at the collar.

'Hey, you. Hey, I'm talking to you!' He glanced up and down the street, and then gestured with his hand. 'Come on! What are you doing? Hey!' Again his head swivelled left and right to see no one was watching, and at the same time a gun materialized in his hand.

I let go of Laura's arm and stepped away from her.

'I'm coming, Tony.' She turned to me and grimaced eloquently. 'Sorry, Thomas. I had to make sure. You know how it is.'

'A girl's got to protect herself. Absolutely.' I kept my eyes on the gun pointed at me. It seemed less frightening than looking at her face. I didn't bother to look at the guy holding it. He could have been anyone. He could have been me.

'Good-bye, Thomas.' She waited for me to answer, and when I didn't, she walked to Tony's car and let herself into the passenger side. He put up his gun and shrugged good-naturedly, as if to say it was nothing personal, just the way things had to be sometimes. I watched him climb in next to Laura and wait for an opening in the traffic. In a moment they pulled out and within seconds it was impossible to distinguish their car from the stream of other tail-lights.

I thought of the planning and organization that had gone into getting me to go to that house in the Hollywood Hills. Also the kind of sophistication and nerve required to hire some professional muscle like Tony to follow her in case I tried to hand her to the police. She had gone to considerable trouble. It was what you might do if you loved someone. But was that love? And if she loved me, why didn't she trust me? But then I could see her asking the same question of me. Why had I insisted on calling her bluff? Why couldn't I have trusted *her* and driven to the airport and broken the pattern of my life? God knows, I'd wanted to. She had still promised the richest kind of excitement. She was still the only woman whose name mentioned in a room brought me to a standstill. So why hadn't I taken that ride?

They say any day now Los Angeles is going to slide into the ocean. But it will never happen: southern California is at least twenty miles thick and the Pacific is only two miles deep.

It was for some such reason that I didn't go with Laura, though she would have been good company for any apocalypse.

Timothy Harris
Kyd for Hire £1.50

'After three days I had one suicide, three murders and a case that had about as much symmetry as a half-digested pizza ...'

A rich man with a suicide in the closet and a missing daughter on his hands. For Thomas Kyd, Private Investigator, a client is a client even when the case carries unsavoury added attractions like a professional killer with no fingerprints and a bent cop who wants private enterprise kept out of crimefighting ...

'A new talent has come through the door gun in hand'
GUARDIAN

Raymond Chandler
The Little Sister £1.50

When she walked into Marlowe's office she looked just like the pathetic but appealing small-town girl from Manhattan, Kansas He sensed something phoney about her – then all of a sudden Marlowe's telephone came alive with the sultry voices of movie stars, the slurred tones of gangsters, the clipped phrases of the police. Every call led him into something deeper than the last maybe he'd be better off without clients from Manhattan, Kansas ...

Playback 95p

6.30 a.m. wasn't Marlowe's best hour for being woken up, especially by some crummy lawyer called Umney Umney's assistant was more interesting A sharp tongue, blue-grey eyes and more curves than a scenic railway The brief was vague A strange lady called Betty Mayfield was being blackmailed by a guy with a mind as straight as a stale banana What started as a standard tail job ended up with something even Marlowe didn't understand.

James M. Cain
The Postman Always Rings Twice £1.25

'Hell could have opened for me and it wouldn't have made any difference. I had to have her, even if I hung for it . . .'

He was halfway to a hobo, kicked off a hay truck on a California road to nowhere. She was a woman who had dreamed of Hollywood but settled for a dead-end husband in a greasy-spoon eating house. All they had to do was kill her husband and hit out for tomorrow.

'A raw blast of a book' EVENING STANDARD

'Dramatic . . . brutal and shocking' SUNDAY TIMES

Serenade £1.25

Juana was a three-peso whore with all the passion and violence of the streets she worked. Sharp had to steal her away from a bullfighter before he took her to bed and made her his woman. From Mexico City to Acapulco, and on to Hollywood and New York, their love burned itself out and left only the scalding ashes of tragedy . . .

'*Serenade* is a masterpiece of its kind' NEW STATESMAN

'Superb . . . this book stands in the front rank'
DAILY TELEGRAPH

The Butterfly £1.25

'All the time my heart was pounding at the way she made me feel, and all the time she knew how she made me feel and didn't care . . .'

Jess Tyler was a simple and honest man, a god-fearing man tortured into crimes of surging passion and chilling violence.

He was tortured by his love for two wayward women – his wife and his daughter . . .

Ed McBain
Calypso £1.25

What a lousy way to die. Calypso King George Chadderton, murdered on a wet September street in the 87th Precinct. Brains spattered on a sidewalk on a wet city night is something detectives Carella and Meyer can do without. And then Clara Hawkins, a leggy black hooker, ends up the same way. Carella and Meyer figure the connection between some tall, crazy killer with a Smith & Wesson and a weird lady in black living on an island with a caged-up man and an alsatian . . .

'Gothic hair-raiser . . . leaves the reader twitching' GUARDIAN

Let's Hear It for the Deaf Man   90p

If you happen to be a cop, there are some people you don't need — like a guy with an arrow in his chest, a burgular who leaves a kitten as his calling-card, a hippie crucified on a tenement wall — and the Deaf Man, who announced he was going to steal half-a-million dollars then needled Steve Carella with a series of cryptic picture clues.

'. . . the climax is ecstatically satisfying' OBSERVER

Eighty Million Eyes £1.25

When top TV comic Stan Gifford died there were plenty of witnesses. Forty million viewers plus 212 people in the studio. Detectives Meyer and Carella had never had it so good . . . When pretty Cindy Forrest, pert-breasted and wide-hipped, undressed for bed there was no one to watch — except her attacker. Detective Kling had never had it so bad . . .

'Fast . . . exciting . . . realistic' OBSERVER

Fiction

☐	**Options**	Freda Bright	£1.50p
☐	**The Thirty-nine Steps**	John Buchan	£1.50p
☐	**Secret of Blackoaks**	Ashley Carter	£1.50p
☐	**The Sittaford Mystery**	Agatha Christie	£1.00p
☐	**Dupe**	Liza Cody	£1.25p
☐	**Lovers and Gamblers**	Jackie Collins	£2.50p
☐	**Sphinx**	Robin Cook	£1.25p
☐	**Ragtime**	E. L. Doctorow	£1.50p
☐	**The Rendezvous**	Daphne du Maurier	£1.50p
☐	**Flashman**	George Macdonald Fraser	£1.50p
☐	**The Moneychangers**	Arthur Hailey	£2.25p
☐	**Secrets**	Unity Hall	£1.50p
☐	**Simon the Coldheart**	Georgette Heyer	95p
☐	**The Eagle Has Landed**	Jack Higgins	£1.95p
☐	**Sins of the Fathers**	Susan Howatch	£2.50p
☐	**The Master Sniper**	Stephen Hunter	£1.50p
☐	**Smiley's People**	John le Carré	£1.95p
☐	**To Kill a Mockingbird**	Harper Lee	£1.75p
☐	**Ghosts**	Ed McBain	£1.25p
☐	**Gone with the Wind**	Margaret Mitchell	£2.95p
☐	**The Totem**	David Morrell	£1.25p
☐	**Platinum Logic**	Tony Parsons	£1.75p
☐	**Wilt**	Tom Sharpe	£1.50p
☐	**Rage of Angels**	Sidney Sheldon	£1.75p
☐	**The Unborn**	David Shobin	£1.50p
☐	**A Town Like Alice**	Nevile Shute	£1.75p
☐	**A Falcon Flies**	Wilbur Smith	£1.95p
☐	**The Deep Well at Noon**	Jessica Stirling	£1.95p
☐	**The Ironmaster**	Jean Stubbs	£1.75p
☐	**The Music Makers**	E. V. Thompson	£1.75p

Non-fiction

☐	**Extraterrestrial Civilizations**	Isaac Asimov	£1.50p
☐	**Pregnancy**	Gordon Bourne	£2.95p
☐	**Jogging from Memory**	Rob Buckman	£1.25p
☐	**The 35mm Photographer's Handbook**	Julian Calder and John Garrett	£5.95p
☐	**Travellers' Britain** } **Travellers' Italy** }	Arthur Eperon	£2.95p £2.50p
☐	**The Complete Calorie Counter**	Eileen Fowler	75p

☐	The Diary of Anne Frank	Anne Frank	£1.50p
☐	Linda Goodman's Sun Signs	Linda Goodman	£2.50p
☐	Mountbatten	Richard Hough	£2.50p
☐	How to be a Gifted Parent	David Lewis	£1.95p
☐	Symptoms	Sigmund Stephen Miller	£2.50p
☐	Book of Worries	Robert Morley	£1.50p
☐	The Hangover Handbook	David Outerbridge	£1.25p
☐	The Alternative Holiday Catalogue	edited by Harriet Peacock	£1.95p
☐	The Pan Book of Card Games	Hubert Phillips	£1.75p
☐	Food for All the Family	Magnus Pyke	£1.50p
☐	Everything Your Doctor Would Tell You If He Had the Time	Claire Rayner	£4.95p
☐	Just Off for the Weekend	John Slater	£2.50p
☐	An Unfinished History of the World	Hugh Thomas	£3.95p
☐	The Third Wave	Alvin Toffler	£1.95p
☐	The Flier's Handbook		£5.95p

All these books are available at your local bookshop or newsagent, or
can be ordered direct from the publisher. Indicate the number of copies
required and fill in the form below

7

Name_____
(Block letters please)

Address_____

Send to Pan Books (CS Department), Cavaye Place, London SW10 9PG
Please enclose remittance to the value of the cover price plus:
35p for the first book plus 15p per copy for each additional book ordered
to a maximum charge of £1.25 to cover postage and packing
Applicable only in the UK

While every effort is made to keep prices low, it is sometimes
necessary to increase prices at short notice. Pan Books reserve
the right to show on covers and charge new retail prices which
may differ from those advertised in the text or elsewhere